Her Shadows

From The Past

Maria Milliner

Prologue

She sits quietly gazing out of the window. The night is cold. A forming frost is slowly transforming the grass below into a carpet of crushed diamonds which sparkle magically, glistening under the reflecting light cast by the moon, the heavenly orb of the night. He smiles down, full and bright, his milky path tempting her to follow it. It reminds her of her college days when she'd sit alone in her room, lost in the mysticism of the night sky as it gradually filled with bright golden stars and contributed to the ethereal atmosphere which had already surrounded her. The full moon, encircled by a misty halo, would call out to her, compelling her to venture down to the sea front. Here, she witnessed for the first time the mystical, silvery path forming across the otherwise dark surface of the sea. The moon had teasingly beckoned, tempting her to follow his shimmering light that was mirrored gently across the water. She'd called it her suicide path – it looked beautiful and appeared to offer her a sense of peace and tranquillity. She'd never intended to follow it, no matter how tempting it looked, but had often wondered where it would lead. The dancing path oozed with an ethereal and spiritual aura, offering her a sense of escapism and mystery. She'd often used it, and continued to do so, as a path of prayer, hoping that her prayers would flow along the moonlit ripples and be answered. She'd frequently wondered if the path would lead her to the magical fairy tale castle that she'd dreamed of as a child, where the handsome Prince would be waiting for her. They would fall in love and live happily ever after. Childhood dreams – life has taught her that. Or is it possible for some of those dreams to come true?

A feeling of loneliness and melancholy suddenly sweeps over her, bringing her thoughts away from the magnetic moonlight and back to the present. It's the same feeling she experienced as a little girl, alone in her own small world, a feeling which she's carried with her for many years, even when surrounded by family and friends. Now, the same sense of aloneness surrounds her, squeezing her so tightly that she feels as if she is suffocating.

The moon silently calls to her. Her friend, her confidant. Oh, how much she has shared with the little man up there – good times and bad. The smiling face looks down, giving her the courage and strength to revisit her shadows from the past and finally bring closure to enable her soul to heal. She, like the moon, begins to reflect, to review her life, her experiences. She feels again the pain, the suffering, the hurt, the loss. Emotions buried for years now surface onto the moon's path below. Slowly, they arise from deep within her heart and soul, filling her with so much pain that it feels as if she is being stabbed at soul level. Tears begin to flow gently down her cheeks – tears for all the hurt she has suffered, for the joy she has felt, as she thinks about what was, what is and what might have been.

It is time. Time to let go. Time to release. Time to heal. Wrapping herself in a soft, comforting blanket, she allows her shadows to come to the fore. One by one, they come under the spotlight of the moon, ready to take part in her stories on the floodlit stage below. She has no option except to witness the narrative being presented to her, although now she is being given the chance to change the script, beginning with her childhood.

Chapter 1

Trudi was the second child in a family of four children. She had an elder sister Fran, a younger sister Alice and a younger brother Thomas. Her father was in the Navy and consequently away for months, even years, and so her early life was spent with her mum and Fran, until Alice was born. The small family occasionally visited their father's ship when it was in dock, which was a great adventure to the young Trudi. After an exciting train ride and a walk where little legs struggled to climb over giant railway sleepers, an enormous metal ship that resembled a monster surfacing from the depths of the water confronted her. A long steep gangplank, which, to the little girl, seemed to rest unsteadily against the ship, led her into the helping arms of a strong, handsome man dressed in white. Trudi recollects staring in awe and wonder at the man in white, captivated by his smile and twinkling blue eyes. There he was, her dad; he pulled her to safety and into his arms, making her feel loved and secure.

Despite the feeling of adoration she had after those visits, it felt as if there was a stranger in the house when he was on leave. It was particularly so when he finally returned home for good, creating an ambience of unfamiliarity. Trudi was nearly eight by this time, Fran was twelve and Alice four. They were accustomed to being a family of four and suddenly there was another person, an intruder, in their lives. A 'stranger' with whom they must become acquainted. A new set of rules by which they must abide. Fran especially was finding it increasingly difficult to develop a relationship with their father, whereas Trudi welcomed this man into her life with open, if a little uncertain, arms.

Then little Thomas was born into the family. She'd longed for the baby to come so that she could love and comfort it in the way that she yearned for herself. She knew that she was loved by her family, but her mum never seemed to have time to give her the attention for which she craved. She was always too busy, looking after Alice or too tired to spend time with her. Fran was often out with her friends and so Trudi was left, alone, wondering where her place was within the family. Consequently, she lived in her own little fairy tale world, acting out her dreams, speaking in her own special language that nobody else understood. No one was able to intrude into her world and destroy it – she felt safe. The outside world was something she simply had to bear. 'How is it?' she asks herself, 'that a little girl's thinking can affect the way she lives her life?' But it had and she'd gone on to live her life accepting whatever experiences came her way. However, it had also given her a belief that the right thing would usually happen, for all concerned.

Trudi was the good girl: reliable and dependable. Her childhood days were filled with pleasing others and, when able, escaping into her fantasy world. Summer nights were spent alone in the garden where she played around the little fairy ring that had grown in the grass. She talked to the fairies, hoping that one would pop up to say hello. She spun round and round, waiting to be whisked away into that make believe land, just as the whirlwind had lifted Dorothy away in the Wizard of Oz. 'Oh yes, the Wizard of Oz! How I loved that film!' She feels that she, like Dorothy, is following her own yellow brick road, highlighted by the moon, in search of whatever is missing in her life, looking for answers.

The story continues and Trudi sees before her a shy, introverted girl who lacked in confidence and found it difficult to mix with others. Even though she'd made friends at school, she carried a feeling of not belonging, just one of the items placed inside her endless invisible bag which was ready to receive her negative beliefs, concerns and unanswered questions. Her first day at Primary school draws her attention, a day she can remember explicitly. Fran took her to school and escorted her to her first classroom, where she was confronted by a room of sobbing children all wanting their mummy. Why were they crying? It was something they *'had to do'*, so just get on with it. It was as if she was cut off from all the natural feelings and emotions which were hiding deep inside, too frightened to come out and be acknowledged. She felt unnoticed, the odd one out and so began to use her safeguard tactics of trying to please others. 'Another thread starting to be woven in the pattern of my life' she thinks.

The 'good girl' was quickly recognised by the teacher who gave Trudi jobs of responsibility to carry out. She was responsible for putting straws into small bottles of creamy milk and handing them out to each pupil. She also gave out the hard coarse mats for their after-lunch nap, but there was one responsibility that had a negative impact on her and began the expectation of good things turning bad. A new girl had joined the class. Trudi was asked to be her friend, to look after her, play with her and take her to the toilet. Her chest puffed out with pride as she promised the teacher that she would do her very best. Everything was great until her new friend had a little accident. She didn't tell Trudi that she needed the toilet, consequently, the contents of the girl's bladder emptied all over the floor. The teacher was not amused and, with a face like thunder, told Trudi that if it ever happened again, she would be made to wipe it up with her bare hands. The pride swollen chest deflated like a balloon that had been stabbed with a pin. She felt sick and tears were burning the back of her eyes. She tried to explain that the girl hadn't told her that she needed the toilet, but the teacher dismissed her. Trudi was five years old and accepted, without question, what the teacher said. Even today, she can't recall if she'd told her mum, who would probably have dismissed it anyway with an 'oh well, you'll know next time.' She wasn't old enough to describe what she was feeling, or give it a name; now, she knows exactly: unjust! She'd been treated unfairly, sentenced without her side of the story being heard. She'd been trampled on, squashed into the ground like a piece of dirt and all positive thoughts about herself flattened too. She recognises this feeling, only too well, having experienced it many times since that day, and it is only recently that she's had the guts to stand up and say, 'who the hell do you think you are talking to?' Trudi searches for that little girl inside herself, so that she can tell her how brave and confident she is. She feels her chest beginning to swell, just a little.

Life changed rapidly after her father's return. Not only was there this 'stranger' and a new baby in the house, but Trudi also found herself being taken away from her safety net, the place she'd come to know as home. Her dad's new job brought about a house move – they were moving to Nottinghamshire, her mum's home county. Trudi wasn't looking forward to living closer to her mum's parents, especially grandma who had, in a young girl's opinion, the characteristics of a witch. She often felt frightened of her and thought of her as the wicked witch of the west. She wished she possessed a pair of Dorothy's red shoes so that she could click the heels and disappear, or make her grandma disappear! There were never any cuddles and she certainly didn't have the qualities a grandmother should have. Trudi believed that her grandma was always comparing her to her sisters and didn't think she could live up to their qualities – Fran who was lively and chatty and Alice, the pretty one. After all, she was told often enough how quiet she was and what a plain Jane she was. There was one time when a family member referred to her as the ugly duckling who'd turned into a swan, but she only heard the ugly duckling; the damage had been done. The seeds that she was worthless and unattractive had been planted.

The house move was quickly upon them. Even though Trudi was excited about moving to a new house, she was also afraid of the newness this would bring. It was unsettling, especially as she and Fran were staying with her dad's parents until the new house was ready. Her parents, Alice and Thomas, were going to stay with the 'witch'. Not that she wanted to stay there, but she naturally wanted to be with her parents. As the scene unfolds, Trudi becomes aware of the familiar feeling of being cast aside showing itself and realises that, even at eight years old, how adept she was at burying all feelings and just 'getting on with it.'

The removal van had been and gone. The car was slowly filled with the leftovers, squashed into every nook and cranny until there was only just about enough room for the air they breathed. A little chuckle rises inside her as she envisages her dad's car filled to the brim with the family of six, carry cot, two rabbits, guinea pigs and suitcases. How it managed to move she has no idea!

The overloaded car successfully managed the journey to her grandparents' house. Trudi was fond of these grandparents and had invariably enjoyed spending time with them. They both had space for her. She often sat on her grandpa's knee listening to the stories that he made up, sometimes a little scary, but usually fun. He wore his shirt with sleeves rolled up to just above the elbow, exposing his wiry arm and the legs of a lady tattoo which travelled from just below the elbow to the top of his arm. He reminded her of Popeye. He didn't smoke a pipe, instead he enjoyed a packet of woodbines, his hand and fingers stained yellow from the way he held his cigarettes. He sat in his chair, smoking his woodbines, telling stories and toasting bread on the open fire, whilst she sat watching the smoke rise around the bread, mesmerised as the flames slowly turned the bread brown and the toasty aroma wafted around her nostrils. Butter was thickly spread on the warm toast and the dripping result handed to her, her mouth eagerly anticipating the taste that had been conjured up by her taste buds. Complete satisfaction hit as the first bite was taken and her lips licked to make sure she captured the escaping butter. She concentrated on savouring every mouthful whilst listening to the stories intently and preparing for the moment when either laughter, or screams, would burst out.

Her grandma, on the other hand, was a sturdy woman who, although appearing a little overbearing, had a heart of gold and was very protective of her family. She always took an interest in Trudi's life and was more of the grandmother figure Trudi had imagined. She was a full-figured lady and far from the figure or personality of Popeye's Olive! She covered her ample body with a full-length pinny, worn over her clothes for most of the day, only removing it when venturing out. She wore thick brown stockings to cover her legs and long bloomers that occasionally peeped out from under her skirt, especially when she stood with her hands on her hips, ready to tell her husband what he'd done wrong! She was an astute lady, full of words of wisdom or sayings. She was also a very good cook, especially her roast dinners. Her roast potatoes were to die for: crisp and full of flavour, with maybe a little too much fat dripping from them, but that's what made them special. Despite being a peculiar match, the couple always seemed to be happy, showing each other affection in their own special way. Trudi felt welcome and safe in their house, even with the underlying insecurity of being away from her parents. And so began her adventure – several months away from her family and the start of a new school, albeit only for a few weeks.

Oh yes! The school. The school where she experienced the same unjustness as she had once before. Another incident of not understanding the reasons behind an action. Extreme anger rises from within as she sees herself, as that child, standing in front of the formidable teacher. She imagines what it must have been like for Oliver Twist when he'd asked for more, yet she wasn't asking for more, she simply asked to take home the woven basket she'd made for her mum. The little wicker basket that she'd lovingly woven with ribbons and taken care to create a perfect present. However, it wasn't the end of term and so it wasn't permitted for her to take it. She recalls thinking how stupid the rule was and not being able to understand why she couldn't take it with her. After all, what use would it be to anyone else? Nonetheless, she kept quiet, simply tolerating that that was the way it was. Trudi notices how the little girl adds the event and accompanying emotions to the unseen bottomless bag. She sees that the shadows had started to form, lying in wait, ready to influence her throughout her life. The basket was such a small event but it is now apparent just how deeply it had upset her at the time. It was a gift for her mum, a gift she'd worked hard on and it was taken away. Trudi contemplates this thought for a while – the similarities to the loss and hurt she has suffered on and off throughout her life. To a little girl those feelings were just as deep as those she has felt as a woman, but no one had acknowledged them, then or now, not even Trudi. She'd tucked them away in her invisible bag, not knowing that over the years the bag would fill to bursting, until one day her shadows from the past would overflow into the moonlight with an urgency to be faced and healed.

Chapter 2

Her attention is drawn to the day when she and Fran re-joined the family in their new home, the family having travelled down to collect them. The arrival at the new house was filled with an air of excitement. It was a new build chalet bungalow, set on the edge of a small rural village, with a path that ran down the side of the house leading to a big open field. The field became a play area for Trudi and her younger siblings where they could run freely, taking care not to disturb the local farmer's cows, mainly out of fright than regard for the four legged occupants!

Trudi watches as her younger self entered the house, breathing in the odour of the newly painted magnolia walls and the new green carpet that ran the length of the hall and stairs. She looked around in wonder. There were radiators for the first time! No more cold mornings with Jack Frost's paintings on the window, inside and out, or sleeping with clothes under the eiderdown to warm them ready for dressing the following morning. She ran upstairs and set about exploring the bedroom she was to share with Alice. Sitting on the bed, she gazed around the room, her eyes and hands searching for anything familiar which would bring her a sense of comfort. She felt the softness of her bedspread beneath her and smelt the comforting soapy fragrance of familiar washing powder. Her searching hands found her row of dolls and teddies, arranged on her bed, waiting for her. Her eyes fell upon the chest of drawers and wardrobe, empty apart from a few clothes which her mum had already put there. She started putting away the remainder of her clothes and added a few personal touches. Then, slowly, Trudi walked around the room, touching each wall, marking her territory as if she were a cat, helping her to feel at home. She walked towards the door, turned and with hands on hips gave a satisfied smile. She was home and very happy to be among her family again except she had the anxious task of starting another new school. She didn't allow herself the self-indulgence of considering her own feelings for long as she'd the responsibility of caring for

Alice who was starting school for the first time; they were placed in her invisible bag and became part of the shadows already hiding within.

The school itself was a tiny Victorian school, where Mr Evans was Headteacher as well as teacher of the older children. It was positioned in the heart of the small village, where there was only one little village shop, a pub, the school, the Church, and the village green. The Church played an important role in school life and village life itself, which was a close-knit community, where everyone knew everyone else. Families had lived in the village for generations and, consequently, some resented newcomers. It was as if Trudi had stepped back in time. Life was much slower and the locals' outlook on life completely different to the one to which she was accustomed. As the school was next to the Church, the normal school sounds were often interrupted by the loud pealing of the bells situated high in the Church tower. Playtimes and even outside P.E. lessons were halted as a hearse slowly drove passed the school and into the Churchyard. She'd been brought up to be polite and to respect others, even so the experience of standing still when a hearse went by was totally new to her. The first time this happened was at a playtime: suddenly all the children stood still, an uncanny silence falling all around. She followed suit, not knowing why until she quietly asked what everyone was doing. She stood in silence to show the required courtesy as the hearse drove slowly by and entered the gates of the Church. Then, as quickly as the silence had come, it was gone.

There were two playgrounds, one for girls and one for boys. The memory of these is painted in her mind's eye. She sees the picture of the two playgrounds as clear as day. They were on different levels and she, as a little girl, would peer over the wall to watch the boys as they kicked a ball around below. The girls were in the top playground with skipping ropes, reciting rhymes as they skipped either on their own or in pairs and, sometimes, they sat on the hard ground playing Jacks or five stones. Trudi also recalls the many cold P.E. lessons outside which had consisted of very basic exercises such as star jumps and running on the spot!

In the summer, P.E. was moved to a field situated behind the school which was accessed by a little path running alongside the neighbouring houses. The pupils filed along the path in an orderly fashion, adorned in their varying P.E. outfits and carrying the necessary equipment. The girls played rounders and the boys played cricket. Trudi giggles as she calls to mind the rounders lessons which the girls supervised themselves whilst Mr Evans played cricket with the boys! There was only one rounders bat. After each turn, the girls were required to drop the bat at the start, leaving it on the ground ready to be picked up by the next in the team. One summer's day, the girl preceding her neglected to drop the bat. Trudi, who was standing at the starting point, shouted for the bat so that she could take her hit. The only hit to be taken was the one received by Trudi as the air born bat flew from one side of the rounders field to the other, with her head being the only obstacle to stop the bat's journey. It was a few minutes later that Mr Evans honoured the girls with his presence. She, with an egg-shaped lump forming on her forehead, was escorted back to school by a friend.

There were two classrooms, one for the Infants and one for the Juniors. The Infant classroom was set at the back of a larger wooden floored room, which, after each holiday, shone brightly following an extreme polishing, but the attempts to hide the scars set deep within the wood were in vain. 'I bet the scars could tell a few stories', she thinks. There were small wooden desks where little children would sit ready to begin their learning and a supply of well used toys which provided some respite from the very formal teaching. This room doubled up as the hall. Every morning, a curtain was pulled across to hide the classroom, and the whole school congregated for assembly which began with a standing choral of the National Anthem and closed with the Lord's Prayer.

Trudi was in the Juniors' classroom which was accessed by crossing a little outside quadrangle. The three toilets were also found here, tucked away in an outside building, which were dark, cold and housed many spiders. It was here that the girls, on approaching the age of ten, changed for P.E. to protect their modesty. If given the choice, she'd rather have changed in the classroom. The desks were all in single rows, four in total, and fixed to the floor with metal strips. Seven year olds began by sitting in the first row and, each year, moved along a row until the time came to say goodbye and move on to the big wide world of Secondary School. Each desktop was wooden and, like the floor, revealed markings buried deeply into the wood, left there by past pupils. Metal legs supported the desk and attached a wooden seat to make a complete outfit. An ink well was set in one corner of the desktop, waiting to be filled when a pupil showed the necessary skills for the long awaited nib pen. As the picture evolves, Trudi summons up the thrill she'd felt when she was given her first pen, a long shaped wooden stick, ending with a metal nib which had two points and a little hole. 'It really wasn't that far removed from a feather pen!' she laughs. Ink was poured into the well, the pen dipped, and she carefully attempted to write. As the pen eased across the paper, a feeling of sophistication flowed through her, just like the ink flowing from the pen and magically forming beautiful copperplate writing before her eyes. One line finished and then came the important task of blotting. She delicately placed the pink blotting paper over the ink and then cautiously lifted it, waiting with bated breath for the result to be revealed. Perfect! The image reminds her of how desperate she was to run home from school that afternoon, full of pride and wanting to share this great achievement with her mum. She also hears that little voice inside her which said, 'what's the point?'

The teacher's desk was completely different to the ones she'd seen previously. This was a true Victorian desk, big and sturdy. It too was wooden and so highly polished that it gleamed brightly when the sunlight cascaded through the high windows. The desk and accompanying seat were positioned on a high platform, at least if felt high to Trudi. When presenting work to Mr Evans, it was like climbing onto a stage with an audience of children and friends below. Trudi thinks back on the friends she'd made at the school, two of whom became good friends, despite the occasional falling out, with one especially. She wonders what has become of them, after all, it is over forty years since she has seen them. She would love to know if they have experienced the same as she has, if they have walked a similar rocky path. She hopes it has been a smoother journey for them.

One of the friends, Susan, lived on a farm, a walk of about two miles from Trudi's house, down a long, country lane. She considers the many times she'd walked alone to the farm and shudders at the thought of a child undertaking it nowadays. It was a walk she always enjoyed, especially on a summer's day when she stopped to admire the wildflowers growing in the hedgerow and watch the butterflies bobbing in and out. They sometimes rested close by, their wings fluttering gently, the colours and patterns flickering as the wings slowly opened and shut, similar to the illustrations of a flicker book. Bees buzzed around, busy carrying on with their work as they flew from one flower to another. As she walked, she dreamily ran her fingers through the soft grasses, picked dandelion heads and watched as the seeds blew away on the gentle summer breeze. Her mind was empty, focussed completely on the present moment. She was caught up in the wonderment of it all and excited in the knowledge that on arriving at the farm, good times awaited her.

Susan had two older brothers and all four children played together for hours in the haystacks, swinging on rubber tyres in the barn. The brothers pushed the girls higher and higher until they reached the rafters of the barn. Then, with squeals of delight, they threw themselves off the tyres into the haystacks below. Trudi felt happy and carefree on the farm, spending her time having fun and feeling totally safe to let herself go. She was able to be herself, to laugh and was free to be a child. Then an irrepressible heaviness engulfed her as the time to leave came round, far too soon. Trudi started the long, lonely walk home, cocooning herself in the memories of a fun filled day and daydreaming about being a farmer's wife.

Her other friend, Ann, lived in the village, just a small walk from Trudi's home. Her family were part of the 'old villagers', some of whom were members of the 'reluctant to welcome change into *their* village' group! Trudi spent a great deal of time with Ann, despite the friendship not always running smoothly, especially in the summer when rounders was played at school. Trudi was the captain of one team and Ann the captain of the other. Everything was fine if Ann's team won, but woe betide if Trudi's team were the winners – Ann didn't speak to her all weekend, ingraining her feelings of being rejected and treated unfairly. Nevertheless, she did share some fond and precious moments with Ann. Ann's dad was a sheep farmer. One day a lamb, which had been abandoned by its mother, was brought home to be bottle fed by the family. The lamb slept by the kitchen range, in a small basket, covered by a soft blanket. Ann fed the baby lamb each day, sometimes allowing Trudi this privilege. It was beautiful, and satisfying, to watch as the little mouth sucked the bottle of milk dry. Its coat was soft and curly, smelling of caramel toffee – hence its name, Toffee. The memory of the sweet fragrance rising from Toffee causes Trudi's nostrils to twitch and activate her taste buds as if she is waiting for a square of her dad's homemade toffee. It amazes her that she can still, even now, recapture the perfume as if the little lamb is in the room with her.

The two girls spent time wandering through the fields behind Trudi's house, fields that changed with the seasons. She loved the spring when they would wander through the field and occasionally stop to pick the beautiful yellow primroses growing in the hedgerow and along the banks. They arranged them into bouquets of small yellow faces which were taken home to their mothers. In the winter, the fields were covered in snow, particularly Trudi's first year in Nottinghamshire when the snow fell thick and heavy. They had great fun on Ann's homemade toboggan. Squeals of delight rang out across the snow-clad field as the taboggan moved faster and faster, gathering speed as it flew across the undulations hidden under the white blanket. Then disaster struck. A nail on the toboggan came loose. Ann asked her to stand on the toboggan whilst she tried to hit the nail back in with a stone. Trudi, keen to return to the frivolity in the snow, happily, and ignorantly, obliged. Suddenly, the toboggan moved from under her, and she fell forward into the snow. Ann's squeals of laughter echoed in Trudi's ears as she lay on the cold blanket beneath her and watched as the toboggan was pulled away. An excruciating pain then soared through her fingers, into her hand and rested in her wrist. Her whole hand and wrist were throbbing. It felt as if someone was inside thumping her hard with a hammer. Trudi pictures the young girl struggling to get up and calling out to Ann for help who, realising that her friend was hurt and that it was down to her antics, had run off. Trudi was left alone to climb the stile and walk up the path to her home, nursing an increasingly throbbing wrist. Luckily the wrist wasn't broken, just severely sprained. As the days passed, the swelling reduced and her wrist displayed various hues of blue and green, changing colour like a chameleon. Hints of yellow ran through, altering the overall effect of the colours until, after what seemed to be an interminable amount of time, her wrist was once again pink.

Trudi gives thought to how she'd been hurt by her friend, physically and emotionally. Yes, it was an accident, but would a true friend treat you in that way? She makes a connection between the feeling then and similar feelings she has experienced through the years. So many times, she has felt let down, betrayed and badly treated by friends, colleagues, family and partners. Is there a pattern, a reason or is she to blame? Hopefully, the story she is witnessing will enlighten her!

Chapter 3

The toboggan incident takes her back to the first Christmas in their new home, the fluttering butterflies in her stomach and the little bounce that was evident in her walk. Her eyes shone brightly with the growing excitement except there'd seemed to her child-based senses, an unsettling feeling.

Trudi was aware that her mum was tired all the time and was becoming more and more impatient. She thought it was due to the move and a new baby and so decided to help in any way she could. She put up the Christmas decorations and decorated the tree. She hung up the cards around the lounge but of course, as this was Trudi, the good deed turned into a wrong. The cards fell and in the process of putting them back up, she broke her mum's best vase. She was reprimanded and left with the familiar feeling of being treated, or punished, unjustly.

Christmas Eve arrived. Off to bed with an empty pillow slip as a sack which was duly placed at the end of the bed, awaiting the arrival of Father Christmas. Trudi lay in bed, closing her eyes ready for sleep, her shoulders giving an excited shrug and her body a little shiver in anticipation of the following morning. She felt as snug as a bug, wrapped up warmly in her bed and ignoring the occasional excited twitch, she drifted into a peaceful sleep.

Christmas Day. She was woken by excited squeals from her sister which informed her that Santa had been. She quickly sat up in bed, looked at Alice and then they both eagerly grabbed for their sacks which were now bulging with various shapes and sizes. Inside they found the obligatory oranges and nuts which Father Christmas left every year, along with a chocolate selection box, pants and socks, soap and other smelly stuff. Father Christmas also left clothes for their dolls, games and other little bits and bobs that contributed to their toy collection. The presents from their parents were under the Christmas tree waiting to be opened after breakfast, which was eaten faster than the speed of light. Once done, Trudi and her sisters excitedly opened their presents, wrapping paper being thrown everywhere. Shrieks of delight escaped as the long-wanted baby doll, game, or record single was found.

Whilst dinner was prepared, the three girls entertained themselves and watched Top of the Pops, singing along to the year's chart music with their voices filling the house as they joined in with Elvis singing 'Return to Sender,' the Christmas number one. Trudi's dad helped cook the Christmas dinner and the house gradually filled with the smell of roasting turkey and potatoes, the windows misting with heat from the oven. Tension between Trudi's parents rose at this time, and the heavy clattering of pans were heard; all the same, nothing could take away the joyful bliss of Christmas. Finally, dinner was served. They waited eagerly for permission to pull the crackers and to start eating the mouth-watering meal which had been placed in front of them. The dinner was followed by a rich homemade Christmas pudding, full of brandy soaked fruit which was covered in thick yellow custard or scoopings of brandy butter. Each mouthful was eaten cautiously just in case the hidden sixpence was found. A loud scream echoed around the room as the lucky person found the hidden coin, cleaning it thoroughly before placing it in their money box. Once the meal was finished, Trudi and Fran helped to clear the table and wash up, as was expected of them, whilst their parents sat in front of the television, waiting for the Queen's speech. When their chores were completed, the sisters sat quietly until the speech was over. It was at this time that their father fell asleep, helped along by the couple of rums he'd drunk with dinner. Nevertheless, he had the uncanny knack of knowing when anyone tried to change the television channel! One eye opened, his head shook from side to side and his mouth uttered a 'tutt tutt.' Operation television channel was defeated! Her mum also took herself off to bed, along with Thomas, leaving the siblings to occupy themselves as quietly as they could, so as not to disturb the sleeping parents.

Christmas tea consisted of sandwiches made from leftover turkey and home cooked ham, a variety box of special Christmas biscuits, trifle and a cake covered in white icing which stood up in points, representing the snow on the ground. Resting on the icing were the figurines of Father Christmas, a snowman and a tree, with the words 'Christmas Greetings' in silver letters standing upright on the edge of the cake. The cake had been made and decorated by Trudi's Dad. After leaving the Navy, he'd started a catering course which he was unable to finish due to finances, although the family were reaping the benefits of his newfound culinary expertise. Not just that Christmas, but nearly every following Christmas, he made fudge which melted in the mouth and toffee which stuck your teeth together as it was chewed. In addition, each Guy Fawkes' Night, he made delicious sticky apples covered in sweet gooey toffee, the sweetness of which clung to the lips long after the apple had disappeared. 'Yes, we were very lucky,' she thinks.

Christmas Day drew to a close. Trudi sat by the lounge fire, drinking a cup of hot chocolate and, as she watched the steam from the cup wafting into the air, she thought about the day that had just passed. All in all, it had been a lovely day. There was just one thing missing that would have made the day magical: snow! It was very cold, snow being forecast and falling in some areas before Christmas, but theirs had been totally missed. Feeling a little cheated, she said 'good night' to her parents and took herself to bed.

Boxing Day. Trudi awoke, shivering. She looked around the room and saw that Alice was still asleep. There was a different light in the room, a silvery glow that twinkled like tiny little white stars. She stepped out of bed, feeling the cold because the heating wasn't on yet. There seemed to be a magical air mixed in with the twinkling light. Could it be? She slowly pulled back the curtain and, holding her breath eagerly, gazed out of the window. She watched breathlessly as tiny white flakes quietly fell from a sky which looked ready to let go of its heavy contents at any moment. The snowflakes increased in size, falling with more intensity. They gently hit the ground where they formed a soft white blanket which looked clean and smooth, waiting for someone to disturb it. Trudi turned to Alice. She shook her excitedly and shouted at the top of her voice, 'it's snowing!' The day was spent wrapped up warm in coats, scarves and gloves, throwing snowballs and making snowmen. Trudi and her sisters wanted to make the most of this before school started back.

Then, Christmas was over, the New Year had begun and the start of the new term was round the corner, regardless of the snow, as the pupils and teachers all lived within walking distance of the school. Trudi thinks of the freezing walk she did four times a day, morning, lunchtime and afternoon. School dinners weren't provided in the small village schools, making it necessary to go home for lunch. It was a mad scramble, especially with a little sister in tow who preferred to walk lazily along and capture the wonders of nature. Time was also dependent upon the day of the week and the chores her mum had to do.

Mondays are the days that Trudi remembers the most. She has an image of herself walking through the kitchen door and her nose being greeted by the aroma of the evening meal on the cooker, usually one made from leftovers from the Sunday joint. This mingled with the soapy perfume of washing powder escaping from the twin tub washing machine. Her mum was standing on a wet floor, surrounded by washing that was waiting to be placed in the machine. A two tub machine sat in front of the sink with hoses, which, after being attached to the taps, hung precariously over the tubs. Hot water poured from one into the larger tub, where the machine heated it further, and soap powder was sprinkled in. The soapy fragrance was enhanced as the rotary arms kicked into action, mixing vigorously until froth began to form. In went the washing, churning round and round, water spilling onto the floor as it splashed over the sides. Tongs were used to lift the washing into the spinning tub, which was filled with cold water using the other hose. More water on the floor! The lid was closed and the not so gentle hum of the spinner began. As it spun faster, the noise became louder, as water was pumped through a hose into the sink; meanwhile the next load of washing was placed into the machine. So, the process continued, until the washing on the floor had disappeared, the machine emptied of all signs of water, leaving an ever growing puddle to be mopped up. Trudi and her sister sat eating their lunch in silence, taking in the scene around them until school beckoned.

Trudi thinks of those days with fondness and notices for the first time how happy she was back then. Maybe she just isn't allowed to experience happiness, for, once again, it had been taken away. Change was around the corner, in the form of another move. Her dad had the opportunity of a job transfer, back to the South of England, and it was felt that this would be a good opportunity for all the family. And so, the upheaval began.

To begin with, until their house was sold and a new one found, her dad lived away during the week, and it felt to Trudi as if he was being taken away again. Even as a mature woman, she can recapture the eagerness she felt as a child, whilst she waited impatiently for his return. 'Wow! It also reminds me of the times I waited for Robert to come back,' she suddenly realises. She would sit by the window, waiting impatiently for the sound of her dad's car wheels on the drive and watch eagerly for that familiar figure to walk towards the front door. Occasionally, as he was home later than expected, she was in bed when he finally arrived, even so he always popped into her room to say goodnight. She detects him standing next to her bed and it feels as if he's back in the room with her. She senses his presence, the unspoken love and the invisible hugs. How she wishes the words had been spoken and the hugs given. Now it's too late, or is it? She shivers as she feels an energy close by and whispers 'I love you, Dad;' a voice whispers back 'and **I** love you.' 'Ok. Back to the story,' she says firmly.

The house was filled with boxes which were piled everywhere. Some of them were already full, others empty, one of which was waiting to carry the precious toys that Trudi had so recently unpacked. She picked up her teddies and dolls one by one, kissing them tenderly before placing them into the dark box. She leaned inside and quietly said, 'don't be afraid. I'll see you all soon' and closed the lid. Her room was empty apart from the furniture and the melancholy air lingering close by, waiting to be transported too.

The day of the move arrived. She'd already said goodbye to her friends. All that remained for her to do was to say goodbye to the house and wipe away the territorial markings that she'd made on first arriving. She silently climbed the stairs and entered her bedroom. She walked slowly around the room placing a gentle kiss on each wall as she passed by. She allowed a tear to fall as she whispered 'goodbye' to each one in turn. One last look out of the window that had brought her the magical snow that first Christmas and then she descended the stairs.

Trudi immerses herself in the heart ache as she watches the little girl wandering through the house kissing each wall in turn as she said her fond farewells. Perhaps all these goodbyes and changes had affected her more than she realised. Is this why she always became attached to houses, to people, to places? Is this why she is still frightened that things or people will be taken away? She can see how past events map the future, how the shadows darken the path. Perhaps if she'd had the insight as a child she could have prevented, or at least been prepared for, some of the experiences she's had to endure. Back then she was ten years old, unaware of what the future held and had been preparing for the next stage of her life. Stage? Yes, that is exactly how Trudi now perceives her life. A stage dramatising the events of a character's life from the tragic novels that she's read. She's often laughed disbelievingly, when reading these types of novels, wondering if it is truly possible for so many things to happen to one person. She now knows it is. Her life is definitely a stage, a stage set with romance, humour and tragedy. Shakespeare comes in to her mind - 'all the world's a stage, and all the men and women merely players.......' No truer words had ever been spoken. Her moonlit stage below is now set for the next scene. She takes a deep breath and waits for it to begin. The move.

Trudi has memories of the move going smoothly and being a completely different scenario to the previous! This time there were no guinea pigs, no carrycot, just the family and a few bags. All other belongings and treasured items were in a big removal van which she, with mixed emotions, had watched being loaded into the big removal truck. There was sorrow at leaving the familiarity of her surroundings and the friends she'd made, as well as a thrill when she considered the new adventures awaiting her. What the new chapter in her life would bring was anybody's guess; she hoped beyond all hope that it would bring cheer and contentment, safety and security. Trudi witnesses a little girl who was slowly hiding away, becoming a shadow herself, whilst desperately seeking a solid base on which she could build her future. A firm base on which her family could stand strong, sharing a future which was filled with the love she so desperately needed.

Chapter 4

The story continues with the family car pulling into the drive of their new home. Trudi was gazing out of the car window, admiring the view that was being presented to her. The first thing she noticed was the beautiful roses in the front garden and, as she stepped from the car, she detected their sweet, fresh perfume filling the air. There was a large expanse of lawn from which semi-circular stone steps opened on to a path which led to the front door. From the driveway the path ran all the way round the house and through a black wrought iron gate to the rear. The gate called to Trudi, tempting her to open it. She went through and followed the path which took her along the side of a pebble dashed garage and continued until she came upon a large garden that was split into two levels. There was a hedge running along the length of the garden, acting as a dividing screen. On one side of the screen there was a soft carpet of green grass edged with flower beds and on the other an expanse of earth, waiting to become her father's vegetable plot. To one side of the garden, a washing line ran along the whole length of another path, attaching itself to two concrete posts at either end. The paths joined at the bottom, forming a T junction, and continued around the other side of the house. Here she found a wooden gate leading to the front, completing a full circle around the house. This circular route, she recollects, soon became a running circuit and a great source of amusement as the three younger siblings chased each other round and round, squeals of delight echoing as the sound bounced off the surrounding walls.

The house itself was another, older, chalet bungalow. On entering the front door, a narrow hallway led to the lounge, a spare room, a bedroom, bathroom and kitchen. In the middle of one kitchen wall there was a deep hollow in which sat a coke boiler; a black pipe rose from it, acting as a means of escape for the emerging smoke. During the winter, coke was shovelled into the top to keep the fire burning, providing the family with hot water and feeding heat to the one and only radiator which could be found in the hallway. The boiler was very often used as a seat by bodies desperately seeking warmth from the outside cold air. Trudi gives a chuckle. 'I remember fighting over who was going to get there first. I was back to warming clothes under my eiderdown and, if I'm right, Jack Frost also returned!'

Upstairs was accessed by a steep wooden staircase along which ran a black wrought iron banister with a wooden handrail sitting on top, to ease the somewhat unnerving climb. The stairs began with a little twist and each step was open at the back. 'Oh yes, that horrible staircase!' As the picture materialises in Trudi's mind, nausea forms in her stomach as she relives the day she slipped from top to bottom. She was fourteen at the time. The incident followed a day at the fair where she was propelled round and round on a Waltzer by a young male attendant who pushed her chair vigorously as the ride took its circular route. On the chair went, up and down, round and round, until it slowed and finally stopped. Her head was spinning faster than the ride itself! Her legs wobbled like jelly as she climbed off with the feeling of liquid rising from the pit of her stomach and a burning sensation as it formed a puddle in the back of her throat. The contents of her stomach emptied where she stood, and her head continued to spin as she was led back to the car by her parents. This affected Trudi's balance for several days after, hence the stair incident. One minute she was standing at the top, feeling like the bee's knees dressed in her new mini skirt and heeled shoes, the next she was at the bottom nursing her wounded pride!

At the top of the stairs, a small landing led to two bedrooms on either side. The bedrooms had sloping ceilings, which became a useful display area for her posters of the pop group she idolised. One room was smaller than the other, but large enough for Trudi and Alice to share. It felt cosy and she loved gazing out of the window onto the neighbouring field below. The field gave her a sense of comfort and familiarity, reminding her of the one she'd left behind. It didn't actually resemble that field in any way. There were no animals, only long grass and wildflowers but it gave her mind a place in which to escape.

Once settled in her new home, Trudi began to explore the neighbourhood, which was a complete contrast to the village life she'd so recently experienced. There were signs of an old village hidden amongst the previously extensive gardens of large older properties and, with effort and close attention, traces could be found in the new housing estates that were popping up in the once green fields. The past was blending with the present, concealing secrets that were waiting to be discovered. 'Now that is so apt,' she shares with the moon. 'My past is blending with my future. I hope, Mr Moon, that my hidden secrets will be revealed and healed!'

Alongside the neighbouring field ran a dirt track where evidence of long ago could be found. On one side, a few large very old houses bordered the length of the track whilst on the other a small babbling stream wound its way in search of its journey's end. The dirt track led its way through an avenue of trees which enriched the hints of the past, with wildflowers and long grass decorating the stream's bank. The track continued its journey until a small stile appeared. Climbing over the stile, Trudi found herself on a narrow grassy path, enclosed by hedgerows and brambles with tall ancient trees towering above her. The light was dimmed by them and cast shadows over the track which danced as the sun broke through, lighting the path with waving patterns. As she walked, she thought of the journey she used to make to her friend's farm, the fun she'd had and hoped she would make new friends when she started the new school. Her wandering mind stopped as she found herself inside a dark tunnel, with light tantalisingly beckoning to her at either end. As she was deciding whether to continue or turn back, a thundering sound echoed around her as what she could only describe as a monster rattling its way across the tunnel. The echo was almost deafening and the tunnel walls seemed to tremble as the monster made its way above her. Trudi peeped her head out, gazing cautiously as the thundering monster travelled on. She breathed a sigh of relief. A train! Her gaze was then caught by the wildflowers growing on the embankment, bringing beauty to the metal track which had transported the roaring monster. She clambered up the grassy bank, picking flowers as she went. She sat on the grass, arranging the flowers into a small bouquet for her mum, just as she had with Ann. Holding the bouquet carefully in her hand, Trudi made her way back down to the path; it was time to return home. The adventure could be finished another day.

The day of starting school was soon upon her and Trudi braced herself for the unknown. It wasn't completely unfamiliar as she was returning to the school at which she'd begun her education, but this time Fran wouldn't accompany her, Trudi would be taking Alice. The school, like her surroundings, was a deep contrast to the Victorian village school with its polished wood and fixed desks. This was more modern and far bigger. There were two entrances, one for the Infant pupils and another for the Juniors. The Infants' door opened onto a long narrow corridor, along which two classrooms could be found. Outside the classroom sat the crates of small silver foiled topped glass bottles filled with milk ready for the morning break, milk which was becoming warmer by the minute. In the hotter months, the cream sitting on top of the milk thickened which gave off a rich creamy odour once the bottles were opened. In the winter, the cream froze, pushing the silver foil lid away from the top of the bottle, revealing the frozen cover which had formed over the milk. There were usually tell-tale signs of birds having attacked the foil with their sharp beaks, leaving little holes as they attempted to steal some of the cream. It was supposed to be an honour when asked to be milk monitor, but it was one which Trudi had disliked immensely, mainly because of the smell. She feels nauseous as she calls to mind the putrid stench of warm, creamy milk which awakens in her nostrils as if it has been lying dormant for many years. The odour which seemed to linger in the room for eternity. The sickening stench which became entrenched in any piece of carpeting after a child brought up the contents of the bottle that had previously been swallowed. Luckily for her, she'd been given permission not to have the milk and spent the rest of her life avoiding creamy milk wherever possible! 'Thank goodness for skimmed milk' she mutters.

The first classroom had, just five years ago, been her very first and was for those children just starting school; the second was for the older Infants. The tables were formica topped, behind which were set little wooden chairs with metal legs, so different to those she'd used before. The floors were covered in vinyl with a large mat resting in one corner waiting for wooden bricks, cars and children to spill on to it once they were released from the grips of the morning session of the three R's. Another mat acted as a home corner containing a cooker, sink, utensils, table and chairs. On the walls the alphabet was displayed, accompanied by a few words from the reading book that was being introduced to the class. The windows in the rooms were lower and larger than in her previous school, allowing the light to illuminate the room and from which the playground could be seen, displaying various painted markings on which the children could play.

Further down the corridor were the toilets and cloakroom. Golden hooks protruded from the wall waiting to be cluttered with bags and coats. Metal mesh baskets sat under a wooden bench into which P.E. bags were pushed. Trudi takes a deep breath and conjures up the childhood smell that hung in the air. The odour of sweaty plimsoles mixing with the disinfectant used to disguise, unsuccessfully, the smell oozing from the toilets. The Infants' section was separated from the Juniors by two big glazed wooden doors which led to the school hall, positioned directly opposite. This was a large room. It was used for whole school assemblies as well as P.E. Ropes were tied back against the wall and other equipment was stored in a cupboard nearby, all biding time with expectation of giving Trudi an experience which was very different to the old-fashioned star jumps outside. The floor was polished wood only made with smaller strips than the Victorian school. The hall was surrounded on each side by long glass windows from which hung heavy curtains. Similar curtains hung on either side of a wooden stage on which, during assembly, the Headteacher took centre, speaking his words of wisdom and glowering at anyone who dared to move.

The corridor then turned, opening into a larger reception area where the Headteacher's office and staff room could be found. The external Juniors' door also led into this area before the corridor narrowed and made its way to the two Junior classrooms. In these rooms, wooden desks sat in rows of two, each having a top which lifted, presenting a space in which to store books. A ridge for holding pens ran along the top of the desk, stopping at a redundant ink well as fountain pens with ink cartridges were now in use. At the front sat the teacher's wooden table, the top of which was cluttered with an array of pens and exercise books. On the wall behind, a blackboard stretched across, the blackness waiting to be disturbed by the screech of white chalk. It was in front of the blackboard that her teacher stood, hand poised ready to portray his verbal words on the board or write a list of mathematical sums which had to be copied into an exercise book and answered before the end of the lesson. He moved along the front row of desks, talking as he walked, emphasising each word as a bubbly wetness formed at the corner of his mouth as he spoke. Trudi chuckles as she recollects sitting in the front row and dodging the spittle that sprayed from the teacher's mouth with each word he uttered. Not a pleasant experience!

She is shown the two doors at either end of the building. One led on to a tarmac quadrangle which was used at playtime, where, hidden in the corners, were netball posts, ready to be placed in position during a lesson. A gap opened on to a playing field which was used for Sport's Day as well as P.E. It was here that Trudi experienced apprehension about playing rounders again, a worry that was unfounded. This time there were no flying bats hurling towards her head. There were enough bats for the whole team! More importantly, there was no competition between friends. Each team had a set captain. All anxieties put aside, she was able to show that she had developing skills in both rounders and netball and exhibited a competence in sport she didn't know she had. She also proved herself to be an excellent sprinter, taking part in local team races and feeling very proud when, having won a race, she appeared in the local paper. It gave her an inkling of self-worth.

The second door was in the Infants' section which led across a tarmac drive to the dinner hall that could only be described as a Nissen hut. It was a long dark concrete building, with a curved metal roof and windows so small, light had to fight to find a way through. Inside was a hard, painted, concrete floor which sparkled occasionally when sunlight successfully found an opening through which to shine and illuminate the coloured particles mixed within the flooring. Formica tables were set in rows on each side of a gangway, anticipating the hungry children that would fill them. At the far end was the dreaded hatch from which hard-faced ladies served tasteless dinners that Trudi would gladly have missed. She recaptures the feeling of dread that she experienced as she walked down the cold dark gangway to face the expressionless woman waiting to thrust the meal into her hands. The unappetising meal, served on a hardening plastic plate, a meal she was expected to eat, not one scrap left. Bile rises in her throat as she imagines the wilting salad served with warm processed mashed potato. A round scoop of potato, falling fiercely on to the plate as the dinner lady emptied the contents of a spoon from a great height. Once, Trudi recalls having found the courage to ask not to have any potato which she then discovered hiding under a warm wilting piece of lettuce.

Trudi is reminded of another incident where she was again treated unfairly. It was forbidden to go through the door leading to the dinner hut without being escorted by a teacher. She knew that this was for the children's safety and abided by the rules, something she always did, which made it increasingly difficult for her to understand why her 'goodness' led to trouble. Wet playtimes, pupils were permitted to play with toys and puzzles in the corridor which housed the forbidden door. On one occasion, a boy threw Trudi's puzzle on to the step, just outside the prohibited door. The 'good girl' sprang into action. With one foot inside and the other on the step, she began to pick up the pieces. The next moment, she was standing outside the Headteacher's room. No questions. No investigation. Her 'good girl' was dealt yet another unjustified blow and the culprit got away scot-free. Trudi thinks back to when she was 'responsible' for the girl wetting herself and when she'd broken her mum's favourite vase. Then, the incident of breaking the window in the door also pops into her mind. It had happened in Nottinghamshire. She was being the exemplary child, clearing the Sunday tea plates, washing up and ensuring that the teapot was emptied and cleaned. It was customary for the teapot to be emptied in the garden as the tea leaves functioned as a food for the plants. Knowing this was the case, Trudi went to the backdoor, her hands carrying the teapot very carefully. She pushed the handle down with her elbow and, as the door tended to stick, used her bottom to help the door open. Unfortunately, her bottom went through the window and another good deed ended with her in trouble.

The memoires resume. Trudi, despite the continued uncomfortable rumblings beneath, was enjoying school life and had become friends with a girl who lived close by. At the start of their friendship, she and Sarah were inseparable. They usually spent time at Sarah's house after school, listening to music and chatting endlessly about anything and everything. Occasionally, if allowed, the two girls would while away the time at Trudi's house. This didn't happen often as her mum was 'too tired to cope', words that were being uttered more and more frequently. Then the twosome became three as Julie joined the friendship. They often spent time at Julie's enormous house that was set in a vast garden where an area of gigantic bamboo plants could be found. This became a den, a little hideaway, where the girls would sit for hours, hidden from the outside world. She was happier sharing her time with just Julie but withdrew when they were a three as she often felt pushed aside. She was more contented in a one-to-one situation where she felt her presence was acknowledged and that she was seen as a person in her own right. In a larger group, she merged with everyone else until she completely faded into the shadows.

Feelings of anger grow within Trudi as she becomes overwhelmed by those childhood feelings which she's continued to experience in her adult life. Here she is, a grown woman, still allowing her shadows from the past to affect her and her life. Like Mr Moon told her at the start of the journey, it is time to release and free herself. It is time to let go and fly.

Chapter 5

The curtain on the moonlit stage opens on the next part of Trudi's life – Secondary school. It was larger than her Primary school, with a sizeable playground at the front and a sport field at the rear. Classrooms were spread over two floors, with additional concrete buildings in the playground. Pupils were streamed according to their ability and placed on the appropriate level for registration, 'O' level pupils upstairs, CSE pupils downstairs and those not working at exam level were in the playground's concrete buildings, known as the M stream. No one seemed to know what the M stood for. All Trudi knew was that she must not be in that stream and so, was relieved when she discovered her tutor room was to be upstairs. She encountered the new experience of having a different teacher for each lesson which brought about the necessity to move swiftly around the school in order to arrive at the next lesson on time. Bustling from one room to another made her feel 'grown-up', taking it all very seriously as she hurried along weighed down by her brown satchel which was bursting with books. The movement and over laden satchel created an air of importance for her. A chuckle escapes as she realises that this air of importance has continued into adult life in her role as a teacher. The more overloaded she is, the more important she feels. Or is this symbolic of her life and the heavy, hidden bag of emotions?

The school smelt similar to the Primary school: polish mixing with disinfectant accompanied by the addition of cigarette smoke which could be seen billowing from the staff room each break. The cloakrooms held the same odour of sweaty plimsoles and P.E. kit except it was far stronger, the number and size of the pupils intensifying the stench that was hanging in the air. Opposite the cloakroom was a large hall with another stage stretching across its width. It was upon this stage, she remembers, that she once nervously stood during assembly, waiting to read a passage from the Bible. Her nervousness deepened as she looked upon the sea of faces below her, knowing that many of them would laugh. After taking a deep breath she began to read. She was fine until she had to read **that** word. A word so innocent yet to a naive eleven year old a word so embarrassing. Naked. It slipped out of her mouth very quietly but loud enough to fall upon the ears of those who found it highly amusing. Sniggers began to reverberate around the hall, moving along the lines like a Mexican wave. '**Silence**' boomed from the Headteacher. Trudi quickly finished her reading and slipped silently back into her place with a face as red as a beetroot. 'Another example of something good turning bad,' she mutters.

A path ran alongside the outside wall of the hall which, with the help from the wall opposite, formed a large quadrangle in the middle of which sat a wooden hut. The wooden hut was Trudi's French classroom and became a minefield of frustration waiting to explode. She enjoyed French and was determined to pass the 'O' level exam. Unfortunately, the teacher wasn't fully committed to his profession, preferring to listen to cricket matches rather than teach. This riled her to such a degree that the smouldering embers within ignited and a fire began to rage. Like an erupting volcano, she opened her mouth allowing the molten lava of words to flow with such force that even she was surprised. Courageously, she accused him of being an appalling teacher. She had a reply for every comment he threw at her, stating that respect had to be earned and that listening to cricket instead of teaching wasn't the way. The teacher ordered her to leave and present herself to the Head. This she duly did, slamming the rotting wooden door as she marched forcefully from the room. She left behind her a split door hanging on by a hinge, a teacher with smoke coming out of his ears and a classroom of bemused faces. Although she was severely spoken to for being rude to a teacher, it was worth it as, for the first time, she felt strong. She'd found a hidden strength and courage which she could call upon when needed. 'I was completely unaware that I would need those qualities quite as soon as I did and, again, in the far-off future,' she mutters.

Trudi didn't enjoy the time at Secondary school. She found most of the teachers intimidating and unapproachable; they filled her with panic, making her want to hide. Chalk or blackboard rubbers were frequently hurled at pupils who weren't paying attention or answered questions incorrectly. She often found herself breaking out in a nervous sweat, her stomach churning in dread of the teacher asking her a question. Geography was the worst. A map of England was drawn, by the teacher, on the blackboard with red dots representing towns or rivers. The whole class had to stand. One by one they were asked to give a name to a red dot indicated by the teacher's cane which hovered menacingly over it. On giving the correct answer, the pupil was allowed to sit. The last one standing was named the class doughnut, a title Trudi was determined to avoid, her willpower being driven by fear rather than the prospect of success.

Then there were the horrendous P.E. lessons or at least the ensuing showers. She enjoyed P.E. itself, just not the showers! After each P.E. lesson it was obligatory to have one. The girls all filed into a cold changing room where, behind a dark green brick wall, a row of showers waited. It was all so undignified to Trudi. She found it embarrassing to strip naked, shower with a group of girls whilst the teacher watched over them. 'This wouldn't be allowed nowadays,' she utters in disgust. She shudders as she is transported back into the shower room, remembering how it became a mission to head to the showers as quickly as her legs would carry her to reach them before the teacher arrived. Trudi thinks how deceptive, but clever, she was when she, and a few other girls, fully clothed, splashed water appropriately over their hair as well as the floor, to successfully give the appearance of having showered. A thumbs up and a pat on the back for being strong and standing in the power!

Trudi always concentrated on her schoolwork, keeping her head down to evade trouble, both at school and at home. There were constant arguments between her parents and Fran. Her mum cried a great deal, for no apparent reason, and always appeared to be exhausted, finding it hard to carry out normal daily tasks. She'd recently taken an evening job, working for a couple of hours each evening after school. As Fran was also working, it became, at the age of twelve, Trudi's responsibility to look after her younger brother and sister until her mum returned. Consequently, her social life dwindled. Whilst her friends were out enjoying life and being young, she was becoming a young adult with responsibilities.

A lump climbs in Trudi's throat as the night a man came knocking on the door springs to mind and she feels the same panic inside her stomach she felt at the age of twelve. He was looking for his son and was convinced that Thomas, whom he'd seen playing, was he. No matter how much Trudi argued, the man wouldn't believe that Thomas wasn't his son. There she was, twelve years old, with a madman at the door, a sister with chickenpox and a brother playing outside. She felt totally helpless. Suddenly Thomas appeared from around the corner of the house. Time seemed to stand still as she leapt forward, grabbed Thomas, pulled him inside and slammed the door, which she locked as fast as her fingers would allow. Running round the house in a frenzy, she locked all the doors and windows. What should she do now? Her mother wasn't expected back for at least another hour and there was no phone. She decided her only option was to ask her neighbour for help. Her brother and sister were instructed to stay in the lounge and not to open any doors whilst she went for help. The Police were contacted who duly arrived, along with her mum. The man was escorted away and their neighbour took Trudi's mum back to her house for a drink to calm her nerves; she returned home an hour later, a little merrier than when she'd left! Although it is presently amusing to remember her mum's return to the house, Trudi suddenly realises that in it all she, herself, had been forgotten. She can't remember anyone asking how she was or even saying 'well done'. No one had considered this little girl's feelings or given a thought to how she was affected by the traumatic event that had happened. She was invisible, like the moon behind a cloud, an invisibility which was thickening with each passing experience.

The weekends brought respite from her childcare duties which enabled her to spend time with Julie and Sarah, except she became aware of a change in their friendship. She wasn't in their stream at school and so the friendship between Julie and Sarah deepened, leaving her an outsider. She'd made friends with three other girls who were in her tutor group and decided to concentrate on building a friendship with them. She thought it was going well; however, Georgia, Bryony and Isla were strong personalities, more worldly wise than she. Trudi also found that her family responsibilities were affecting her friendship as, nine times out of ten, she was unable to accompany her friends when they went out and before long, they stopped asking her to join them.

As a woman she can fully understand the reasoning behind the behaviour of her friends; as a young girl it had been another rejection. She realises that she'd also, subconsciously, felt anger towards her friends, but more so towards her mum and the situation she'd found herself in. Life seemed so unfair. Trudi shouts out at life, 'I was waiting for you to offer me experiences full of fun and laughter that I, as a young girl, should have been allowed. Instead, I was forced to carry a burden which, I can now see, was weighing me down. I was wearing a cloak of heavy lead on my shoulders, which became heavier as each day passed.' The grown woman feels the fury welling inside her, twisting around her stomach, gathering momentum like the energy inside that old sleeping volcano before it erupts. She feels sick to the core as she becomes aware of the anger she'd obviously felt as a child which mixes with the lethal mixture of rejection and loneliness that has accumulated over the years. A mixture she's swallowed which has turned into a hard lump and clings as it tries, unsuccessfully, to manoeuvre its way down the oesophagus. It sticks and sits firm waiting to be forcefully spewed into the universe, to be released and forgotten, bringing Trudi the emotional freedom she craves. She looks questioningly at the moon. 'Is this what you're helping me do?'

At the time, she contented herself with the fact that she at least wouldn't be alone at school, spending as much time as she was able with her friends. Her mum, though, was becoming increasingly tired, in fact, too tired to get up in the mornings. This meant Trudi had to take Thomas to playschool, resulting in her arriving late for school. Even with a letter of explanation from her parents, she was frequently questioned about her late arrival by teachers and friends. All she knew was that her mum was too tired, which painted a picture of a very lazy parent. She, herself, had begun to wonder why although thought it unwise to voice her curiosity. She simply did as requested by her parents and asked no questions. Often, her mother would be resting in the afternoons when she returned from school. She was still able to prepare and cook meals for the family, with Trudi's help, even though she found it exhausting. She'd stopped working in the evenings and was gradually spending more and more time in bed, her role as 'mum' diminishing day by day. She found eating difficult and when she did eat, it didn't stay inside her for long and her bodily weight was disappearing as quickly as ice melts. Life, nevertheless, carried on regardless. No concern was voiced by anyone, not even by the Doctor who informed the family it was a bad tummy bug and she'd get over it. Trudi and her siblings carried on to the best of their ability, being left to their own devices with strict instructions not to disturb their mother. An unspoken air of despondency and anguish seeped from every nook and cranny in the house, which was slowly being absorbed by Trudi's life force and soul.

The illness worsened. Trudi's mum was now unable to keep any food down and was finding it increasingly difficult to get out of bed. Weeks had passed by. Weight continued to disappear and soon she became completely bedridden, having no energy to lift herself up. She was carried from room to room like a weightless feather by her husband. He cradled her in his arms, looking as if he was carrying a bag of bones as well as the weight of the world on his shoulders. He appeared lost, not knowing which way to turn and there were no signs of her mum's health improving. Then, an angel, in the form of Trudi's Aunt May, stepped in to help.

Aunt May was a positive, determined, strong lady and was the type of person who easily took control of situations with such a presence of command that no one questioned or doubted. She brought a sense of peace, a feeling that at last someone was steering a lost ship back on course. She began by attempting to improve the energy levels of Trudi's mum by feeding her steamed fish, a smell that filled the whole house. An odour which, even in the present time, makes Trudi gag as the memories associated with the fishy smell flood her mind and nostrils. The steamed fish worked for a while, but soon her mum's stomach was refusing that too. Aunt May then insisted that another opinion was sought because she was adamant that it was more than gastro enteritis. She was the one who demanded for a consultant to visit. She was the one who was strong and forceful and without whom Trudi would have lost her mum forever.

The episode opens on bonfire night. People around were busily preparing for the night's festivities and the early evening sky was already filling with a mixture of sounds and exploding colours. Except in Trudi's house, the family were preparing for the unknown. Her mum was in bed, the family quietly occupying themselves, waiting for their dad to begin the firework display. There was a knock on the door. It was an eerie knock which filled the house with a sense of foreboding. As the door opened, Trudi saw a tall man in a suit carrying a black bag bulging at the sides due to the contents hidden within. He disappeared into her mum's bedroom. Time slowly passed. The tall man reappeared, his gaze falling briefly on the young faces peering up at him. He smiled hesitantly before fixing his eyes firmly on their dad and asked to speak to him alone. Minutes later, the man stood by their dad who informed them that their mum had to go to hospital immediately. The words being uttered rang around the outside of Trudi's ears, waiting for permission to enter. She furtively glanced at her brother and sisters. Fran was standing rigid and motionless, the weight already bearing down on her shoulders. Thomas had wrapped his arms around the legs of Fran, his eyes wide as he stared at his dad, not really understanding the situation. Alice looked pale, her beautiful blue eyes misting with the wetness induced by the tears beginning to form. As quickly as they appeared, they were gone, wiped away by her little hand leaving no trace of emotion's brief visit. The words then fell upon Trudi, as if falling upon deaf ears. Despite hearing a muffled sound, she didn't allow the words to absorb into her consciousness. The moment froze, until the tall man began to move. Slowly, very slowly, she watched helplessly as her mum was taken. Taken on a bed with wheels. Taken through the door, leaving a cavernous hole behind her. There were no tears, no protests, just acceptance as she watched her mum being put in an ambulance, not knowing when, or if, she would see her again. The family stared silently in the doorway as the ambulance faded into the distance, the flashing blue lights merging with the exploding colours already present in the sky.

Time that had stood still suddenly sprang back into life, as if it had abruptly woken from a dream. The family spilled into the back garden, the recent event brushed safely under the carpet or placed in invisible bags, ready to watch the firework display and eat the gooey toffee apples made earlier by her dad. Thunderous noise echoed around the neighbourhood as the fireworks emptied their contents across the night sky, painting beautiful patterns as they exploded in the atmosphere. Trails of smoke appeared as the colours faded from view, reminding Trudi of how her mum had so recently disappeared from her life like a puff of smoke. She looked around at her family wondering if they too felt as empty as she did, vacant of all emotion yet a yearning to know that the future was bright. A longing to know that her mum would return, that the family would be complete once more.

Trudi visualises that night with perfect clarity. She sees herself looking at her dad and finding no expression, no feelings visible except for a veil of despondency over his eyes. A wretchedness he was unable to share which later escaped in the form of anger and intolerance. She recollects how she knew instinctively that she must withdraw, keep her head down and plod her way through the darkening tunnel that had formed in front of her. She senses the chaos, the pain of that little girl who was praying hard that there would be a glimmer of light waiting at the end. She also remembers the uneasy feeling she'd had in Nottinghamshire and realises that, even back then, it had been her intuition attempting to warn her that something wasn't right. Now she knows what that was.

Chapter 6

The months that followed are portrayed with her inside a tunnel that only welcomed darkness and teased the miniscule fragments of light to cast shadows along its wall. The emptiness within her had grown and created an ever deepening cavity at the bottom of which her invisible bag was waiting eagerly to receive the unexpressed emotions that were hurtling towards it.

Life was carrying on as normally as possible except there were additional responsibilities being put on to the already heavy burden. Tension was forever present between Fran and her dad whilst Trudi was walking on eggshells, somehow aware that the slightest trigger would cause an explosion. Fran, at sixteen years old, had left her job so that she could look after the family. She did her utmost to keep the family fed and watered, except this didn't always meet the expectations of their dad. It was at these times that despondency and nervousness reared their ugly heads from the abyss below, in the form of anger and added more fuel to the already burning fire. Fran had put her life on hold to care for them all. In fact, the upheaval had distressed the whole family, but not one of them voiced how they were feeling. Each family member was burying their head in the sand, along with unshared emotions which would hide there until released sometime in the future.

Fran tried her best to keep the household running smoothly, something that Trudi has only recently fully appreciated. Her sister's escape from the turmoil and pressures was seeing her boyfriend which helped her to keep some sense of sanity; Trudi's escape was to withdraw. She sank more and more into herself, performing in a robotic fashion – a robot that had been programmed to function and cope with any eventuality. Her dad was tired and lifeless; he was also short-tempered and it was Fran who received the brunt of it. Everyone learnt not to upset their father and avoidance tactics were put in place, usually in the form of keeping quiet, keeping out of the way and doing as requested. Unless you were Fran who stood her ground, which resulted in she and her dad poised like two animals preparing to fight for survival. Head to head combats became more and more frequent whilst Trudi attempted to shield her younger siblings to protect them from more anguish. Her need to withdraw was intensifying, to protect herself just as a tortoise seeks protection by retreating into its shell.

Trudi finds herself shrouded by a dark cloak, enveloped by the shadows in the room, but the moonlight is persistent in its attempt to reveal her and her shadows. She is unable to hide or resist. The memories flood in and the wave hits her with such a force that she has the sensation of drowning. It's as if she is being pulled under by a tumultuous swell which fills her ears with a thunderous noise as she tries to surface, gasping for air. Each breath she takes crushes her soul as the images from the past and present flash before her eyes and create a collage of the experiences she's had to endure. The pain stabs teasingly at her body, working its way deeper until the sharp sword like presence pierces her heart and releases a tiny piece of the suffering that she's buried for so many years. Tears pour from her eyes, forming a cascading waterfall as they stream down her cheeks and bring with them a small sense of relief. She acknowledges the familiar feelings of aloneness and helplessness and how no one had shown comfort or support to the young girl, or any of the children. No one had been there to justify the inexplicable emotions that were penetrating her little body or help her understand and grasp that it was okay to feel that way. No one had shown her how to manage the unknown emotions and so the only thing she could do was to hide them away, ignored, but not forgotten. She reaches out to that young girl and comforts her as a mother would in an attempt to ease the pain. She tells her that everything is fine and how proud she is of the way the small girl has managed; she can let go in the knowledge that she is loved and cared for. The flood disperses and her breathing slows. A feeling of comfort washes over her and brings a sense of release.

Trudi's thoughts take her to when she visited her mum in hospital and the very mixed emotions that accompanied her. A long white, clinical corridor filled with the overpowering aroma of antiseptic led to her mum's ward. She trotted down the corridor, humming a little tune as her footsteps tapped out a rhythm on the concrete floor. The impression of being a carefree five year old joined the rhythm of her walking causing her to give way to the occasional skip. The little child inside was glimpsed briefly, but she was gradually being enveloped by the ever darkening clouds. The little girl was brought back with a jolt into the body of the burdened twelve year old as, on entering the ward, she became overwhelmed by the picture presented to her.

It was the smell she noticed first. Urine combining with disinfectant, creating an overpowering stench which churned her stomach as she struggled not to pinch her nose. The noise of snoring from sleeping patients. The incessant coughing and pitiful moans from others. Beds, once neat, ruffled by the bodies restlessly tossing and turning. Then her eyes found a woman who looked familiar. A lady who looked older than she remembered, lying in bed, surrounded by tubes and bags. Mum. She looked so frail and weak, with hardly any flesh on her bones. She managed to smile, was so pleased to see them although found talking tiring. Her bed was situated at the entrance to the ward which they later discovered was the position for patients who weren't expected to live. She'd undergone major surgery for a perforated stomach ulcer which had also shown other complications. The doctor informed them that their mum was a strong and very lucky lady. She'd fought and survived surgery against all odds. The future was looking positive, a flicker of light shining at the end of the tunnel.

It was two years later that Trudi discovered the truth. Her mum had had bowel cancer. A shocking revelation that explained why her mum had been incessantly tired for so long, why she hadn't been able to be a 'proper' mum. To this day, she still doesn't know whether her dad had known the truth from the beginning and protected his family from knowing. If he had, what a burden he'd carried whilst trying to keep a family together. What a man of great love and strength, something that Trudi has only come to realise since his passing. She wonders who'd been there for him? Who knew the feelings he'd had, how he was suffering? Everyone was quick to label him 'the big bad ogre', but she knows now that he was a man of deep feeling who was just never able to show it.

Days passed. Weeks passed. Gradually, little by little, signs of improvement were visible. The hospital bed was moved from just inside the door, to further up the ward, an indication that she was no longer at death's beckoning. There was more colour in her cheeks, her whole body was looking stronger and fuller. She was eating well and all bags and tubes had been removed. During her time in hospital, a visiting friend introduced her to a spiritual route, opening her up to the energies and healing of Guardian Angels, Spiritual Guides and prayer. It gave Trudi's mum a strength and belief which helped her through a very dark time. The doctors themselves couldn't figure out the miraculous turn around. She always said it was a miracle she pulled through, that it was the hand of God. There were certainly enough prayers said for her. Whatever the reason, she'd survived and the time came for her to return to the family nest.

Trudi's mum was finally home, with a long road of recovery ahead, including numerous sessions of chemotherapy that left her feeling drained and nauseous. However, apart from her hair thinning, her body was responding well and she gradually appeared fuller in figure. Naturally, she needed time to convalesce and recuperate from her long battle, spending a great deal of time resting in the bed that, what appeared to be a lifetime ago, had once held a frail and dying woman. Trudi is surprised to notice an element of resentfulness, as she thinks of how, on her return home from school, she would find her mum still in bed. She now perceives this as the child needing her mum back to normal, but she also recognises how desperately she'd craved for the security of a mother's love. Trudi pauses her thoughts. 'You were there when I really needed you though. You gave me love and support at the most difficult time of my life. Thank you, Mum.'

Trudi wonders if Fran too had felt angry, for their mum's return impacted greatly on her life. Due to the family commitments, Fran didn't return to work. She stayed at home doing housework, washing and cooking dinners and continued in her role as surrogate mum. However, if things were not done their mum's way it resulted in constant criticism being hurled towards Fran. She may not have had the energy to carry out the tasks herself, but she certainly had enough to oversee. Occasionally she mustered up enough strength to heave herself out of bed to check Fran's work. Fear became a silent intruder. Worry about duties not being done correctly, of their dad's wrath on finding out that Fran had allowed her mum to get up, of being too noisy or of their mum falling. Trudi presses pause. Perhaps the fear they'd felt had actually been anger. Anger for not being appreciated, thanked or treated fairly. Anger for not being given the opportunity to explain their side of the story after their dad had heard their mum's version. It was Fran, though, who became a release for her parents' frustrations, anxieties and anger. This fuelled the desperation within Fran and culminated in one heated argument after another. She was fighting for her life just as their mum had fought for hers. She desperately wanted her life back and at seventeen, who could blame her? Trudi now admires the way that Fran had fought for survival and found the courage to challenge her parents. She now understands but hadn't at the time. Back then she'd wished it would stop, that Fran would just do as she was told and not argue. She catches sight of her younger self withdrawing more, learning not to argue nor answer back – anything for a peaceful life, to be loved and embraced. She recognises the insecurity and glimpses her self-esteem disappearing like grains of sand blown by the wind.

Trudi is shown herself at thirteen years old. She was a well-developed young lady, with a curvaceous figure, which she hated. She was by no means overweight, all the same, she felt huge and the curves, to her eyes, were fat. Her sisters were both of a more slender build than she and Trudi assumed a great deal more attractive. She was teased, by family and friends, about her cleavage, the spots on her face and not forgetting the dark hair which was beginning to show on her top lip. Her legs were shapely although was told by her mum that they looked like footballer's legs. She was uncertain of the meaning behind the comment: was it the shape, the size or the hair? She began to wear baggy clothes to hide behind, grew her hair to cover her face and out came the razor. Despite being very tempted to swipe it gently across her lip, common sense prevailed and she concentrated on attacking the thick black carpet covering her legs. Instead of improving the image she held about herself, it merely emphasised the negative qualities she felt she had. It was reinforced by the fact that her friends had boyfriends, she did not. Boys weren't interested in her, so she buried herself in schoolwork and home life, feeling totally unattractive and wishing desperately that she could be like her friends. Her low self-esteem was being reinforced everywhere she turned and she felt lonelier than ever.

The summer after her mum's operation, Trudi's dad decided to take them on a family holiday to help with her mum's recovery. A cottage was rented in the Southwest of England and the family spent an enjoyable week lazing on the beach and exploring the scenery around. Her mum was looking much healthier, benefitting from the sun and Trudi was feeling happier about life. She started to allow a little contentment to filter in, to touch the outer skin of her soul which was accompanied by a sense of security in the knowledge that the family were together again. Yet, as if life would not allow her this indulgence, it dealt another blow. About a year after the major operation, her mum was taken into hospital for another one, once more the children not knowing why. She wasn't in hospital for long, but the troops were required to pick up the household responsibilities once more. In between the ironing and general housework, Trudi somehow managed to find the time to complete homework and revise for the upcoming mock exams. There was no time to wallow in self-pity or to allow emotions to take hold. The whole family appeared to resign themselves to this being the way of life. A life without their mum, full of responsibilities and unanswered questions.

It was many years later that the question was answered. Her mum had had to have an abortion. Due to the major surgery she'd previously undergone, the doctors insisted that the pregnancy was terminated and demanded upon sterilisation which had resulted in her stomach being opened up yet again. Trudi recalls the conversation she had with her mum, quite a few years later. From the way her mum had spoken, she gave the distinct impression that she blamed her husband, and not truly forgiven him, neither for the pregnancy nor for the way she felt he had treated her throughout their married life. She'd experienced a lonely marriage, one which was based on fear, or at least that was how it had been described. It wasn't as if she was mal treated or physically abused in anyway. It was his selfishness, the words he spoke, the tone of his voice, his argumentativeness. Trudi believes that it was more probable that it was based on her mum's own insecurities and shadows because she knows that this man had loved her mum deeply.

This thought reminds her of the time she found her dad out in the garden, clutching the drainpipe and crying, after her mum had another minor cancer scare. That wasn't a major problem for Trudi, it was witnessing her dad tremendously upset that caused her pain. It was by accident that she saw him as she was taking the rubbish to the dustbin. She stood still in her tracks, her heart going out to him, but did nothing. She quietly retreated into the house and pretended that she hadn't seen him. Her father had appeared so lost in his own pain and grief that she didn't think it right to intrude. Now, she wishes she had reached out to him, even silently. She wishes he'd known that she'd been there for him. Perhaps if she had he would have been able to reach out in her times of need and there've been many moments when she would have done anything to feel the love and comfort from her dad.

As if a light has been switched on inside her, she notices the similarities to her own married life. She too has felt lonely at times and is sensitive to the tone of her husband's voice. She lives with an unease brought about by her own shadows and the experiences within her marriage, though she also knows that her husband loves her beyond all doubt. The light within shines brighter as she realises that she hasn't truly forgiven. Forgiveness. An easy word to speak out loud except how does one truly forgive someone who has provoked pain so deep that it feels as if your heart is splitting into pieces and left as a broken jigsaw puzzle waiting to be put back together. Life has led her along a spiritual path, like her mum, and introduced her to spiritual teachings; she knows that if she is going to move forward in her own journey she must forgive and release all. She must forgive her dad, her mum, her husband, herself and life in general.

Chapter 7

The last part of the story has been concentrating on her dad's emotions and she is almost silently defending him, yet what about her mum? She was thought to be a moaning, demanding and unappreciative woman, but was she? Were these traits being driven by unrecognised and unhealed emotions? Were these the same as the ones recently brought to light in Trudi's own life? As she recalls listening to the words shared by her mum, she recollects how her mind had absorbed them like a sponge soaking up water, which was then left heavy with its contents ready to spill. She thinks about the sentiment hidden within the spoken words and, as she does, the heavy sponge begins to drip its contents, soaking her in its absorbed emotions. She senses the pain that her mum must have felt, the terror, the anger. Unspoken and hidden away. The pattern of her mum's life manifesting itself in her own. As the common threads in their stories form in Trudi's mind, she begins to find empathy. She makes comparisons between their two lives, a connection slowly becoming apparent. Different experiences with similar emotions and reactions. She's beginning to understand how circumstances affected her mum, from childhood through to adult. She is being pushed to consider how her mum must have felt as a child as well as a grown woman and how her mums' shadows have blended with her own, and maybe the family as a whole.

Her mum had often spoken about her childhood, the fear that she and her siblings had of their mother and it was after listening to her mum's stories, Trudi became aware of how life's experiences had affected her grandma too. Grandma Violet was a clever lady and very talented on the piano except she hadn't been able to achieve all of which she was capable. It was during the First World War that she met Fred, whom she married a few years later. He was a kind, gentle man who would dodge confrontation at all costs. This was his personality although it may also have been determined by his experiences during the war. He was fifteen at the time of subscribing into the army, falsifying his age, and had undergone horrendous conditions in the trenches, resulting in trench feet. Due to this condition, he found working difficult, thus requiring time off; money became short and soon they owed payment on the mortgage. The house was reclaimed and the family were moved into a council house, much to the dismay of Violet who was a very proud lady and felt ashamed.

Violet had an air of superiority and snobbishness about her and Trudi often wondered if her grandma had been some great lady in a previous life. The table for afternoon tea was always set as if Royalty was expected, with a lace cloth covering a highly polished wooden table. Matching china tea plates, cups and saucers were neatly arranged, waiting patiently for food to be placed upon them. It had almost seemed sacrilege to allow a crumb to fall upon them, let alone place a whole sandwich! Appropriate silver cutlery sat by the side of each plate, resting quietly on top of pretty cotton serviettes, folded in such a way that there was an uncertainty as whether it was permitted to disturb them. In the centre of the table a tiered china cake stand was placed, carrying a variety of cream cakes waiting to be devoured by lips eagerly anticipating the delicious, sweet taste. Carefully cut triangular sandwiches offering a selection of fillings were positioned on larger plates. Buttered triangular pieces of bread were presented on another, awaiting the arrival of the jam which was sitting in small glass bowls around the table. There was, of course, a small silver spoon positioned inside each bowl ready to carry the jam to the side of a tea plate where a knife would be used to spread it on to the bread. Also present were milk in a china jug, sugar cubes in a glass bowl accompanied by silver tongs and a tea pot, filled with tea, looking comfortable and cosy in its woollen coat which had been knitted by Violet. A silver strainer sat over a silver bowl ready to complete its job of catching the tea leaves as the tea was poured into the cups. 'Everything was laid out so properly, unlike mine, unless guests are expected!' she laughs.

Violet had three children: Grace (Trudi's mum), Barbara who was three years younger and Charles, born around one year later. She always made sure her children were dressed appropriately, usually in beautifully sewn or knitted home-made clothes. Their leather shoes shone brightly after being intensely polished, after all, there were appearances to keep up! All three children were brought up to present themselves well, to always behave correctly and display good manners at all times. In fact, they lived under a cloud of unrest and high expectations which simply managed to create an air of self-doubt and very low self-worth.

Whether her grandma had suffered from depression, no one knew, although her behaviour certainly pointed in that direction. She found it difficult to cope with everyday life, especially the children. She was intolerant of them, often inflicting which, nowadays, would be classed as physical abuse. Trudi's mum had told countless times how, as children, she and her siblings had cowered under the table as Violet headed towards them, leather belt in hand. Then there were the occasions when Grace was sent to her room without food or drink, for no apparent reason, receiving some comfort from Fred who secretly took her a sandwich when he returned home from work. Trudi imagines herself as that little girl and empathises as she notices the aloneness, the abandonment, the anxiety, all the feelings that she herself has felt through the years. 'No wonder,' she sighs, 'it's been passed down the line! The shadows have stayed firmly within the family. But this is where it ends!'

Trudi's mum also spoke of the fond memories that had also been made, and she is able to take solace in the fact that her mum had experienced some warmth, yet she is conscious that the damage had already been done. The jigsaw puzzle of her own life is beginning to fit together, missing pieces being replaced by pieces from her mum's as if acknowledging how lives are all interlinked and how shadows from the past linger until they are faced.

Grace attended the best school in the area where she showed great aptitude in art, something she'd revealed at a very early age. This, along with many other attributes, weren't acknowledged by Violet who merely commented on the successes and abilities of others. 'Hmmm! Who does that remind me of?' Trudi asks herself. Grace was believing herself to be incapable, worthless, beliefs with which Trudi truly empathises. After finishing school, she became a Nurse. It was the beginning of the Second World War, but this didn't prevent the young girl from enjoying life and often referred to it as 'the best time of her life.' She was living in the Nurses' home which had a strict curfew. Consequently, there were a number of occasions after a late evening's dancing, when she had to throw stones at the bedroom window and ask to be let in by another Nurse! She spent many evenings dancing in the local ballroom and it was here that she met her first true love, William. He was an American soldier who was based nearby. She was besotted with him and he with her. Many a night he took her dancing, spending as much time together as his duties would allow. Then came the day when he had to return to America. She was heart-broken, and hid in her room, not eating. Trudi recalls Grace saying that, during this emotionally difficult time, Violet unexpectedly showed support and reassurance. She takes comfort from these words which tell her that her mum had been loved by Violet. She also perceives additional links to her life emerging, a connection to when her own mother showed support and love towards her at a time when it was most needed. More and more understanding is dawning. The moon is shining brighter with each acknowledgment she makes, as if to signal that she is on the right path. This gives her the incentive to continue with her story, to discover more connections and bring healing to the line of pain and torment that has been carried for generations.

A look into Grace's life story continues at the end of the war with life trying to return to normality as much as the aftermath of war could allow. Despite rations still being enforced, Grace wasn't prevented from finding the occasional pleasures in life. One year, she and her friends embarked on a camping holiday when they spent days lazing on the beach, nights dancing and time relishing in their young carefree life. It was during this holiday that Grace met James. Whilst walking along the path, she stopped to fasten a shoe strap when a voice called out 'do you need help?' She looked round to see a shortish man with a very receding hairline. He appeared to be a complete show off and she wasn't attracted to him at all. He just wasn't her type, nevertheless, she knew that this was the man she would marry; they married one year later.

Grace's married life began by living separately from her new husband. He was in the Navy and his Naval Station was in the South of England but they had no house to call their own. Consequently, she remained with her parents and he with his, meeting only at the weekends. Within a few months, Grace discovered that she was pregnant which made it even more important for the couple to be together. James' parents offered to buy a larger house that could be split in to two flats; they would live upstairs, James and Grace downstairs, to which the couple agreed. Although grateful, she found it very difficult to feel part of the new family and missed her own incredibly. Her husband's family appeared overbearing and a complete contrast to her own. She felt more and more alone and was immensely homesick which deepened as each day passed. Then baby Fran was born, filling part of the gap in Grace's life. A little baby so innocent and pure, unaware of the part she would play in creating a triangle of conflicting affection and emotions.

Just a few weeks after the birth of his daughter, James was called away on duty. He sailed away, leaving his wife and baby Fran in the suffocating bosom of his family. Grace did later come to realise that his family's 'interference' had been delivered with good intentions, at the time, though, she received it with resentment. Advice on how to feed, how to stop Fran crying and other general comments were forcefully shared by Victoria, James's mum. His siblings were constantly in the house creating havoc and frivolity with Arthur, James' dad, which reinforced her feeling of not being part of *their* family. She was slowly being swallowed by a snake, its widening mouth closing over her and its powerful muscles forcing her to travel the length of its throat until she reached its stomach. She had no fight in her and decided to spend as much time away from the family as she possibly could. A large town was just a bus journey away and became a frequent place for Grace to visit. Once there, she pushed baby Fran, who was sleeping peacefully in her pram, through the bustling streets and lost herself amongst the crowd of people. This, unfortunately, resulted in intensifying the need to see her own family and prompted her to embark on a homeward bound train journey. She stayed with her parents for weeks on end, returning to her 'home' only if she deemed it necessary.

Fran was an important part of Grace's life, often sleeping in her mother's bed whilst James was away. When he returned, Fran was too young to understand why she suddenly had to sleep in her own bed and why she was unable to have her mum's undivided attention. Being of strong character even at that early age, she fought for attention, thus creating the beginnings of a divide between her and her dad. He wanted attention from his wife, but this little person created a block and a split between father and daughter had begun. It wasn't always obvious that James was fond of his daughter. His jealousy of the bond between his wife and daughter affected his ability to understand, or welcome, this newcomer into his life. This was only natural, Trudi surmises, after all, her parents hadn't long been married before Fran arrived and were then separated for months on end. Time to build their relationship was interrupted by separation and a new baby. A baby whose connection with her father would be affected by his absence, as would his to her.

Trudi pauses and takes her concentration away from the scenes being played out in the moonlight. She is confused because these aren't her memories. What she is seeing is the story of her parents. Why? She allows herself to absorb them and asks Mr Moon to give her clarity. As if he has pushed a rewind button, the images flash backwards at highspeed and stop at a point in her life that is deemed of importance. At slow speed, her life and her parents' play out, sometimes side by side and sometimes merging. They interconnect and similarities are highlighted. The pattern within their lives is almost repeated within hers and she suspects that this is an important piece of information. Why else is she being shown this? Perhaps she can heal her parents as well as herself. 'Maybe a little far-fetched,' she muses, 'although anything is possible! There are too many similarities for me to ignore them. It's time to shine light on the shadows, so Mr Moon do your work!'

Chapter 8

The story picks up at the point where Trudi was born, four years after the birth of Fran. According to Grace, James welcomed the birth of Trudi and formed a bond with her more easily than with Fran. Perhaps he'd had time to adjust to his life and didn't see her as a threat, but Trudi also had more of an opportunity to build an attachment with him as he wasn't away from home as often. Certainly, the grown woman can only feel love towards her father, despite having been fearful of upsetting him or letting him down.

She was only a few months old when the first move for the family was on the horizon. Her dad's ship was stationed in a Scottish dock and so the first two years of Trudi's life was spent in Scotland. They lived there until James was re-stationed to the South of England, two years later, where her parents bought a bungalow, very near to the coast. It was a small bungalow with a large front garden, or at least it had appeared large to the small Trudi. She calls to mind the perfume of the rose bushes that decorated a semi-circular bed, the petals from which she used to make rose smelling scent. She visualises herself gathering the fallen petals, placing them in a jar, adding enough water to cover them, fastening the lid and then waiting patiently. A few days later, the lid would be removed for the contents to be inspected, the aroma of rose water rising into the air. The scent was usually pleasing, although it occasionally exuded an odour of rotting petals and stagnant water, especially if left too long! She may not have been an entrepreneur, but she thoroughly enjoyed experimenting.

The rose bed sat behind a low brick wall, on which she would often sit, lost in her own world, kicking her legs to and fro, whilst she waited for Fran to return home from school. Other times she rode her little tricycle as fast as her legs could go, round the driveway and going in and out of the two entrances, making her own little racing circuit. Her trike! Trudi has fond memories of her trike which was a far cry from the ones of today. As far as she can recall, her trike's wheels were far bigger than modern ones. The frame was a large red metal one with handlebars that curved round with two handles pointing towards the rider. On the left side there was a bell and, on the right, there was a brake lever, hidden under the handle. Above all, the thing that she loved most was the boot at the back. A large boot which looked very much like a bread bin, with a door that opened downwards to reveal a space large enough to carry dolls and teddies. Naturally, she did exactly that! She smiles as she visualises her little trike, with dolls and teddies hanging from the boot as she cycled furiously to nowhere in particular. 'Those were happy days,' she sighs.

Picturing the back garden has brought back many memories, some happy, some sad, some lonely and some a concoction of all three. She remembers spending a great deal of time playing on her own in the garden, occupying herself and making sure that she wasn't a nuisance. She often spun round and round on the lawn with arms open wide whilst her eyes gazed up towards the sky, watching the world spin by. Feelings of downheartedness would sometimes briefly surface as the sense of being alone overwhelmed her. Then, fluffy clouds merged into one big cotton wool ball as she spun faster and faster until dizziness set in, making her fall to the ground in fits of giggles, changing the initial feelings into ones of happiness. She also spent many hours skipping with joy as her friend, skipping along with her as she turned the rope in time to the rhymes she was chanting. Her body wiggled as she sang out 'jelly on the plate, jelly on the plate, wibble wobble……' The rope whipped over her head, hitting the ground with a tap before it carried on its journey. She turned the rope faster and her legs jumped more quickly as they tried not to become entangled with the rope. Yes, she'd been alone. She'd been sad. Yet, she was able to change the emotions and feel pleasure. She used the time, unwittingly, as a learning experience. This, Trudi realises, is exactly what she must do now. It's time to stop being the victim and focussing on the negative. It is time to look at the lessons life has given her, to find the happy inner child and move forward confidently.

She returns to the story. Feelings of warmth and love flood her whole being as she pictures the walkie talkie doll her dad had brought back from abroad. The doll was about half a metre tall and was dressed in a knee length white lace dress. She wore a lace bonnet on her head and little white shoes on her feet. How she adored that doll. Unfortunately, the doll met a horrific ending; her cousin removed the head. All the same, it didn't stopped Trudi from taking her everywhere, pushing the headless doll proudly into town and giving her very special rides in the trike.

She relives the thrill of her fifth Christmas. On entering the lounge, she saw a large, peculiar shape hidden under a big white sheet. She slowly pulled back the covering, awe and wonder making her eyes shine as a magnificent doll's house was revealed. It was a large white house with trellis on the walls. Two large doors opened to reveal the inside and all the tiny furniture arranged in the rooms. Miniature people were placed in various positions and food was set out in the kitchen. She thinks of how, over the years, she's refurbished the house by decorating inside, adding carpet and various items. The house was very special to her. 'It still is special,' she thinks, as she pictures it sitting in its own little corner in the attic. It has sat there for many years, Trudi being unable to let it go; she's even had the urge to live in a similar house. She gives a smug grin to herself. The house in which she is now living has similarities to her doll's house and it was that which had drawn her to the property. The house had beckoned and silently called her; she'd known that they were meant to be, just like two lovers.

Her mind wanders back when, at the age of four, she underwent the horrendous experience of having her tonsils removed. It wasn't the operation itself because her only memory of that was being told by a doctor to count to ten; she only reached one before falling fast asleep. No, it was the nurses, or at least one nurse in particular. She pictures the stern nurse in detail, dressed in her blue uniform with a stiff, white apron. A long nurse's cap perched firmly on her head, the length of which fell behind and covered her hair which had been neatly tied into a bun. She was there to do her job and didn't show any compassion towards one very scared little girl. The nurse insisted that this small being, with a very sore post operation throat, ate every single sharp chip on her plate. When Trudi said she couldn't eat them because they hurt her throat, the nurse, with a voice as sharp as the chips, told her to cut off the pointed ends. Besides the chips, there was also the pyjama incident. Her parents had bought her new pyjamas for her stay in the local cottage hospital. They were blue, covered in printed white bows and she was told that she mustn't get them dirty. She didn't realise that her parents meant before her hospital stay and so she was mortified when, after the operation, she was sick all down them. The stern-faced nurse was not impressed either and demanded to know why Trudi hadn't requested a sick bowl! It was a very traumatic time for her which was eased by the delight she felt on the day she went home. Her parents arrived to take her home, bearing a gift of a sailor's dress, made by her mum. A blue dress with a full skirt, a large sailor's collar trimmed with white and a belt to fit round her waist. There hadn't been time for her mum to finish the belt with fasteners and so it was secured with a safety pin. This didn't spoil the moment in any way because she loved the dress and was completely overcome by the affection shown by her parents. As she imagines the dress, she can feel the love oozing from every stitch made by her mum and recollects how the emotions of that day sparked a sense of belonging within her. She was loved by her parents and she was worthy. Acknowledging this for perhaps the first time fills her with a warmth and compassion towards them she hasn't noticed before. They'd both been victims of their own experiences. They weren't to blame for the events that she's met in her life. She has had her own journey to make as they'd had theirs. She is gaining understanding which is helping to bring forgiveness to the front door. Beyond doubt, she knows that without her parents she wouldn't have been given the opportunity to learn from the lessons that life has thrown her way. She wouldn't have had the inner strength to call on in times of need. She can now say thank you.

Her memories have been taken in a full circle, she notices, and returned to the bungalow where Alice and Thomas were born, where her father had returned to the family and the divide between Fran and her father widened. Back to the bungalow, from which her life's bumpy path had opened in front of her and where the impending future events were waiting to take their toll on the whole family. None of them to blame. Simply circumstances and the shadows from their parents' life journeys. She can see more acutely how the journeys each one of them has made have all been part of the same jigsaw puzzle. Somewhere amongst the puzzle of turmoil and tangled emotions there was a common thread. A thread waiting to be unravelled. Perhaps if she can find the end of her own thread it might help to release them all? At the very least she hopes it will enable her to let go and step freely into the future and follow the moonlit path with strength, knowledge and wisdom, leaving her shadows from the past firmly behind.

Trudi's attention is taken back to the chalet bungalow where the family had nearly lost their mum, only it is now portraying a family who are more settled, with each day being filled with 'normal' routines and events. The young family had grown, interests and experiences had changed and friendships had widened.

Alice and Trudi often played with their dolls together. Alice had a Barbie and Trudi's walkie-talkie doll had been replaced with a Tressy doll, whose hair magically grew and shortened with the turn of a key. Tressy and Barbie would spend a long time getting ready for an evening out or a party at home. Various hairstyles were attempted and several outfits put on, until they, or the two girls, were satisfied with their appearance. As Trudi was four years older than Alice, her interest in playing 'dolls' diminished or at least took on a different role. Overtime, she became fashion designer and dress maker for the two dolls who were used as models, displaying the various outfits she created. She found scraps of materials left over from the many outfits her mum had made and turned them into mini-skirts, dresses and coats. A sense of pride and accomplishment rose as she dressed the dolls in her new creations which gave her the urge to attempt making something for herself. She was given permission to use the sewing machine, her mum's pride and joy, and was shown how to thread the cotton and use the machine correctly. It was set inside a highly polished wooden table, the top of which lifted, revealing the machine within, and folded out to create a work area. The appliance was lifted and secured in place, standing by for the necessary cotton and bobbin to be threaded. The electric foot pedal sat under the table waiting for pressure to be applied, gently at first. The slow whirring sound of the motor vibrated into the room as the machine kicked into action, becoming louder as more pressure was applied causing the machine to work faster. Stitches appeared as the machine took the fabric on a journey, guided by her hands as she made sure that the guiding foot was the correct distance from the fabric's edge. The end of the fabric arrived and two pieces had successfully been joined by a seam. Little by little, pieces of different sized and shaped fabric were joined, until the finished garment was sitting before her. She became a perfectionist, taking care over every stitch, and every detail. Each subsequent item she made was finished to the highest standard she could achieve; people often commented on how professional they looked. Sewing became her new past time, only it was more than that to her. It was an accomplishment in which she excelled. This prompted her decision to take needlework as an 'O' level where she learnt new skills and techniques to improve her work. She also studied 'A' level textiles and dress, which was when she first encountered the smooth running of a different machine, one which offered the choice of a variety of stitches.

Trudi no longer played with Tressy, instead she became her, wearing the various items she created. She pictures one dress that was part of her father's checks before she ventured out: a short (very short!) blue floral 'A' line dress with bell bottom sleeves which were edged in lace. She felt sensational when wearing it. Other outfits she has made, step out of an imaginary wardrobe in front of her and parade along the moonlit stage. The pair of striped hipster flared trousers which fitted tight across the hips and thigh, before flaring out widely from the knee. Accompanying them was a homemade, midriff blouse which finished a few inches under the bust line, exposing flesh from there to the top of the trousers. Then, the dress that she loved above all, was standing before her, her prom gown. She glimpses her tanned body wearing a long-fitted halter neck dress made in a bluebell blue coloured fabric. A dress in which she'd felt beautiful and happy.

It was whilst she was at training college that her creativity experience expanded. She chose to study dress and textiles which provided opportunities to experience working with various forms of printing, collage and clay. However, it was the process of screen printing and tie dye that interested her the most. There was something satisfying about gently smoothing the ink across the mesh, followed by anticipation as the stencil underneath allowed the design to successfully appear on the fabric laid out below. Tie dye, on the other hand, offered her a sense of awe and wonder. Even though string was tied to stop dye penetrating the required areas, there was no real way of knowing if it had been successful until the string was removed. Her beautiful and beguiling friend, the moon, inspired her to create a tie dye cushion that represented the magical sphere with its misty halo which had bewitched her on many occasions. It reflected the colours, the halo and magic of the orb in the sky and was a perfect tribute to her friend in the sky.

She is then shown a picture of herself sitting alone in her college room, gazing at the moon or starlit sky and lost in the deep, ethereal music to which she was listening. It was at that point, she recalls, that writing became a different channel for her to express herself creatively. She found words coming into her mind and felt urged to put pen to paper, not knowing what would appear. Words naturally and easily flowed and lines of writing emerged on the paper right under her nose, sometimes in the form of poetry. Poems with feeling and depth, poems with meaning, some rhyming, some not. What she remembers the most about the writing is the meaning and teachings behind the words. There were words of comfort, words of joy and words of encouragement. Looking back, she can see that it had been her initiation into guided writing, a spiritual tool which she has developed and used on numerous occasions over the years.

Trudi looks out of the window and gazes at the moon. 'Well, my friend, this is all very interesting and positive. Life has obviously helped me to develop in so many ways, and my shadows haven't always forced my hand. I know there's still a whammy to come, though. What are you going to reveal next?' He shines down, almost smiling, and highlights one of her happiest moments.

Chapter 9

At last, the family appeared happy and settled. Their mum was strengthening day by day and Trudi was able to fully concentrate on revising for her 'O' levels which were approaching fast. A revision timetable was made and the whole family were aware of the times she needed to be alone in peace. Time was also allocated in the timetable for herself, not only for relaxing but also for her job. She'd worked on a Saturday since she was thirteen years old and, before that, had washed cars for family and friends, earning enough money for her favourite band's LP. Her first Saturday job was cleaning the rooms in a hotel. She rode her bike the two mile journey, arriving at the seafront hotel at eight in the morning. Carpets were waiting to be hoovered, furniture required polishing, sinks and baths needed to be cleaned, the taps on which had to be polished until they gleamed, and all toilets had to be spotless before the final chore of washing the lino floors. It usually took her until midday, when, twelve shillings in hand, she began her journey home.

The hotel job was put behind her when her neighbour, for whom she babysat, offered her a job in their bakery and cake shop. It meant longer hours, eight thirty until five thirty, but she would be earning more money, a grand total of one pound and fifteen shillings! It was hard work at times, especially all the cleaning, although she enjoyed every minute, especially the fruits of the day. She was allowed one treat at lunchtime and, at the end of the day, any fresh cream cakes remaining were shared between the staff. Sunday tea was supplied with an indulgence of meringues, chocolate eclairs and strawberry tarts, which were all gratefully received by her family.

Serving customers was the most enjoyable part of the job as she could join in with the light-hearted banter provided by the regulars. At times, she amused herself by playing spot the newcomers who were usually holidaymakers from various parts of the country and sometimes the world. She took delight in trying to figure out where their accent was from, occasionally finding it hard not to copy it when replying. Every so often, she came across the odd customer who would have tested the patience of a saint. Customers who perused, for a great length of time, the trays of small cakes displayed in the cabinet before choosing a selection which was placed carefully in the fold out cardboard box. The price was totalled and the lid was about to be closed, when the words 'I've changed my mind,' were uttered from the customer's lips. Smiling, Trudi would open the box and ask, 'what would you like to change?' This process didn't happen just once, but several times before the customer finally made a decision with which they were happy. 'They were lucky to leave the shop without the remnants of a thrown cream bun on their clothes,' she laughs to herself.

These occurrences became even more exasperating with the introduction of decimal coins when customers insisted on being told the total in 'old money'. This resulted in several different totals for her brain to calculate, 'without a calculator or self-totalling tills like the youngsters of today,' she grunts emphatically. At the time, she sympathised with the older generation needing to know the 'real' price of a loaf of bread, as they referred to it. She also had no qualms about rummaging through their purses to help find the 'new' money. It was when they changed their minds about the purchase that was the problem as this affected the end total, in 'old' and 'new' money! The customers seemed to be unmindful of the fact that it was different for her as well. Even with these small annoyances, the time spent at work was full of fun and laughter. She felt part of the team, in the shop front as well as in the bakery at the back of the shop where the bakers teased her with harmless flirtation. She smiles impishly as the words and jokes come back to her and she admits, with a laugh, how much she'd enjoyed the attention.

During the school holidays, Tracy, her neighbour and boss, employed Trudi as a house cleaner, twice a week. The skills she'd learnt whilst working at the hotel were put into action as she worked around the house. Every single piece of fluff was removed from the carpets, each surface polished until it shone and all specs of dust removed. Cushions were plumped, the beds made and the bathroom taps gleamed from the vigorous rubbing. Washing that was sitting in the machine was hung on the line and, when dry, removed and folded neatly, ready for ironing. As she mulls over the amount of work she'd undertaken at fourteen years old, she recollects the summer afternoon when Tracy and children had come home to find a pile of dried washing on the hall floor and her 'housekeeper' nowhere to be seen. Whilst folding a bed sheet she'd removed from the line, she experienced a sharp prick in her finger, followed by a throbbing which made the pain more excruciating with each pulse. In agony, she dropped the pile of washing and glimpsed the culprit, a bee, hidden amongst a sheet. The pile, and offending bee, were left where they'd fallen as she ran round to her house in a panic. The sting was removed by her mum and a cold compress applied, followed by vinegar. A stern-faced Tracy greeted her as she walked back into the next-door house. She was standing with her hands on her hips and looking at the pile of washing with a displeased expression on her face. Trudi felt obliged to apologise profusely before explaining what had happened. At least words of sympathy were expressed prior to asking her to finish folding the washing before she went home.

Trudi was also continuing the social life upon which she'd recently embarked, attending the school club which was held twice a week. It took place from 7.30 until 10 on a Wednesday and Friday evening, the latter being 'the' one to attend as a disco was held on that session. The memory of the checks she had to go through before was allowed out of the house, makes her laugh out loud, such as bending over so that her parents could check if her skirt was too short. She recalls the night when she was unsure about which part to hold, which would be the lesser of the two evils – too much thigh or too much cleavage! Another time, despite being dressed in a short, black shirtdress, accompanied by bright red platform shoes, her dad wouldn't let her go unless she cut her nails, which, in his eyes, were far too long! 'Why?' she thinks. 'What was his reasoning? At least mum stepped in and saved my nails!'

Her thoughts travel back to the social club for it was there that she met, unbeknown at the time, her future husband. He was the boyfriend of Georgia, one of her friends, who decided that she no longer wanted to go out with him. Robert was very upset and Trudi offered him a shoulder to cry on, not realising that she, herself, had feelings for him, until he planted a thank you kiss on her cheek. A kiss that she cherished and held hidden deep within her heart. He ignited an unknown feeling inside her and her heart felt as if it was going to explode. Butterflies swirled in the pit of her stomach which contributed to the intensity of the warmth building inside. It was as if an invisible force had reached out and touched her soul, making a bond between his soul and hers. They'd connected. He was her soul mate. That was, however, the last time she saw him for many years.

Trudi looks back on that time and realises how much she enjoyed that part of her life, but she also recalls how she desperately wanted a boyfriend. The impression of her feeling like a withering wall flower when she was out with her friends, pushes its way to the fore. Her friends all had a boyfriend, but boys were just not interested in her. Then she is reminded of the night that a lad told her she was beautiful. She calls to mind feeling as if she was air born, floating in a beautiful bubble as she walked home, desperate to tell her mum. She also recollects the bump as she was brought back down to earth when her mum said, 'he must have been drunk.' There was no 'that was nice' or 'well, you are.' Simply shot down by the invisible arrows which burst her bubble and emptied its contents with a thud on the hard floor below. She settled in her bed listening to Radio Luxembourg, when, to her surprise, she heard her name being mentioned. The warmth and happiness she'd felt was reawakened as the DJ read out a request for her, wishing her good luck for the impending exams. It was from the very boy who had been brave enough to tell her she was beautiful. She snuggled under the covers, hugging herself contentedly, at the same time wishing it was someone she liked in return!

As she reminisces, her mind is taken to the parties that she'd occasionally been allowed to attend but, in particular, the one she wished she'd avoided. She thinks of the mixed feelings she had, excitement as well as trepidation, and can see how her intuition, even then, was trying to warn her. Her friends would be there with their boyfriends and she would be alone. Would she find a boyfriend? Not that she would know how to behave, or what was expected, if she was approached. It was all alien to her. All she could do was watch, observe and learn. 'Oh Trudi,' she reprimands herself, 'your naivety didn't work in your favour. If only you'd followed your guts!'

The party was an all-night one, not that her parents were aware of that little bit of information. As far as they were concerned, Trudi was going to a sleepover. She walked the mile and a half to Bryony's house, whose parents were away, with her elder brother being left in charge. On arriving at the house, it was obvious that the party was already in full flow, but Bryony's brother was nowhere to be seen. Bryony took her into the lounge where music was blasting out and cider flowing freely. She began to relax, albeit deep inside she had the feeling that she should leave except she was also battling with a great desire to be welcomed into the group. The latter won. Her friends were the popular ones, the in crowd and she was desperate to be part of it. If only she'd listened to that small inner voice. Trudi trembles as the event opens before her eyes; it's as if she is watching a remake of an old movie. One minute she was sitting minding her own business and the next she was dragged from her seat and pinned down by a group of boys. Nausea rises as she observes the way she kicked out violently in vain. Gradually, piece by piece, her clothes were removed, whilst her 'friends' watched on, laughing and cheering. The picture changes to her sitting in her pants, coiled up like a snake in shame and trying to hide her semi naked body. She's unable to recall how she saved her dignity but, somehow, she managed, amongst her tears of shame and anger, to retrieve some of her clothing which she quickly returned to her shaking body. Her jeans, though, had disappeared. The scene shows her shyly and quietly leaving the room with the laughter and occasional rebuff about the attackers' actions echoing in her ears. She positioned herself on a kitchen stool where she was found sobbing by Bryony's brother. Whether he said anything to the assailants, Trudi was never made aware, he simply brought back her jeans and looked very embarrassed as he left her to dress.

She relives the sensation of desperately wanting to run out, to find a phone box from which she could phone her dad and ask him to collect her, knowing that in all probability her request would be turned down. Also, questions would be asked and more likely than not, she would be blamed. Tears well in her eyes as she becomes overwhelmed again by the horror, anger and desperation of that night so long ago, as well as the craving for the comfort of her parents. She knew it wouldn't be offered and it was that belief that made her decide to put on a brave front. Despite feeling compromised and unwelcome, as well as totally humiliated she chose to remain at the party.

The evening progressed. Music, dancing, laughter, but she didn't feel part of it. Then, at a vulnerable moment, a lad approached her and started to talk to her. Thinking he was attracted to her and wanted to find somewhere quieter to talk, she naively allowed him to lead her to another room. He, on the other hand, had other ideas. Total innocence and a desire to belong opened her up to a situation where she began to feel out of her depth. It started with gentle kisses, followed by unfamiliar hands touching her body, touching her in places no one had ever touched her before. Her hands were then introduced to a part of the male body she'd only seen in Human Biology books. Panic took hold. She wasn't that sort of girl and was not going to be forced to do anything she didn't want to. She was saving herself for her Knight in shining armour. From somewhere, she found the inner strength she needed. Pushing the lad as hard as she could, she shouted 'no' in such a way that he had no choice but to leave. She decided to remove herself from the party and quietly took herself upstairs to bed. The memory of seeing groping bodies in every room and her friends among them, brings to mind the words she'd emphatically thought, 'if that's how they get boyfriends, I don't want to know!'

That night, despite her body being heavy with an emotional exhaustion, she had difficulty sleeping. She could hear quite plainly the voices below, discussing her and the night's events. When asked by Bryony why they had stripped Trudi, they replied, 'for a laugh.' Despite one of them saying that her body was 'surprisingly good', anger and hurt was welling inside, so the 'compliment' was ignored. How dare they humiliate her?

In the morning, she was greeted by her friends in a subdued manner, but the night's event wasn't mentioned. Trudi left, vowing to herself that she would never attend another party. The vision of her walking the long road home is revealed on the moonlit path below her window. As she walked, she talked to herself. There were words of regret, disgust, anger and blame, mostly directed at herself. She was nursing her pride whilst wondering if she could have averted the abhorrent deeds of others. She did consider informing her parents except the worry of meeting their wrath and disappointment made her decide to hide the event away and keep it hidden amongst her bag of rubbish. It was another shadow that would follow her into the future.

Chapter 10

The party scene comes to an end and the void that had been created in the friendship with Bryony, Georgia and Isla is opening wide before her. Trudi hadn't succeeded in becoming part of the in crowd, however, she is now able to understand that this had been for the best and can see how life presents new opportunities.

She is reminded of how a new friend, Glenda, came into her life; she was a gentle soul who offered her a true friendship of understanding, compassion and loyalty. Glenda had a magical quality and the air of a fairy or an imp; she didn't have a bad bone in her body. As she reflects on the relationship, Trudi realises that Glenda was her first introduction to spirituality, albeit in a very different way to her experiences now. She was a free soul and had touched Trudi's; the inner children within them both became friends and played out in reality. The friendship gave Trudi the experience of life as a teenager. It was through this acquaintance that she experienced joy, laughter and permission to be carefree. Most importantly, it was through this friendship that she gained confidence in herself. She began to see herself with new eyes and appreciate her own beauty. Glenda helped Trudi to begin to love herself.

The memory of the weekends and holidays shared with Glenda fills her heart with a warm glow. The two young teenagers would catch a train to the nearby seaside town and spend their time wandering, barefooted through the town streets, or along the beach. They were usually adorned in bell bottom trousers and mid-drift tops and, as they walked, they listened to the latest chart music which blasted out from a radio being carried by one of them. Trudi smiles as she thinks of how many times recently, she has turned her nose up in disgust as youngsters have gone past with rap, R and B or some other loud music blasting out from their boombox or cars. Enjoyment doesn't seem to change, just the music and equipment!

On Friday and Saturday evenings, she and Glenda headed off to hit the town's night spots. Their Saturday jobs gave them enough money to venture out, only to make it stretch further, they bought a half price child's train ticket on the outward journey. She giggles as she thinks of how they made sure that the necessary make-up was at hand on arriving at their destination, where the first port of call was the station toilets. Here make-up was applied, transforming their young faces into ones that were more suited for entry into the disco. When the preparations were complete, they made their way to the disco where they danced the night away without a care in the world. As she immerses herself in the memory of the experience, she recollects the night she was approached by a lady who asked her if she would like to perform on the disco stage. The stage was raised and situated at the front of the dance floor where she would be on full show. An invitation to be one of the local Pan's People! Yet, despite being elated and her confidence having received a huge boost, it was not quite enough for her to accept the offer.

The story pauses, which allows her mind to ponder over this for a while. 'Why didn't I have the confidence to say yes? Why didn't I tell anyone? I suppose I never mentioned it to mum because I knew it would have been ignored or laughed at.' She realises that each time she's taken a step towards building her confidence, she's been knocked back. A glimmer of moonlight shines on the emerging realisations which provokes the start of an understanding. She can perceive how it was impossible for her to accept any compliments because they were always spurned by others. She could only give credence to negative comments thus impounding the black picture she had of herself. A picture that had begun to emerge many years ago and has been developed over the years. A negative picture of herself, edged with a dark coloured frame, hanging on a wall in her mind as a reminder of just how useless, ugly and fat she is. It is time to capture a new image, one that captures self-respect. It will be framed in such a way as to illuminate all the good qualities, the beauty lying within waiting to be portrayed by the commissioned artist: Trudi.

Her mind travels back to the evenings out and especially the journey home. This was usually via the very last train of the evening, which was followed by a lonely, but happy, walk home in the dark. Their finances didn't stretch to a taxi and her dad would certainly not be used as one! In fact, sometimes there was a need to be more creative with their money at the start of the evening, when they occasionally skipped the outward train and hitched a lift instead. They walked together along the main road with thumbs out in the hope of someone stopping. She recalls that they were usually successful in obtaining a lift and managed to keep it secret from those who would not be amused. That was, until one night a lady stopped and, as Trudi settled herself into the car, the lady said, 'you look very much like a nurse I work with.' Without thinking Trudi replied, 'my sister's a nurse.' After an exchange of details, it became apparent that the lady worked with Fran. Fran was informed of the escapade, who, in turn, informed her parents. Trudi was in big trouble, although she can't remember being 'grounded', she can remember the anger she'd felt towards her sister. Fran had betrayed her and interfered in her life. Trudi smiles to herself. 'If only teenagers understood the reasoning behind the handiwork of their elders!' Fran had been looking out for her younger sister, just as she herself would her children. Regret rises as she considers the potential outcome of her teenage activities. 'How stupid you were,' she chastises her younger self. 'Though' she muses, 'it was all worth it and certainly helped me to relax. It definitely took my mind of the exam results.'

Her attention drifts to the day that her exam results arrived. She knew she'd worked so very hard but never presumed she would succeed in achieving the results she required. Another characteristic that had been knocked deeply inside with a hammer forcefully hitting a nail to ensure it stayed firmly in place. Intellectual achievement and understanding hadn't come naturally or easily. Her sisters were clever, she had to work hard. She was told time and time again that she was daft like her mother and not good with words like her sisters and father. It was this belief that affected her desire to open the letter in case it displayed the truth: failure.

An image appears of the younger Trudi sitting in bed on results' morning, turning the unopened envelope over and over within her hands. Then, as suddenly as it had been turning, it stopped, as if frozen in time. She watches as her fingers slowly came back to life and gently prized the envelope open. She holds her breath, just as she had back then and watches her fingers grab the offending piece of paper which held the key to her future. As she observes, Trudi senses the same feeling of disbelief that she'd felt at that time, except now, she also feels proud. She'd passed and was one step nearer to being a teacher, a longing she'd had since the age of five. Okay, the grades were not the highest but she'd passed and achieved the grades she needed! She sees herself apprehensively climb out of bed and make her way downstairs to the kitchen where her mum was busy cleaning. There were no signs of anticipation or eagerness to know the results or even acknowledgement of her presence, so she simply said, 'I've passed!' Her mum turned and smiled, saying 'well done. That's good,' only Trudi didn't feel the warmth and enthusiasm that she'd been hoping for. There was no praise for being able to pursue her desired career, instead her parents insisted that she looked into other career opportunities and not concentrate fully on teaching. Trudi remembers feeling as if they were trying to manage her life, except she'd still agreed to investigate alternative opportunities. They accompanied her to career events, but she knew that teaching was the only career for her. Having satisfied the request of her parents, she felt in a stronger position to tell them that she was going to be a teacher and nothing else, which she did with a strength that she still has difficulty believing. All she had to do was pass her A levels, the pressures of which came only too soon.

Before the next set of exams there was Fran's wedding to prepare for. She was marrying Paul, her childhood sweetheart; Alice and Trudi were going to be bridesmaids. Trudi had been asked to make the dresses and so was able to put her sewing skills to good use, however her sewing ability was tested to the full when making Fran's wedding dress. The dress was made from a delicate, sparkling organza with an underskirt made from a white silky material. There was a slight opening at the neck of the bodice which itself fitted tightly across the chest before nipping into a small waistline. From here the dress fell delicately, forming a long train at the back which sparkled as the light reflected on the frail gauzy material. 'Quite a task for a seventeen year old to undertake,' she says out loud, 'but even if I say so myself, I made a jolly good job of it.'

The bridesmaids were dressed in Edwardian style dresses made in a purple and pink striped fabric with flowers evident here and there. The fabric's pattern resembled the designs worn in the Edwardian time and the shades of colour were enhanced by the baskets of sweet peas held in their hands. It was a flower that is now one of Trudi's favourites. She loves the colours and the perfume that fills the air. It is a flower which gives a sense of joy, only, like so many things, is gone too soon. Just like the wedding day: over in a flash, yet a day that was filled with love and happiness.

Summer turned to autumn, autumn to winter, winter to spring. Spring is a special time for Trudi. It is a time for growth, new life and new beginnings, the relevance of which has been shown to her more recently. She sits and paints a spring picture in her mind's eye, depicting the snowdrops that she waits to appear with anticipation, indicating that spring is around the corner. Then come daffodils, their glorious heads bobbing gently in the garden and their trumpets blasting a golden light all around. It is a time of hope, the sleepiness of winter over, bringing a freshness and lightness to the world which leads into the warmth and colours of summer. The shoots of the tender new plants gently push their way up through the soil, the buds form and finally burst into spectacular flowers that shine in a magnificence of colour, a sign that summer has arrived. 'Summer! My favourite time of the year.' Her picture captures the heat, sun, warm light evenings and lazy days. Carefree days of lying in the sun. Days filled with a sense of happiness, of hope and fulfilment that seem to radiate from the sun itself.

The summer, one year after Fran's wedding, brought Trudi the chance to fulfil her long-life dream. She managed to obtain the qualifications needed to embark upon her teaching career and, in the autumn, was to leave home to begin this new stage in her life. This is where Mr Moon takes her.

Chapter 11

Trudi woke early. She propped herself against the pillows in her bed and slowly gazed around the room, taking in the view as if it was the last time she would see it. She breathed in deeply and absorbed the smells: the residue of perfume and deodorant that had been sprayed, soap powder on the bed linen and the lingering odour of sandalwood joss sticks that had been burned by Alice. Rays of sunlight peeped through the curtains, illuminating various objects which she'd decided not to pack. The faces of her favourite band smiled at her from the wall, filling her with a reassurance that they would keep her place safe until she returned. Piled in one corner were the boxes and suitcases containing some of her possessions and clothes, as well as the books and resources needed for her new adventure. She knew she should remove herself from her bed, but it was offering her a sense of comfort of which she was reluctant to let go. Her eyes fell upon Alice who was still sleeping, tucked up safe and warm in her own bed. 'Oh, how I'm going to miss her,' she thought. The noise of her parents' movements reached her ears. The familiar sound of her father's voice as he playfully provoked her mum. The kettle being filled with water, the clanking of the cups as they were placed on the table, waiting to be filled with tea. The smell of toast cooking under the grill wafted up the stairs, bringing with it the knowledge that the time had come. Sitting on the edge of the bed, she allowed her toes to play with the carpet beneath her feet, squeezing the soft pile as if to crush the memory into her senses. Then, pushing herself up from the bed, she walked towards the window and pulled back the curtains. The light cascaded into the room, rousing Alice from her slumber, who looked at her sister and asked, 'are you ready to go?' Ready? Trudi was ready in terms of being packed, just not emotionally. There was a mixture of anticipation and fear. Fear! Why should she be frightened? Hadn't she managed to travel to France on her own?

It was just over a year ago when she had the opportunity to stay with a French family, a family she didn't know from Adam.

Her parents had taken her to the airport where she found her own way through customs and to the boarding gate. At seventeen years old, she managed the flight and the bus journey from Nice to Cannes where an unknown family were waiting her arrival. She survived a month within this family, speaking a foreign language and struggling to keep up with the deep conversations held each night. The opportunity had, in spite of her struggles, allowed her to gain in confidence and strength and introduced her to a whole new experience of living.

The house itself was a small French Villa which had been the family's holiday home for a number of years. The rooms were large and kept cool from the heat of the sun by large wooden shutters which also acted as a shield against any flying insects, especially those with a bite! In the garden a few orange and lemon trees were growing, the leaves of which gave off a citrusy perfume when scratched. The house was situated close to the beach at Cannes and days were usually spent lounging under a blazing sun as the warmth of the soft sand below her seeped into her gradually darkening body. When the heat of the sun became too extreme, relief could be found in the large tepid bath of sea water which stretched welcomingly in front of her. Lying on the water's surface, the gentle waves massaged her body as they lapped around. It was a beautiful place and Trudi totally understood how the famous stars were attracted to the area. It was certainly magical. In the evenings she and the family sometimes strolled along the promenade in Cannes, the port of which was home to some luxurious boats. The family also took her on excursions to visit some of the local sights including Monaco and the complete contrasting mountain village of Saint Paul. The area was absolutely stunning and something she would never forget, but she was glad when the time came to return home. Trudi laughs as she recalls the complete sense of relief that had washed over her on seeing the familiar faces of her parents waiting for her in the arrival lounge. She also remembers desperately trying to convince herself that if she'd undertaken that adventure on her own, she should be able to embrace leaving home for college without panicking. She observes herself standing tall in her bedroom and smiling at Alice as she replied to her sister's question. With a Mary Poppin's hmph, she said 'nearly. I've got to get dressed and have breakfast, then I'll be off.'

The boxes and suitcases were loaded into the car. It reminded Trudi of the day they'd moved house when she was eight and the same feelings of being lost that she'd experienced when her parents had left her at her grandparents' house, only this time it was her choice. She said 'au revoir' to her bedroom and her home in the way she always did, her mind taking photos of each room so that she wouldn't forget. Then she climbed into the car, waving to Alice and Thomas as her dad pulled out of the drive. This was it. No turning back. Her new life was about to begin.

The college was situated on the south coast. It appeared huge and was swarming with a mass of people, some who seemed to know exactly where they were going and others who looked just as lost as Trudi. Students were filing into a great big hall where established students were there to meet and greet, pointing the lost souls in the right direction. First came the process of admittance where proof of name and placement offer were required. Information, rules, more information, schedules, lists of places to go for help were all handed out. Then finally came the hall of residence details. Trudi was beginning to feel flustered. Anxiety rose as the realisation hit that she was about to be given details of her new home for the next three years and the time was coming for her parents to leave.

Her accommodation was in a house close by the college, not in the main halls of residence. It was an old Victorian house with a path leading to a crescent shaped tiled step, on which sat a pair of big double front doors. A large brass knocker invited you to announce your arrival and two round brass knobs waited to be turned. Trudi and her parents were greeted by the student in charge of the house, who showed them around the building. It was a house steeped in history, holding evidence of having been a large home for a relatively wealthy family. The front doors opened onto a large hallway from which a wide staircase led upstairs. She remembers the staircase as a place where she often imagined herself as the lady of the house, dressed in Victorian attire, walking gracefully down the stairs where her smartly dressed husband would be waiting! Trudi smiles, 'the house certainly caught my imagination.'

From the hallway, double doors opened to reveal the communal sitting room. Further along the hallway there was a student's bedroom and the shared kitchen, which was set out with kettle, a few pots and pans, ironing board and iron. A little utility room was alongside where a washing machine was positioned ready for use and an indoor line stretched across the length of the room. As Trudi recollects, she found it difficult to concentrate on the information that was being given to her because her attention was drawn to the historical tell tell signs of the original kitchen and adjoining scullery. The large, deep sink was still present, as were the servants' bells which would have rung to notify that a servant was required in one of the rooms. The floor was the original red tiles which at one time would have been highly polished by hands that showed evidence of hard work. Tucked away in a corner was a door which, on opening, revealed a steep, narrow staircase leading to the servants' quarters. She was absorbing the memories oozing from the walls, listening to the bricks tell their stories and sensing the hustle and bustle of everyday life in the kitchen. Her mind created images of the weary servants climbing the stairs after a long, busy day, ready for sleep. She couldn't decide which role she would have preferred, servant or lady of the house, although both had a sense of appeal, of romanticism. She was so preoccupied by her fantasising that she completely forgot the purpose of her being in the house. A voice talking to her caught her attention and she saw the ghostly apparition of a girl who was leading her back along the hall and up the wide staircase. It was as if two different times had merged.

A large landing presented itself from which three well sized bedrooms could be accessed and tucked in a corner, hidden by a narrower flight of stairs, was the old servants' door which led down to the kitchen below. The narrow stairs also led up to the servants' quarters and it was there that Trudi found her room. It was quite a small room compared to the others which was still expected to house four students, although they did later succeed in getting it changed to a double. The original Victorian fireplace was still visible with a gas fire set inside it. There was a bay window and accompanying seat, which offered a view over the streets below and a distant hint of the sea. This became the place where she spent contemplative moments, staring at the night sky and began forging a friendship with the moon.

Her parents stayed to help her settle and then they were gone. Trudi was left, on her own, in a strange new world, full of people she didn't know. The feelings of her first day at school resurfaced: vulnerability mixed with acceptance. She swallowed deeply as her roommates entered one by one, Sarah, Gill and Anne. The next few hours were spent becoming acquainted and investigating the college grounds, with the first port of call being the food hall. As the weeks passed, the foursome became six when Susan and Beth joined the friendship group. They became very good friends and remained so for the rest of her life. She smiles. 'I don't know where I would be now, without their love and support.'

Trudi found college life liberating. It opened her up to whole new experiences and learning. She was independent, able to make her own decisions and learn from the mistakes. Her first mistake springs to mind: drinking far too much at her first college party! Each student had been given a 'college parent' as a means of support during the first year. She'd been allocated a third year student as her 'mum', who was of the opinion that the first piece of support should be to widen her social field by inviting her to a party. She certainly made an impression, not only on the other guests, but also on her roommates who helped her to bed that night. The room was still swimming the following morning. That was the first, and last, time at college she allowed herself to become so intoxicated.

She thinks back on her second mistake. Besides her main subject of Art and Design and tutorials on teaching and child development, she had to choose another one as part of her learning timetable. Instead of choosing a subject which she'd enjoy, she allowed her anxiety of being alone to make the choice. She opted for World Affairs, a subject about which she knew nothing, instead of dance and drama, something she would have thoroughly enjoyed. Even so, she'd be with Sarah, guaranteeing her someone she knew. It involved debates about politics, solving world problems, gathering information and reporting back, which were all alien to her. She struggled and was convinced that she was unable to contribute. Her shadows of 'you're not good with words' and 'it doesn't come easily to you' stepped to the fore, making her feel less intelligent and pushing her deeper into her shell. Her fear manifested the very thing she'd been trying to avoid, loneliness; at least it only had to be endured for one year. It was at lunchtime that anxiety really hit, when the thought of entering the cafeteria alone terrified her. The friends always agreed to meet for lunch, although lecture timings dictated if this was possible. Even if she had to wait, or dash away from a lecture as quickly as she could, Trudi did her utmost to make sure she wouldn't be alone. She's transported back in time and feels as if she's standing alone amongst the swarm of people buzzing around her whilst her eyes search anxiously for a familiar face. She senses the anxiety which had caused her stomach to churn, followed closely by relief as the waving arms beckoned her to join her friends.

Teaching practice played a major role in building her confidence. She never knew where her placement would be, or who would accompany her. Her first practice was miles away from the college, requiring her to stay, Monday to Friday, with a host family. The coach left from outside the college at seven on a Monday morning, full of students anticipating their first teaching experience. There were various drop off points along the way until Trudi arrived at her destination, along with another student who was attending the same school, as well as boarding with the same family. The family were very welcoming and she found the girl with whom she was sharing, friendly and easy to get along with, which made the whole experience more pleasant than she'd expected. It also meant she'd another person she could pick out of the crowd at college mealtimes. Initially, she was eased into the teacher role by reading a story to eagerly waiting children sitting on the floor around her, but by the final week she was happily teaching the whole class. Trudi felt at home and confident in front of the class, a point that the teacher herself highlighted. Weekends were spent preparing lessons, writing evaluative reflections and compiling evidential assessment reports on pupils of differing abilities. This would, along with her aptitude as a teacher, determine a pass or fail. Fail she would not!

Despite the workload that the weekends brought, there was always time to take part in college social life. For the next four weeks, the coach picked her up from outside the school every Friday at around four o'clock, for what seemed to be a never-ending journey back to college. Depleted, but excited students filed onto the coach at each stop, chatter filling the inside as they all shared their week's experiences and made plans for that night. They usually arrived back by half past five, traffic permitting, which allowed enough time to eat and prepare for the evening's event. Friday night was college bar night. It was open every night, with Friday being the most popular as there was often music or a disco. Hordes of students piled into the hall, fighting their way to the bar in desperate need of a very reasonably priced drink. Drink in hand, the evening began. Laughter and incessant babble grew in intensity as more people joined the already heavy congregation. By the end of the evening, the sound was almost deafening as alcohol fuelled voices competed with the sound of music blasting out from huge speakers, all part and parcel of college life.

Sadly, it was after the first teaching practice that Anne decided that teaching was not for her and the group of six became five. The famous five! Not because they stood out amongst the crowd, simply because they were such good friends who spent their free time together walking into town, shopping and strolling along the beach. The memory of them ambling along the streets is clear in her mind. They walked and chattered about everything and nothing, taking a pit stop at a café for a well-earned coffee or lunch. In the summer, ice-cream became an obligatory part of the agenda and, as it was a holiday resort, there were a number of ice-cream parlours for them to explore! The resort was once a popular choice of her grandma Victoria, who'd partaken of her favourite knickerbocker glory on each visit and insisted that her granddaughter 'had one for her.' She'd pressed money into Trudi's hand, with instructions to let her know what every mouthful tasted like. Trudi smiles affectionately as she recollects how her grandma had given the exact amount that she'd had to pay herself, many years ago.

She did as her grandma had requested with the additional cost being paid by herself. Much to her friends' amusement, she described the taste out loud so that it was imprinted in her head, ready to be shared with her grandma. There was a topping of thick whipped cream, the fluffiness of which was disturbed as the long-handled spoon burst through the white swirly top to pick up a mixture of ingredients beneath, all held within a long cone shaped glass. The strong vanilla flavour of the layers of smooth white ice cream was evident as it entered the mouth, the coldness sending shivers through her body. Strawberries with their pleasant summer perfume were scattered throughout, their sweet taste noticeable within the melange as it hit the taste buds. It was definitely a request that she was quite willing to carry out again!

The streets became a source of amusement to the young friends where the inner child was released, giving them permission to behave in a very infantile manner. The devilishness within them came alive encouraging them to secretly knock on front doors and run away with stifled giggles before they were spotted. She joins in as she recaptures the laughter that had risen from their bellies as, without a care in the world, they battled against the coastal rain with the child ego encouraging their arms to become windscreen wipers, swaying from side to side as they beat the pelting rain away from their eyes. Oblivious to the amused passers-by, they continued their journey, arms waving in front of their faces, singing 'the wipers on the bus go swish, swish, swish.' On occasion, a seaside storm hit and the girls would stand mesmerised as they watched the sea lash over the protective wall and spill its guts over the road. The thrill of the spectacular water show called the dare devils to battle their wit against the gathering waves and tease the water to come closer, jumping back with shrieks as it threatened to overrun their feet. Foolish but fun!

Evenings brought out the teenager when they headed off to the social bar. Here they met fellow students with whom they'd made acquaintance, in particular a lad called Tony who was huge in personality as well as height, towering above her by two feet. He was loud and vivacious and his presence could be felt even before he entered a room. He often accompanied them home from the bar and attended soirees held by the girls, usually in Trudi's and Sarah's room. The sound of his platform booted feet could be heard thumping their way up the flight of stairs, reverberating between the close walls until he reached the room where they sat until the early hours in deep conversation.

Discussions would continue until their eyes could no longer fight the desire to close and their beds became increasingly alluring. 'Goodnights' were whispered and the girls returned to their own rooms as quietly as they could in order to not disturb the sleeping housemates, but the sound of Tony descending the stairs was unavoidable. Trudi chuckles as she thinks of the thud of his platforms breaking the silence of the night as he made his way back to his lodgings. 'They were fun nights,' she murmurs wistfully.

Trudi stops the image and gazes at the moon quizzically. She mulls over the college years which gave her many experiences, helped her to blossom and brought her out of herself, regardless of a number of knocks along the way. She admits that there had been times when she felt lost and alone, with that old familiar feeling of not belonging haunting her, but, on the whole, they'd been good. 'Perhaps you're showing me how each experience teaches and develops a person. I can see how they all, good or bad, happy and sad, affected me and no doubt, Mr Moon, you're going to show me more!'

Chapter 12

The story resumes at the beginning of her second year at college when Trudi encountered her first 'real' boyfriend. Her roommate Sarah was going out with Mark who had a best friend called David. They often used to hang around in a foursome and before long, David asked her out on a date. In hindsight, she should have queried the fact that they were never alone, but she was bursting with joy and so didn't question. The delight of a boy finding her attractive washed over her like the rays from the warm sun and poured into every cell of her body. She was the happiest she'd been for a while, although she was also aware that the effervescent bubbles of euphoria could just as easily go as flat as an open bottle of lemonade. Life's experiences so far had taught her that contentment is short lived and so that was what she expected. 'Perhaps that way of thinking brought it about. A bit like my fear bringing me aloneness,' she considers, 'but how do you change your thinking when life is dealing out blows?' Trudi certainly doesn't feel she's deserved all that she's suffered. Perhaps these experiences have been life lessons, whether it be from a previous life or the present. 'If this is the case,' she ponders, 'I've had one hell of a lot to learn.'

As if not to disappoint, her belief didn't let her down and, on this occasion, it dealt a double whammy. Trudi's mum was taken back into hospital. Seven years on and lumps were detected in the lymph glands. Prayers and more prayers were sent out, by Trudi and many others. Yet again, her mother had to undergo surgery, only this time Trudi was away from home and felt totally helpless. The flame of guilt was ignited and burned forcefully inside. Finger like sparks hit out sending the sensation of an electric shock coursing through her body which awakened the guilt further, bringing with it a compulsion to return home. Accompanying it was the need to care for and protect her mum as if Trudi herself was the parent, as well as the worry of letting her mum down, but she also had college commitments.

Realistically, she knew that there was nothing she could do and that her mum was receiving all the help she needed. It was her shadows from the past which were continually in the background that were the obstacle. Suddenly, as if the electric shock of the past jolted her into the present, she becomes profoundly aware of how she still has the need to care for people, to the point of exhaustion and detriment to herself. At times, it's as if there is an energy vampire, draining every ounce of life from her body but she still manages to give more. Somehow, she must find a way of preventing her energy being syphoned from her. In her mind's eye, she envisages tentacles reaching out to her and searching for a point of entry. The picture forming is similar to that of a big black octopus with its long arms seeking the life force for which its body craved. As if reason is attempting to portray a different scenario, the image changes. It becomes one of a suckling baby who is hungrily in search of its mother's breast for milk, for comfort and also love. Successfully completing its search, the baby latches on and guzzles fervently as the mother embraces her child. She pulls it in tighter with unconditional love pouring from one soul to another. No expectations, just pure love and it is this that Trudi has never experienced. She has been cared for but unspoken expectations had been set. She has learnt that love comes with conditions that can never be fulfilled. Instead of loving unconditionally she has sought approval and inclusion which she has never achieved, as the invisible goal posts were always moved. She realises how this was the same for her mum. They have travelled in their own vehicles, along their own paths, in search of love. Her mum used the vehicle of illness, fear and emotional control with a silent expectation that her children will provide the fuel. Trudi's transportation has been guilt, the prospect of rejection and a belief that she is responsible for making things right.

She has always believed that she was a compassionate person, only now she begins to query it. A compassionate person wouldn't feel resentful, they would be able to give freely and she's certainly becoming more resentful about the demands being presented. She still wants to offer assistance but also desires time to herself and, above all, the energy to give freely and willingly. It is all pointing to the word NO! A simple word, yet so hard to say when years of programming are dictating otherwise and her guilt buttons are very easy to press, something of which people are uncannily aware. What is the answer? The little inner voice is suddenly there, encouraging her to write as it whispers words into her ears:

'Your life is your own. Own it! You cannot be responsible for the journey that others must take. Live your life and allow others to live theirs. Set your boundaries and be strong. You are a compassionate person, but you have become use to working from your guilt. In order to love unconditionally you must first love yourself. If you love yourself, people will see you as a loving and caring person who is content. They may ask, but you will come from a different base and they will come to appreciate your honesty. They, too, will learn from this for their perception of life will change. Imagine yourself inside a ball of energy that is bright and colourful. The radiant rainbow colours swirl inside, giving you your own source of energy and offer you protection. Although the ball is light and gives the appearance of a bubble, no one can penetrate it. Your energy is locked inside. The key to unlock this is compassion and unconditional love. When presented with a demand, ask yourself: do I really want to say yes? If you have any doubts, or your stomach feels heavy, the answer should be no, but it will be your choice. Remember the times when you have said no and the strength that accompanied it. It is time for you to stand strong again! Keep yourself grounded. If you feel that someone is attempting to unlock your energy ball, surround yourself with a purple cloak of protection and imagine the reaching tentacles being cut away. Life is presenting you this, yet again, for you to act. Do it now! We are with you. Blessings.'

She reads the words and finds it difficult to believe that she has written them. In truth, she hasn't. She has been the vehicle of spiritual guidance, a gift that she's been given. She will endeavour to follow the advice that has been provided and no longer be a victim of the past. She will be a future victor standing tall in the light of the moon.

Her mind returns to the memory and the scene opens with a new understanding. She understands that it was her own belief that she must make things right that had triggered the foundation of guilt. It was upon this firm, yet unstable base that walls of protection had been built. Walls which kept Trudi enclosed in the kingdom where she was responsible for looking after people and solving their problems with the main problem, that time, being her mum.

It was David, who came to the rescue and offered to drive her to the hospital, which she'd no hesitation in accepting. Sarah and Mark went too, helping to keep her mind away from the impending visit. As they travelled along her well-known home bound route, she pointed out familiar landmarks until they finally arrived at her home. She'd pre-warned her family of the visit and her dad had kindly arranged lunch before they set off for the hospital. Her family had met Sarah previously and so all their attention was on Mark and David, especially the latter. Her dad shook hands with the two lads, thanking David for bringing his daughter home whilst his eyes summed up the person standing in front of him. Alice was welcoming; Thomas, on the other hand, found it difficult to hide his amusement about his sister bringing home a boyfriend!

After lunch, they said their goodbyes and made their way to the hospital. As she proceeded down the same corridor that she'd walked down seven years previously, Trudi's stomach turned somersaults and the recently eaten food threatened to find a way out. The strong odour of hospital filled her nostrils, a horrible combination of disinfectant, the remaining odour of a recent meal along with urine, or other bodily fluids and functions. A smell that transported her back to the day that she'd visited a near to death mum.

Even though her dad had told her that her mum was doing well, she didn't really know what to expect. The doors to the ward were standing open and revealed her mum with tubes attached and bags hanging by the side of the bed. The anxiety and numbness felt formerly by the young girl swept over the nineteen year old, causing her legs to weaken. She attempted to take a step forward except her feet refused to budge. Transfixed and glued to the spot, she was unable to move, until David's hand woke Sleeping Beauty and persuaded her feet to step forward. Slowly, with her friends following, she made her way towards her mum and smiled as she said hello. Her mum was totally surprised by her daughter's appearance and embarrassed about her own, especially as she had unknown guests. Carefully sitting herself more upright, she did her utmost to cover the offending bags by her side and to make herself more presentable, needlessly apologising for the way she looked. Trudi and Sarah chatted to the frail looking woman whilst the two lads occupied themselves in a desperate attempt to hide how uncomfortable they were. Trudi suggested that they went for a cup of tea to which they eagerly agreed and Sarah went with them which gave Trudi some time alone with the patient. It also gave Grace time to share her views about David, whom she thought to be nice enough, especially as he'd driven Trudi over. The three friends returned, an indication that the time had arrived for her to say goodbye to her mum. She was reluctant to leave though felt more at peace after seeing her. She was also safe with the knowledge that, unlike the first time, there was a definite indication that Grace would pull through.

It was shortly after the visit that her mum was well enough to go home and Trudi could settle back comfortably into college life, although her relationship with David had changed and she wasn't sure how or why. It seemed to tie in with the break-up of Sarah and Mark. David suddenly became very cool and evasive. No arrangements were made to meet and if they bumped into each other around college, he would ignore her. She felt totally confused as well as angry. At one time, the confusion would have encouraged the submissive Trudi to give in, however, on this occasion, the anger forced a different personality to show. She would not be treated unfairly and cast aside without explanation and, so, she decided to take matters into her own hands and confront him. She still doesn't know how she found the courage to do it, but over the years, she's come to realise that when something matters to her, she always finds the strength and courage to fight. The shadows become a force to be reckoned with, pushing her forward positively.

Appearing more courageous than she felt, she marched over to the pottery room where she knew she would find him. He was sitting at the potter's wheel with his hands carefully moulding a lump of clay into the desired shape. He looked more than a little surprised as she pushed the door open. She laughs out loud as she recalls the forming bowl becoming unstable on the spinning wheel and wobbling dangerously, when she brusquely demanded, 'why are you avoiding me?' She then hears clearly those words of explanation which made her confidence and self-esteem plummet. David explained that he'd only gone out with her in the first place because Mark had asked him to. She felt like the unstable piece of clay that was swaying from side to side as pressure was removed from the pedal, but she also felt cross. She had the urge to hurl a piece of clay in his direction, instead she said, 'don't you think it would have been better to have told me rather than ignore me?' Without waiting for a reply, she turned and quickly left before the threatening tears found their way to the surface. It had come at a time when she was feeling vulnerable and her foundations were like the potter's wheel, spinning and creating an unstable surface on which she was standing. Automatically, she returned to a tortoise state and withdrew into her shell.

She longed for the year to finish when she could be at home with her family, except the security of being at home had to wait. First, she must endure the trials of a twelve week teaching practice. The school she was given was a local school where the pupils were accustomed to students and well versed in ways to test teaching capabilities! She had a class of forty, seven year olds, who were very street wise and advanced for their years. Their teacher kept the children under her thumb and on a very tight leash, consequently, they had a field day when this young, inexperienced student teacher stepped in. There wasn't a problem whilst the teacher was present, it was when Trudi was on her own, that the well-behaved pupils turned into devilish imps. Hysterical laughter takes over as she conjures up a picture of the quiet classroom turning into a rave with pupils dancing on the tables and chairs, whilst she played the guitar and taught songs. Madness had taken over, yet somehow, she managed to restore order! She relives the horror she felt whilst taking a phonics lesson that was being observed by her tutor. The sound of the day was 'f', innocent in itself, but one delightful child gave a totally unsuitable word and then casually asked her tutor how to spell it! Even so, she passed and learnt a great deal, except the experience left her drained and full of cold which turned into painful sinusitis.

It was with throbbing nose, eyes, head and teeth that she made her way home for the holidays. Her legs were heavy and it was with great difficulty that she arrived at her home railway station with a fifteen minute walk to her home. Exhausted, she broke down and put aside her nervousness of asking her dad to collect her. Thankfully, he agreed. Five minutes later, she was home and her aches and pains soothed with a cup of his Navy remedy of hot milk, rum and treacle. The warm, sweet liquid slipped easily down her throat bringing comfort to every part of her body. Relaxed and secure within the bosom of her family, she fell into a peaceful and refreshing sleep.

Chapter 13

The moon shines reassuringly as the story of her final year at college begins. It seemed incredible that there was only one more year to go and then she would be a near qualified teacher. However, there was a dissertation to write, a final presentation of her artwork, one more teaching practice to complete and a teaching post to find. When all had been successfully completed, all that was left was to pass her probationary year and then she would be a fully-fledged teacher. One of her dreams would have been met, leaving only the desire to find her true knight in shining armour.

For the final year, she opted for a room of her own as she felt in need of her own space. The room offered Trudi the chance to dream, to be creative and to find herself a little, only she didn't like what she found. She became more of a recluse, spending increasing time gazing out of her bedroom window at the streetlights below and listening to music that created an ethereal atmosphere in the room. The music transported her to an unknown place, arousing thoughts and emotions within and she found herself using these as a means to manifest her feelings into words, usually in the form of poetry. She also began to intuitively write, being guided by an unseen force that dictated the words and steered the pen across the paper, words which were beautiful and inspiring. The reason for her time alone is now clear in her mind; it had allowed her to become in tune with her spiritual side and develop the gifts she's been given. She's been moved to write on many occasions since then and now embraces the gift of being able to channel guided writing, as well as the gift of clairvoyance. A gift with which she has been blessed that has guided and helped her through many of life's challenges.

It was at that time that she first noticed the 'suicide path' cast by the full moon's reflection across the surface of the sea which led her to her friend in the celestial sky. The beautiful shining sphere, surrounded by a halo of yellows, blues and pinks, that hung in the sky like a Christmas bauble. As it shone, a silver path appeared which danced provocatively as its formation was broken by waves that gently rocked to and fro. It stretched before her and beckoned her, opening a path that would lead her to inner peace and tranquillity. It moved her, both emotionally and spiritually, and offered her a journey to who knew where; she felt that it would be a magical one and lead her to realms beyond her understanding. Now, here she is in the present day, staring out of a window with that self-same moon drawing her back into the past. Her friend the moon, encouraging her to follow the path, to reflect on her experiences and welcome her shadows from the past as friends not foe, as enlightenment not destruction.

For the final teaching practice, she was placed in a little village school which was set in the middle of a beautiful and quiet countryside. During the week she stayed on a farm that was about a ten-minute walk from the school, down a long country lane. The journey to and from the school brought back childhood memories of the times she walked to her friend's farm and lost herself in the wildflowers and grasses. The walk wasn't as carefree as then, due to the heavy bag accessory and the pressures of being a student teacher, yet she still enjoyed every moment. There was something peaceful and uplifting about walking in the fresh, clean air with the beauty of nature all around. It was a warm summer and the rays of sunshine glistened through the leafy trees, casting shadows that moved in position as the day wore on. Later in the day, the change in the sun's position offered some shady respite from the heat, as she slowly made her way back to the farm, whilst reflecting on her day of teaching. Luckily, the experience was proving to be far more enjoyable than the previous! The whole school appeared relaxed and the staff welcoming. The pupils were attentive and keen to learn. Whether that was due to the pupils, or her confidence having grown, she didn't know, she was just thankful for the smooth ride.

The farm was owned by a dear older couple who treated Trudi and the farm hands as part of their own big family. It was a magical time and Trudi felt totally at home. The weather was glorious, the air clean and fresh and she was enjoying the touch of freedom. Perhaps her vivacity was due to the relationship she'd begun with one of the farm hands. Martin was not what you'd call handsome, but there was a quality that had attracted Trudi to him; perhaps it was his bronzed, muscular physique!

Being Trudi, she was caught up in the magic and contemplated the idea of him being her Prince Charming. A giggle breaks the silence in the room as she brings to mind her dreams of him coming to her rescue and the two of them riding off into the sunset on his tractor! Still, that is who she is, always caught up in some magical fantasy or fairy tale. 'Well, why not,' she says to herself, 'it's certainly an escape from the reality of life.'

During the weeks that followed, she and Martin became good friends. To begin with, it was flirtatious banter with all the farm hands, though Martin was the one who was more attentive. He took her out occasionally for a quiet drink and then their connection began to change, becoming more than just friends. She thought that it was probably a 'holiday romance' and when teaching practice was over, she was prepared for a complete and final ending. Martin, however, surprised her by inviting her back to the farm for the odd weekend. He astounded her further by asking if he could accompany her to her final Prom to which she eagerly agreed. Cinderella would go to the ball, but was it with her Prince Charming? She wasn't sure.

For the Prom, Trudi made herself a long, flowing halter neck dress in a cornflower blue material. The dress fitted tightly against her chest and waist which enhanced her shapely figure, before releasing into a softly flowing skirt. The glorious weather had turned her skin to a deep golden brown that set the dress off perfectly and, with help from the corn flower blue, enhanced the blueness of her eyes. She looked and felt stunning, empathising with Cinderella as she changed from the little scullery maid whom no one had noticed, into a beautiful Princess. Unlike Cinders, she'd no need of a carriage, for her bubble awaited which floatingly transported her to the venue, hand in hand with her Prince.

Carried in the intoxicating bubble, she drifted through the evening. For the first time in her three years at college she was noticed by members of the opposite sex, who complimented her on her appearance and asked why they hadn't been aware of her before. Her exhilaration heightened as an electrifying energy surged through her body and responded to the attention she was receiving. Her whole face shone as if a secret light had been switched on that revealed a hidden beauty to the world as well as herself. The thrill within her blended with the exhilarating atmosphere of the whole room which was filled with celebration and relief that everyone had achieved their goal. Even so, there was also an element of sadness at the impending goodbyes which were put on hold until the very last moment. Locked in the arms of Martin, their bodies rubbing softly against each other as they moved to the music, they danced the final dance, oblivious of the people all around. As the music stopped, cheers and clapping echoed around the energised space. Then, slowly, as if reluctant to let go of the vibrant energy surrounding them, final goodbyes were said and the room began to empty. The evening had ended yet, unlike Cinderella, she didn't lose a glass slipper, or return home alone. She was accompanied by her friends and her possible Prince.

He stayed with her that night, carrying the magical evening deep into the early hours of the morning. Wrapped in his arms, she felt happy, at peace but aware that his kisses were becoming more searching and fervent in their quest. She felt his body responding to the closeness of hers, but despite all emotions and feelings, Trudi was unable to give herself completely. This was when she realised that perhaps he wasn't the man of her dreams. He was not her Prince Charming after all.

College was over and a new adventure was about to start. She hadn't been able to find a teaching position because jobs were hard to find, but her intuition told her that the right position would present itself. Martin promised to be in touch and to visit her at home. There was the usual 'keep in touch' from the friends she'd made, but it was her true friends, her college buddies, who kept their promise. Trudi pictures her dear friends and thinks back to the weddings they have shared and how, twenty-five years later, they revisited the old college stomping grounds. It was as if they had never been away! 'Yes, they are true friends. I know communication is the once-a-year letter inside a Christmas card, but you were there for me when I needed you. Thank you for being true friends.'

As Trudi reminisces, the glistening path below brings her attention to the next part of her story: the return home, which was far more difficult than expected. She'd become accustomed to the independent life of college, and now here she was, at nearly twenty-one, having to abide by the house rules once again. Before long, she slipped back into the good little girl and easily picked up her place in the ongoing family dynamics. However, there was also a hidden strength, which was waiting for an opportunity to reveal itself.

Martin kept his promise and visited her on several occasions. One time, he took her to his family home for his birthday celebration. She was nervous about the prospect of meeting his mum, which was heightened by the fact that there was a hundred-mile motorbike journey ahead of her. The closest she'd come to riding a bike was one with pedals! They set off on the journey with Trudi clinging on for dear life as the bike made its way round the winding twisting roads which led to the motorway. The engine vibrated, gently at first, and her body moved with the motion, as instructed, when the bike wound its way round a bend. It was when they were on the long open road that the vibration became more vigorous. Her whole body shook from head to toe, as if she was being mixed in a blender. Gradually, she relaxed and began to enjoy the thrill of feeling the wind blowing across her face as Martin raced along the road. It was on removing her body from the bike that the impact of the experience hit her. Jelly like legs wobbled beneath her and felt so numb that they appeared not to belong to her. Her whole body still vibrated as her bones attempted to reconnect inside, bringing stability to a fragile torso. As the blood began to flow freely once more, the parts of her body that had been deadened by the pressure of the seat awakened. Her body was reacting as if it'd been inside a machine that had tossed it from side to side as well as up and down, but she'd come out of it alive. All she needed to do was survive the weekend and the journey home.

Shortly after the weekend, which had been more enjoyable than she'd expected, Martin joined her to celebrate her twenty first birthday. Her college roommates, much to her delight, attended too, staying the night at her house whilst Martin stayed at Fran's. Her sister had offered to hold the party at her home and it was full to the brim with family and friends. A magical evening of fun and laughter followed, made even more special because Martin was there, except she was still not able to take their intimacy a step further. She saw Martin a few times after that, and then the crunch came. He decided that there was no future for them. This she could have accepted; it was the fact that he discussed it with Fran, which hurt Trudi to the core. Why hadn't he talked to her first? He thought of Fran as being knowledgeable and spiritually guided and she, in her wisdom, advised him to end the relationship. However, what made Trudi truly angry was the fact that Fran couldn't understand why she was upset. In truth, Trudi had known that there was no future with Martin, but what gave her sister the right to interfere?

She presses pause on the scene below to allow herself time to mull over the uncertainty and questions that have been provoked. She can see how control had been taken away from her, and her emotions ignored, which has happened time and time again throughout her life. She brings to mind all the times this has occurred, considers the family dynamics that she'd so easily fallen into and becomes aware of the games they'd all played. She, and her siblings, had each been given a role to play; there was so much worry of getting it wrong buried deep within each of them that it brought about anger and guilt which resulted in conflict and turmoil. There has certainly been much conflict that has caused her pain and heartbreak and so many times that she has been wrongly accused. However, she can see that people had successfully found her Achilles heel: guilt and fear. There is no blame to be apportioned. She can simply learn from her lessons and try to change accordingly. A shiver runs through her body as an unseen voice quietly murmurs in her ear, 'life is the biggest educator of them all and will continue to provide you with the opportunities to learn.'

The moon's light pulls her attention back to the unfolding story. Trudi was twenty-one years old, with no boyfriend and no teaching job. Teaching vacancies were few and far between. She had no worries over this area of her life as she firmly held on to the belief that she'd always been destined to become a teacher. It was as if her soul was leading her along her chosen path. There was a deep, inner knowing that when the time was right, she would be successful, although her dad believed differently and tried to direct her future. Whilst waiting for a teaching position, she was working in a home for children with additional needs, mentally, physically and emotionally. She felt that the job was very rewarding, but her father considered it a complete waste of her qualifications. He wanted her to join the Civil Service, as with her qualifications she'd be able to enter at a high level. She knew that this wouldn't be right for her and her hidden strength came to the fore as she insisted that she would be successful in obtaining a teaching post.

Whilst working in the home, she caught German Measles which affected her quite badly. The rash was tolerable, but the pain in her head and behind her eyes was excruciating. It felt as if someone was hammering pins into her eyeballs and bashing cymbals inside her head. They say things happen for a reason and it was during the time off sick that the phone call of her future came. She was invited to attend an interview at an infant school not far from home. Her life was about to change.

She remembers the feelings of apprehension when she attended the interview as if it was yesterday. A picture of the school is presented to her: a cold, bleak, Victorian building which needed some tender love and care. The head mistress was fairly young, with a stern and unapproachable demeanour which blended in well with the Victorian atmosphere. Trudi visualises herself sitting opposite the hard-faced lady who'd barricaded herself behind a desk as if to prevent anyone from seeing the true person. Question after question was fired, making it more like an interrogation than an interview. All that was missing was the bright light shining menacingly into Trudi's eyes. Aside from that, life dealt her a good hand and the interview was a success; she was offered the post which would begin after Christmas. All she had to do now was learn to drive and find a man, but in which order?

Christmas was knocking on the door, bringing the start of her new career ever closer. She had a mixture of excitement and apprehension bubbling away inside about the forth coming teaching post and her future as a whole. There was still no man in her life. The vision of being the old spinster teacher, forever on the shelf and persistently waiting for her knight in shining armour to come and rescue her was foremost in her mind. The night she was feeling very sorry for herself, lost in her own misery and thoughts, comes to mind and causes her to smile.

Alice had a new boyfriend, which only helped to reinforce Trudi's single status. Alone again at Christmas. The sound of her voice loudly singing the words of 'It'll be lonely this Christmas' was briefly interrupted by the phone ringing, but she quickly resumed the indulgence of self-pity. She ignored the phone and told herself that 'it would be for Alice anyway.' It was for Alice, except the call also involved Trudi and turned out to be the reason for her meeting her gallant saviour. Trudi grins and laughs affectionately as the picture reveals Alice suddenly appearing in her room and presenting her with a fait accompli. She'd arranged a blind date for that night. Orders to dress and put on make-up were swiftly given, followed by a final statement of 'no arguments.' Alice then left, leaving her shaking and nervous sister to get ready for the daunting and unknown events to unfold. She was applying the final touches to her make up when she heard the knock at the front door. Aware of her sister's voice mingling with a male voice, she strained to listen to the words that were being spoken, merely receiving a muffled and indiscernible noise. The voices below stopped and were followed by thundering footsteps up the stairs. The bedroom door burst open revealing a flustered Alice who, after taking a deep breath, uttered 'he's o.k. but put your shoes on.'

When Trudi finally plucked up enough courage to go downstairs, the wisdom of her sister's words registered. Even with her platform shoes on, she was towered over by a tall, slim man standing in the doorway. Shyly, her eyes slowly travelled up the long legs and body to meet a pair of big brown eyes gazing down at her. Her heart skipped a beat as a click of recognition echoed in her mind, accompanied by the sensation of meeting a long-lost love as her soul entwined with his. It was him; the kiss on the cheek that she'd cherished for so many years, was re-awakened. Seven years had passed. She hadn't even passed him in the street and now, there he was, standing in front of her. Robert! She saw the sign of recognition on his face and knew, from the moment their eyes met, that he was the one. No matter what, she knew that she would spend the rest of her life with him. A whirlwind romance followed.

Chapter 14

Christmas had come and gone and a new year was beginning, along with the start of Trudi's new career and a new job for Robert as a tour guide for a local coach business. Their connection was becoming more serious day by day and she was completely overwhelmed by the intensity of the feelings that was burning away inside her. A volcano of passion that had lain dormant for years, waiting to be awakened by her knight, was aroused and became too strong to ignore. She was unable to resist the growing desire and finally succumbed. She willingly, but nervously, surrendered her body to the man who had touched her soul and stolen her heart. Hearing the words 'I think I love you' made her heart pound and these words were shortly followed by promises about their future. A river of jubilation coursed through her veins when he finally asked her to marry him. Neither of them wanted a long engagement and so they decided to marry in the August of the coming summer, which came as no surprise to her parents when they were informed. There were seven months of planning and she would have the school summer holiday to finalise arrangements, as well as have time for a brief honeymoon.

The weeks flew by, with Trudi caught up in the magic and floating through life in her bubble of love. She was settled in her teaching role and life was the happiest it had ever been. Then the first obstacle presented itself – she was pregnant. It wasn't just the pregnancy, she also had to consider her career as well as ask the question, 'were she and Robert actually ready for this commitment?' Warning bells began to ring, alerting her of possible outcomes, but Robert was very supportive when she told him. Her doubts were squashed and she realised what an idiot she was for worrying. The forthcoming baby didn't change anything, except the wedding date, which was brought forward a couple of months.

Trudi's mind is taken to the moment she'd told her parents the news. She sees her mum sitting silently, disappointment evident in her eyes, whereas pure anger was visible in the whole of her dad's body, who also voiced his opinion very loudly. He saw it as a complete waste of her life and qualifications, even though her intention was to return to teaching after the birth of the baby. The anger showed in his voice and the way in which the words were hurled towards her, the ferocity of which hit like cannon balls against her chest. His eyes bulged with a mixture of disappointment and fury. Clenched fists hung tightly at his side and his cheeks developed a redness as his anger was contained. She sighs at the memory and recollects that it was at that point that she decided to uncomfortably leave her parents and the emotive scene behind.

Trudi watches as, with head held low and shoulders slumped, her younger self walked from the kitchen with a picture in her mind of her father's ears letting out steam as the pressure inside his head was discharged. She didn't return until very late into the night in the hope of avoiding her parents, but Alice's warning from the bedroom window told her that she hadn't been successful. After a reassuring hug from Robert, she warily made her way towards the front door. Inhaling deeply, she quietly unlocked the door and paused for a moment before heading towards the kitchen where she found the recipient of her dad's anger. Several of the kitchen doors had been used as a punch bag as angry fists had found release.

He was standing quietly in the corner of the kitchen with his back towards her and the emotional turmoil still evident in his slouching body. It was obvious to her how she'd bitterly disappointed him and she felt so guilty for having let him down. Slowly and silently, she walked over to him, ignoring the fact that he didn't turn. Undeterred, she slipped her arms around him and whispered, 'I'm so sorry Dad,' and, without waiting for a response, she tiptoed away in the hope that sleep would bring some ease to the situation. She now understands that her dad's anger had been frustration more than disappointment. He loved her and only wanted the best for her. Perhaps he'd been able to see into the future and knew of the storm which was heading her way?

Telling her parents was difficult enough, but Trudi still had to inform the school and face her future in laws. Robert's mum was first. He disappeared to bury his head in the sand (a trait of his she's discovered over the years), leaving her alone to break the news. All in all, his mum took the news well, showing no emotion, a characteristic which, Trudi came to learn, was often evident. Practicality was her solution to everything. She offered them assistance in the organisation of the wedding and a room in her house until they were able to find a place of their own. Above all, being a devout Christian, she was pleased that her son was 'doing the right thing' and marrying Trudi.

She looks back on informing the school as having been even more daunting. Not only was there the stigma of being pregnant whilst unmarried, but there was also the big question of how it would affect her whole career. The feeling of being a naughty little schoolgirl swamped every inch of her body as she entered the Headteacher's office. She positioned herself, as requested, in a chair facing the Head who was sitting behind her desk. The very prim and proper single lady who'd originally interviewed her, sat with a straight poker face void of any emotion or thought and listened intently as the problem was relayed. The separating desk gave the same impression of a barrier as it had before and intensified the awkwardness. Trudi relives distinctly how each word made her body squirm in her seat as she informed the Head of the predicament she faced. The expressionless face first spoke words of annoyance at the situation, followed by ones of support. Due to the circumstances and the fact that Trudi had demonstrated that she was a committed and able teacher, arrangements would be made for the probationary time to be shortened. Then, a few weeks later, all the turmoil and trouble seemed to have been pointless and fade into oblivion as new emotions engulfed her whole being, shaking her to the core. Trudi miscarried.

It began with stomach pains at work but was told by a colleague that it was normal to feel the inner changes taking place and so she'd dismissed it. A few days later, she woke early with a pain that stabbed at her internally. Short sharp pains came at first which developed into a deep throb in her abdomen, making her double over in agony. Without mentioning it to a soul, she struggled to the bathroom to prepare for work, where she became aware of a warm, wet sensation forming between her legs. Nervously, she peered between her trembling limbs. Blood!

There was no ignoring it. It was time to talk to her mum, who immediately phoned the doctor and before she had time to think about what was happening, was wheeled into a waiting ambulance. There were no words of reassurance from her parents. She was totally alone with no one there to comfort her or support her as the ambulance whisked her away. Her only companions were trepidation, apprehension and the ambulance crew.

The staff at the hospital weren't any more reassuring. They explained what was happening and that a D and C was required to make sure that the womb was completely clear, but she felt that there was an air of disapproval. She now reckons that it was her guilt. The 'good girl' showed her face and she found herself turning her engagement ring round to make it resemble a wedding ring in the hope that this would lessen the judgemental stares. She desperately wanted Robert, to feel his arms around her, to feel his love and tenderness, but he didn't come. It was her parents who appeared on the ward and took her home. It was her parents who told her that it was all for the best and to pull herself together when she broke.

The suffering and emptiness of that time consumes her body and she feels the hurt that she'd hoped she would never have to endure again. She experiences the sense of abandonment she had that day which was reinforced by the absence of the man she loved. She senses the alarm that had devoured all her common sense, panic that Robert had walked away. Then an overwhelming anger dominates as she is reminded of the reason why he wasn't there. She is shown the picture of Robert as he finally appeared at her bedside, looking worried and concerned. He cradled her in his arms, apologising that he'd not been there for her. His words of explanation had taken a while to register because she was soaking up the love and comfort evident in his touch. She remembers him asking how she was and saying how sorry he was for not being there. She experiences, again, the shock and extreme fury she'd felt as he said that he hadn't known. Her parents hadn't told him. It was Fran who decided that he should be informed. 'Good old Fran,' she thinks, 'this time you did right by me. Thank you.'

The past penetrates her mind and buried emotions are suddenly stirred and awakened to such an intensity that she's unable to prevent it. Anger engulfs her and a hatred towards her parents swamps her, giving a sensation of being sucked under a mass of thick mud. She gasps, desperately seeking air that appears out of reach. How could they have denied Robert, the father of her child, the knowledge that he'd lost his baby? How could they have denied her the comfort she'd so desperately needed? She sits quietly, permitting every emotion to penetrate until she feels she might explode. Her stomach expands with each breath she takes and her mind whirls with each thought that enters. Bile rises in the back of her throat as everything is pushed up to a mirrored surface that reflects it all before her mind's eye. Studying with earnest the images that are forming she asks for answers, for clarity and for release. Words begin to penetrate her head. She is guided to put pen to paper and the words appearing give plausible explanations. Her parents had been suffering too. Their own pain of losing a child had been awakened only they hadn't shared it. They'd identified with her torment yet hadn't been able to acknowledge it. Their shadows from the past had risen and clouded their actions, but they had, in their own way, been trying to give her strength, to protect her. They both had concerns about her future. 'Yes, Mum, you were right to have them, weren't you?' she says to the room. As the answers to her questions are revealed, Trudi feels comforted. The heaviness has lifted, the nausea gone. Understanding and compassion replaces the anger, love replaces hatred and thanks are given to her parents for caring for her so deeply that they had wanted to protect her from the future.

Trudi is taken back to the weeks after the miscarriage when she needed time to recover physically as well as emotionally. She was signed off sick for a few weeks which enabled her to finalise the wedding preparations for, even though she'd given Robert an opportunity to delay the wedding, or even a means of escape, he was still adamant that he loved her and insisted on going ahead as planned.

They couldn't afford an extravagant affair and so found ways to keep the cost as low as possible. Her wedding dress had previously been bought in a style intended to cover any signs of a growing bump and, consequently, wasn't the dress she would have really liked. It wasn't overly fancy, simply delicate with a form of subtle elegance. She'd also chosen a plain long veil which was held in place by a small sparkling white semi-domed cap. She settled on a bouquet of white flowers: a mixture of roses and lily of the valley with green foliage mixed in between which altogether formed a small diamond shaped arrangement. Her friend's daughters were to be bridesmaids and to keep the cost to a minimum, Trudi made their dresses herself. The marriage was taking place in a small local Church with the reception being held in the Church Hall; all catering was being done by the family. Her uncle offered to be wedding photographer and a family friend offered to drive her to the Church in his car, a white saloon which, once polished and decorated with white ribbons, would very much look the part on the day. Trudi settles in her chair as the wedding day starts to play out before her. She recaptures the Cinderella moments, the magic and the love she'd felt all around her.

On the morning of the wedding, she woke to a blaze of glorious sunshine. She was too excited to eat breakfast, but her mum insisted on her eating at least one slice of toast, after which she set about helping with the food preparations. She really did relate to Cinderella. Dressed in rags (well, dressing gown), she helped to prepare, and present, the food for the finger buffet. Time was ticking and the clock struck twelve. Although the ceremony wasn't until three, she must allow herself time to get ready. Cinders left the scullery and went upstairs to her room. She showered and carefully applied make-up. She dried her hair which she styled in the fashionable pageboy mode and changed from her rags into her ball gown before heading back to the kitchen to make sandwiches. In nearly full wedding attire, she stood in the kitchen, knife in hand, poised ready to collect the butter and spread it onto the never ending mounds of bread lying before her. Finally, everything was all set to be taken to the venue whilst she finished her own preparation.

Cinderella went upstairs to finish her transformation from scullery girl to Princess. Final checks were made and then the last piece of the make-over was completed. She brushed her hair under neatly before placing the cap and veil on top of her head, put on her shoes and then made her way downstairs. Her mum had already left with the bridesmaids, leaving her home alone with her dad. The car arrived which had been polished until it gleamed, giving it a reflective surface from which the sun's rays bounced and nearly blinded Trudi as she stepped out of the house. Not a word was spoken as her dad escorted her down the path and helped her into the car. They travelled in silence to the Church. Once there, her dad took her gently by the arm and looked lovingly at his daughter. He spoke the words that she'd always hoped to hear. Not 'I love you,' but words that held so much more. He softly said, 'you look beautiful.' Words so simple yet full of sentiment and admiration, a moment that still fills her with an overpowering sense of love. A moment she holds very close to her heart. There'd been no anger, no reproach, just love. How she wishes he'd shown it before and that she'd told him how much he meant to her but the words never seemed to come.

Carried by the love she was feeling, she floated down the aisle, with her dad by her side, to meet Robert. Their eyes met as her father passed her hand to Robert's, tenderness evident in his as he whispered, 'you look gorgeous.' They turned towards the Vicar ready to make their marriage vows and exchange rings. She would be truly married; the fairy tale would come true and they would live happily ever after. The magic continued into the early evening. Speeches, food, dancing, wine, laughter and love all played their part in the magical concoction that had cast its spell over the couple. She was in a bubble of paradise, gliding through each moment which appeared to last for ever. Then, the day drew to its close and she found herself sitting in her carriage, next to her husband. They were about to embark on their new life as Mr and Mrs, albeit living alongside Robert's parents, something which seemed very similar to her parents' start.

Despite their living arrangements, the romance and magic continued to fill her heart. There was a lightness about her with her feet not touching the ground as she floated through each day. Work had resumed and she enjoyed every moment of teaching skills to those little souls whose parents had entrusted into her care. It was rewarding when pupils began to read or write and she quickly learnt that there was more to teaching than teaching skills. It involved being a mum, a nurse, a counsellor, a psychologist, a friend, but above all, someone who cared enough to listen, have fun and make them feel safe. Building good relationships with the parents was also very important, being there when they needed support, or answers to questions and to give them confidence in her ability to care for their child. She knows without doubt that she'd always achieved this and that she was a very good teacher who was loved by pupils and parents alike. She was a natural and no one can ever take away the pride or sense of achievement she has.

The school in which she was teaching was about twelve miles from her mother-in-law's house. Trudi hadn't yet managed to pass her driving test. She was trying to practise as often as she could although was reliant upon Robert being available. She snorts heavily at the memory of finding him sitting in the car wearing a crash helmet which was comical, just not very encouraging! Until she passed, she relied upon her dad to pick her up on his way to work and drop her at school twenty minutes later. Getting home was not as straight forward. This required a bus journey, a train ride, followed by a thirty-minute walk. Not that she minded the walk, even with the heavy bag of preparation in her hand. She used the time to dream about her married life and make plans for their future. She looked at the gardens and houses she passed, considering which one she would like as a marital home and, as she skipped past people walking along the path, she wondered if they felt as happy as she did.

Even living with her in laws didn't take away her happiness, despite being a little uncomfortable when she arrived at the house. After all, she hadn't known these people for very long and part of her considered herself a guest in their house. She almost jumped for joy if the house was empty when she arrived home. This meant she didn't have to socialise; she could go straight upstairs and prepare for her husband's return. It was on those days that she waited impatiently for his car to pull into the drive and then, with feet as light as a feather, glided down the stairs, leapt from the bottom stair and flung her arms around his neck. Their lips met and she was gently led up the stairs into their room where they made the most of the empty house.

An air of cynicism washes over her and she sighs deeply at the memory. 'Not all empty houses bring heartwarming experiences, some bring heartbreak.' That was then. Times change. People change. Things happen. On reflection, she now realises just how much their start to married life had coloured their future. She admits that her shadows were always hovering in the background, waiting for an excuse to rear their ugly head. They'd had a lightning romance and hadn't had time to truly get to know each other, to become accustomed to each other's ways and to fully understand each other. This develops over time, but their foundation wasn't stable. Emotions and hormones were still reeling after the miscarriage and she's only just perceived how deeply it had affected her. She'd been undergoing the process of grieving and didn't have the insight to learn from the experience. Instead, she continued the habit of pushing unwanted feelings deep down inside and out of sight. Now, through knowledge and spiritual growth, she is wise to how, like the hidden fuel within a car, concealed emotions can drive reactions, especially when confronted with uncomfortable situations. Reactions fuelled by her guilt, her fear of failure, dislike of herself and her need to please. All the emotions that keep her living as a self-made victim, a role which, she's discovered, is another her mum also had.

Perhaps if they'd had a better start, life may have been different. Although, if it was all part of her life's journey, her soul's learning, then it all had to be. She has certainly learnt a great deal about people but, more importantly, about herself. She'd entered married life bringing a dowry of shadows from the past which had fed her insecurities, created vulnerabilities and encouraged her to expect the worse. She'd written the script which was waiting to be enacted with her as the main character, the victim.

Chapter 15

They hadn't been married long when Robert announced that he had the opportunity to become a British tour guide during the tourist seasons. It would mean him staying away for five days a week for as long as a season lasted, the prospect of which Trudi didn't favour. The rejection surfaced from the depths of beyond. He saw it as a good experience, she saw it as a loss, a loss of her new husband. She was being abandoned and no matter how much they discussed it, she knew it was a fait accompli. Her feelings ignored, by Robert as well as herself, she embarked upon the role that was to become part of her newly married life, that of a grass widow.

She finds herself identifying with how her mother must have felt when her dad was in the Navy. She experiences true empathy with her mum's misery and loneliness, but above all with the feeling of not belonging in the house which was supposed to be home. Just as her mum had, she visited her own family as frequently as she could. She caught the bus to her hometown, taking a bag of clothes so that she could stay a few days. Occasionally, if she wanted exercise or fresh air, she walked instead of sitting on a stuffy bus, breathing the air deeply in to every cell of her body with each step taken, until her lungs were filled to bursting. Then, with great strength behind it, she forced the breath into the space around her, as if she was a dragon breathing fire from its nostrils. As the breath escaped, she released the frustrations of life. 'I would have screamed too if I could have,' she murmurs quietly but with a conviction that she feels all the way from her head to her toes.

The weather at that time, was still as glorious as it had been on her wedding day. The sun was shining brightly, the sky a clear blue and there hadn't been any significant rain for months. She spent the summer holidays sunbathing in her parents' garden, absorbing the sun as if her body was a sponge, or on the beach with her mum and Alice as company. She was more secure in the bosom of her own family except she missed Robert desperately. Fridays couldn't come quick enough. She packed her bag, waved goodbye and made the journey back, with butterflies flying in her stomach as the delight at seeing her husband increased.

Back at the house, she waited expectantly for Robert to arrive and to be whisked into his arms as he stepped into the room. She waited for his lips to caress hers, for his body to show how much he had missed her, but his appearance didn't usually live up to her expectations. Her dream was shattered as he walked in, smiled and said 'hello' before taking her hand and sitting beside her on the sofa. Neither of them was able to show their burning desire with an audience, for nine times out of ten, his parents were present. This waited until they were alone in their room, when all her concerns were swept away as their mouths met and their bodies entwined; two souls united in a long-awaited passion. Lying wrapped in Robert's arms, she felt safe, clinging hold of every piece of blissful pleasure before it was time to say goodbye once more.

As the weeks of separation went by, the need for a place of their own intensified. Trudi was yearning to be a 'proper' wife. She wanted to cook meals for her husband and have their own space where they could relax and be themselves. Luck was on their side. A friend knew of a 'granny annexe' flat which was available to rent. It had its own entrance, kitchen, lounge, bathroom and bedroom. It was perfect and affordable; however, the owner needed a quick response and Robert was away. That night, she was hardly able to contain herself whilst she waited for her husband to phone. She paced up and down, like a cat on a hot tin roof, until the phone rang. The receiver was quickly grabbed and, before he had a chance to speak, she shared the news, holding her breath in anticipation of the response. She almost burst with excitement when he agreed to visit the flat on his return, the following day, with the possibility of moving in.

The flat offered them all they needed, but most importantly, the chance to become a 'normal' couple and to have a place of their own. They accepted the tenancy and planned to move in a few weeks later. As the flat was already furnished, the move was straightforward; the only things that required moving were clothes and personal belongings. It didn't take long to arrange the flat as they wanted, which was swiftly followed by the new enthralling experience of a weekly shop to stock the empty cupboards and fridge. She laughs out loud in disbelief at how excited she was over a grocery shop. Nowadays she even finds it soul destroying completing an online shop that is delivered to her kitchen! Back then, there weren't as many supermarkets competing for custom, they weren't as big and certainly didn't offer as much variety. It was a case of driving to the nearest supermarket and doing the shopping yourself. No click and collect! No home deliveries! 'Also, no substitutes,' she sniggers. Even so, she recalls, the novelty of their first shop together soon wearing off as it became part of the regular routine, fitting it in around work. It became even more of a chore if she had to walk the two miles there and back, burdened with heavy bags. 'It's strange,' she ponders, 'how things that once gave pleasure so easily become a chore. People really are fickle and are never completely content!'

The moon calls her mind back to the evolving history of her life and presents her with a bundle of mixed emotions which, at the time, she hadn't been able to understand, or manage.

The autumn months that followed, brought a mixture of sentiments for her, some happy, some sad. She was overjoyed at moving into their own place and becoming a wife in the true sense, or at least as she perceived her role at the time. She laughs as she speaks to her luminous friend, 'my ideas of a wife have changed considerably over the years; I realise how difficult I made life.' Her moods were, at that time, exceptionally changeable. She discovered herself feeling low, even neurotic. She accused Robert of only marrying her because of the baby, a baby she'd lost. One day she would feel fat and ugly and the next was able to find a tiny morsel that she admired. There were times when she wanted to shut herself away and weep, and other times, she was happy, full of fun and enjoying life. She was certainly not easy to live with, yet he stood by her despite the uncertainty of how to best deal with her emotional explosions.

Trudi permits her pal in the sky to encourage her to mull over this part of her life and it suddenly all seems so simple to explain: her body was still recovering from the miscarriage and her emotions affected by changing hormones. She becomes aware of the effect that this also had on Robert, acknowledging perhaps for the first time that he was also grieving. Grieving not only for the loss of their baby, but also for a child he'd lost before they'd met, which had left him with a mass of unaddressed issues. She can make connections between hers and Robert's past experiences, understanding the impact these have had on their life together. There are links between major traumas they have shared and those experienced previously. She can appreciate how their individual bags of hidden emotions have spilled and combined to form a united bag of ingredients. Ingredients for a recipe of a volatile concoction which was just waiting for the necessary seasoning to be included for it to explode. Recipes from the past seasoning the future, bringing to the taste buds of life flavours that possess an added zest, an additional zing and definitely an extra punch. Flavours offering tastes that were bitter and sweet which culminated in an overall sourness, leaving an unpleasant residue that would take time to dissipate. Flavours which would need their ingredients to be sieved and separated, leaving them ready to be freshly combined and create a new recipe for life.

The memory of their first Christmas in their own home emerges from the moonlight. They had decorated the lounge together in a simple way to represent the time of year. In the corner of the room stood a small Christmas tree which emanated its fresh pine fragrance every time she walked by or touched it. During the day, the tinsel lying on the branches glistened as the light shining through the window fell on the silvery threads. In the evening, the tree took on a completely different appearance as the lights were switched on. A mixture of moving colours brought the tree to life as they flickered on and off and encouraged the tinsel and baubles to join in their dance. Sitting on the top of the tree, a golden star shone in the light and displayed the importance of its role in the Christmas story. As she takes in the picture that is being presented, she can't help but think that the changing lights were symbolic of her life at that time. Joy and happiness switching on and off, brightness flickering and emotions dancing, all represented by the Christmas tree.

They couldn't host any festive meals themselves as the flat was too small to accommodate a large gathering. Christmas Eve was spent with her family and she thinks fondly of how a roast dinner was presented by her parents which was always a welcome treat even if there was another to eat the following day. As she focusses on the memory, she detects the aroma of the roast pork with crunchy crackling, the accompanying mouthwatering crispy potatoes, homemade sage and onion stuffing and a sweet apple sauce. Of course, the vegetables always included the obligatory sprouts! Pudding usually consisted of the choice between a homemade apple pie with cream or custard, or, if preferred, a strawberry trifle. She thinks of how the ambience changed over the years. In the early days, the house was filled with adults playing card games or charades. As time passed, it altered, with the contented noise of an ever-growing family buzzing through the building, the laughter of excited children and the crying of over tired little ones. 'Happy times,' she whispers, 'but also sad, especially as you deteriorated more and more Dad.'

Christmas day was spent with Robert's family. It was pleasant enough, except Trudi found the chaos of her mother-in law's cooking almost too much to cope with. The kitchen tops became invisible under the debris from the cooking explosion that had taken place. Almost every cooking utensil had been utilised and abandoned in the place where they'd last seen action, causing the work surfaces to gradually disappear. However, the meal that followed tickled each and every taste bud on the tongue which led everyone to overindulge in the food extravaganza. The main course comprised of turkey, beef and ham with crispy roasted potatoes that crunched under the force of the bite. Sausage stuffing, thyme and parsley, cranberry sauce and light Yorkshire puddings were all available along with a variety of vegetables. But it was the desserts that contributed to the explosive pressure of an already overloaded belly! Puff pastry apple pie, chocolate profiteroles, and a very rich Christmas pudding. All homemade of course and accompanied by thick yellow custard, whipped double cream, pouring single cream or brandy butter.

Once the meal was finished, it was time to put on the combat uniform and head into the war zone where, with stomach feeling heavy and full, the battle commenced. Somehow, working alongside her sister-in-law, they managed to clear the debris and restore order to a once cluttered area. A walk followed to assist in the digestion of food before tea was presented. They gently strolled along a nearby riverside path which was used frequently by the locals and displayed the changes that come with each season. The colours of spring, summer and autumn had all vanished, leaving the sleepy barrenness of winter. As they walked, the warmth of their breath formed a smoky veil as it escaped from their mouths and hit the cool winter air. It was a refreshing and revitalising walk which was appreciated greatly by their overloaded bellies.

Back home, their stomachs began to prepare for the oncoming Christmas tea. They were feeling slightly less uncomfortable, though not fully ready to indulge in the plates of sandwiches and of course, Christmas cake. It was Christmas and so it would be rude not to sample a small tasting. A groaning group of people, who really should have known better, then gathered to play card games and empty glasses of wine until it was time to leave for their own home.

On Boxing Day, the couple met Alice and boyfriend Stuart for a Christmas drink at a local pub where, on entering, a roaring log fire brought respite from the cold winter's night. The flames caught Trudi's attention as they danced joyfully in their yellow and orange clothes and then leapt upwards as they were drawn by the draught from the chimney. Their flickering movements became stronger and brighter. As a new piece of log was thrown on to join the burning embers, smouldering colours with a reddish hue formed which added to the Christmas colours already present. Slowly, it ignited, making crackling sounds as red sparks pirouetted and exploded in the air, the noise joining the heightened voices in the room, voices that were booming out Christmas carols. It was a scene that continued until the final bell was rung and the people started to leave, with singing voices that could still be heard as they wove their merry way back home.

Trudi sighs and closes her eyes so that she can keep the picture alive, not only of that night but of all the nights that they had shared there. She pulls her knees tightly into her chest and hugs the warmth of those nights into her whole being. It wasn't just the warmth from a burning fire, it was the cosiness within the atmosphere and the comfort of shared love, no matter the time of year. 'They were magical evenings, or was it me caught up in the romanticism of it all?' She begins to wonder if she'd lived in a fantasy world, the one she'd imagined as a child, because the feeling she'd had then certainly hadn't continued for long; she knows that the bubble in which she'd been living back then is, at some point in the future scenes, going to burst. It then strikes her how, like the changing lights being a representation of her life at that time, the flames of the fire could easily illustrate it too, not only of that time but also the future. The joyful dance which turned into strong flickering movements and culminated in red sparks exploding. 'Yes, very symbolic, especially my future,' she murmurs.

Chapter 16

Their first year together was swiftly over and another about to begin, bringing with it the possibility of buying their own home. Appointments were made to view a selection of houses. They eagerly followed an estate agent like sheep as he did his utmost to persuade them to buy, managing to make a complete hovel sound like a palace. Then she saw **the** house, a three bedroomed end of terrace set back from the road. It was as if the house was waiting for her, a long-lost lover; she knew instantly that that was the one. She pictures herself walking along the path towards the front door, which opened and invited them to step inside the house. As they walked in Robert squeezed her hand, which instantly told her that he felt the same as she did. This was their future home.

It was only a matter of weeks before they were able to move. There were no complications and no chain, simply a mortgage to arrange and boxes to pack. As they didn't possess any furniture, the move was painless; they could manage with the few odd bits and pieces that people had kindly given them and the rest would come later. The first thing was to scrub the house from top to bottom and try to make a home from the little they had. They might not have had a great deal, but they had a home. The neighbours made them very welcome and there was a real sense of community spirit which became even more apparent when they all worked together to create a street party for the Queen's Silver Jubilee. Tables were placed in a long line down the length of the road and covered with red, white and blue tablecloths. Plates of a variety of foods were set out, including many sandwiches and cakes decorated with red, white and blue icing. Soft drinks were available for the children and wine flowed for those adults who wished to indulge. Union Jack bunting hung between the lamp posts and flags were positioned at differing points along the tables. An extension lead ran from a nearby house, which allowed music to be played from a music centre, enticing the revellers to turn the road into a dance floor. Bodies gyrated, arms and legs lashed out in all directions as they attempted to catch the beat of the music being played, which blasted out well into the night.

All in all, it was a fun day and she should have been feeling content and happy, especially as they'd also recently celebrated their first wedding anniversary. Yet, there was that ever present underlying insecurity, a worry that something was going to happen to burst her bubble, shadows waiting in the background. Thinking back, she considers again the possibility of her fears and negative thinking being the magnet that had drawn the oncoming incidents towards her. Also, as the good girl had let her down, had she mapped out a path of turmoil and suffering as a form of self- punishment? 'Well, life certainly seemed to be dishing out the punishment,' she mutters.

The path below, becomes a vessel for loneliness and heartache as the time for Robert to leave swoops down upon her once more. She witnesses in person the anxiety and insecurity as he continued with the weekly tours, reliving the undeniable apprehension that it was the beginning of something significant over which she had no command. 'And I was right!' she shouts triumphantly, with a little bit of anger mixed in. Her inner feelings had been right and this knowledge led her to later trusting herself more than the people around her.

A positive step forward for her, came with passing her driving test which gave her a newfound independence. She could drive to work, visit family and socialise in the evenings, all of which helped alleviate some of the loneliness she was experiencing whilst Robert was away. In some ways, she recaptured the freedom of her student days, with the addition of an incessant longing for her husband's return. School holidays were the worst because she no longer had work to occupy her mind. She passed her time in the garden, shopping or visiting Fran. Preparations for Alice's impending wedding also kept her busy as her sewing skills were once again called into action, assisting her mum in making the bridesmaids' dresses. She calls to mind her sister's wedding and imagines the young bridesmaids in their pretty pastel dresses following Alice, who'd looked so beautiful, as their dad escorted her down the aisle. 'Why is it,' she asks herself, 'that, other than how beautiful Alice looked, all I can remember of the day is me thinking how fat and ugly I was, when, in truth,

I looked good.' She hurriedly searches through her photos until she finds the one of her on the wedding day. The photo portrays a young woman wearing a light blue A-line midi skirt and a flowery top bearing colours that complemented the skirt. As she looks at the photo, she catches sight of a young, attractive, slim girl who looked radiant and happy. 'Why on earth did I think myself fat and ugly?' she wonders.

She suddenly becomes angry about all the time she has wasted wallowing in negativity, self-destructiveness and self-pity. She no longer has youth on her side and passing time has changed her appearance. Smooth skin has been used as a canvas by the artist called life, adding lines which depict the journey taken and outline parts of the story as it unfolds. Lines which, if read correctly, portray happiness, heartbreak, laughter, tears and suffering but above all, wisdom. Life has continued using its artistic skills to add texture and fullness to the once firm frame, telling a tale of creation, happiness, motherhood and fulfilment. A canvas portraying the beauty and knowledge of life itself. A self-portrait. A portrait to be admired not spurned. A portrait to be looked on with love not contempt.

Trudi knows she should now become the artist and replace the grimace that so often reflects from the mirror with a smile. It is time to allow the wisdom and knowledge hidden between the lines of her story to radiate out and paint her whole face, filling the gaps with beauty and light. It is time to view her image in a new light and change the one she sees and assumes others see. She hesitantly looks into a mirror and smiles shyly at the face staring back at her. The face returns the smile, encouraging her to look more intently. She detects her story unravelling before her, each line, each crease adding depth and meaning. She gazes deeply into the eyes, the mirror of the soul, and senses the wisdom concealed within. Still focussing on the face, she wraps her arms around her, hugging her body tight and says 'thank you. Thank you for helping me to write my story and to paint my picture. Thank you for the wisdom, the lessons learnt, the strength and love. You are me and I am you. We are one. Thank you.'

Trudi breathes deeply, partly in acknowledgement of the last realisation, but also in preparation for what she knows is about to be revealed. She's in need of some Dutch courage and so pours herself a large glass of wine, takes a deep breath and shouts 'bring it on!'

The time for Robert to return on tour arrived, but on this occasion, she suffered a vulnerability that made her stomach churn. She'd no explanation for the rising emotions nor for the doubts that were bubbling under the surface. When she voiced the distress she was experiencing, she was told she was being silly by Robert and also by her family. Despite everyone trying to put her mind at rest, deep inside she knew something was wrong. She had no visible proof, only a gut instinct that became stronger as the weeks went by. Invisible pieces of a jigsaw were being collected, waiting to be put together to create a picture which would give her the reason for her doubts.

Although Robert's affection towards her hadn't changed, there was a tension between them when he returned home each weekend. An explanation of being tired and under pressure was given for the invisible barrier. Arguments became more frequent and for no apparent reason, leaving Trudi with the perception that she was going mad. She couldn't understand where the argument had come from. One minute they were talking and the next she was being accused of only thinking of herself. Arguments over the choice between marmalade and honey or anything equally as trivial were taking place and she began to feel exceedingly insecure. Her dreams were about him having an affair, dreams that were so real she can still, over twenty years on, recall them vividly, especially one. She can bring it to mind as if it is a film she's watched over and over again. One that's been paused at the scene where her husband's body is lying against another woman. The scene then plays out in slow motion, allowing her to observe every movement made by the couple, how their hands caress each other's naked curves, how their lips meet with the passion and hunger that she'd presumed was for her alone. Then, it pauses once again, clearly showing the female's face which glares at her and displays a smile of victory. It is the face of an attractive young girl, with pleading blue eyes and long blonde hair that cascades over her naked shoulders. Yes, the very dream that she had dreamt time and time again, brought alive as if it is happening there and then. She knows she did her best at the time to dismiss it as a nightmare brought about by her anxieties and she never divulged her dream to anyone. Fears, though, were constantly poised under the surface just waiting for the opening to pop out to say hello.

Robert's phone calls became less frequent. Her imagination was encouraged to add to the story that was already forming in her mind and to develop the scenes of her dream further. When he was home, her unrest usually subsided. He told her often enough that she was being silly, that he loved her, that he couldn't always phone because he had to work. There was a good reason for everything, even the cinema ticket she found in his trouser pocket. A ticket for a movie she wanted to see. Not only had he gone without her, but he'd also not told her. He gave the explanation of it being a boys' night out and that he'd forgotten all about it. All feasible, nonetheless, deep-down Trudi didn't believe a word he was saying.

That set of tours came to an end and Trudi put her dreams and worries in her invisible bag. Robert was paying her lots of attention and the tension appeared to have diminished. They were a happy married couple once more and enjoying each other's company until he was given the opportunity to become a European tour guide. This meant he would be away from home three weeks at a time over a period of several months, with weekend breaks in between. She didn't want him to go. He saw it as the chance of a lifetime, job fulfilment and the chance to travel. Arguments resurfaced and she was again blamed for being selfish, thinking only of herself and not giving any consideration to his wishes or job progression. The guilt button had been pressed. Perhaps she was being selfish, even so he hadn't been willing to even consider her. She catches her husband standing adamantly in front of her and can almost picture him stamping his feet like a child. She can laugh at the tantrums now, but back then she'd seen it as a threat and backed off. He'd made up his mind and he would be going.

His time of departure came round quicker than the speed of light. One minute he was there and the next gone. Initially, she was very upset but found that she became accustomed to her own company as the weeks passed. Alice and Stuart often invited her out for a drink in the evenings which eased the solitude she was experiencing; it was at bedtime when she felt the loneliness the most. The whole house felt empty, but it didn't possess the immense emptiness of her marital bed. She'd find a part of the bed, pillow, or failing that an item of clothing which still held his smell. Then, taking comfort from the odour, she curled into a small ball and endeavoured to sleep. The picture of herself curled in the foetal position, brings a smile to her face. 'That's certainly not the case now,' she sniggers, 'I'd love the bed to myself!'

Most of the time apart fell during the summer holidays. She managed to keep herself busy to help the hours pass and even met up with Martin whom she hadn't seen for nearly three years. He was having difficulties in a relationship and had asked for advice and Spiritual guidance from Fran. Trudi was playing with her nephew Gary in the back garden when Martin appeared, still as wiry and tanned as she remembered. She felt a little embarrassed at first, which was soon replaced with chatter and laughter and concluded with an invitation to meet for a drink. Even though it was totally innocent, she felt as if she was betraying Robert and so decided to decline the invitation and head home.

Something out there obviously discerned the part of her that was tempted and decided to give her another chance. Her car broke down on the way home, just outside her parents' house. A phone call to Fran brought Martin to the rescue. He helped fix the problem and followed her home to make sure she arrived safely. She could have invited him in. She could have offered him a drink, but she didn't. She was a one-man girl, faithful to the end. No matter how great the attraction to discover if another man would find her attractive and desirable, it wasn't in her nature to be unfaithful. 'Yep, the good girl prevailed,' a thought that makes her realise that in retrospect, she wishes she'd taken up the opportunity and experienced the assumed thrill that masks the disloyalty of the adulterer. She wishes she'd experienced the body of another man and investigated her ability to arouse and seduce. Perhaps, then, the future would have been easier to endure, to understand. It was not to be. Her loyalty was too strong. She and Martin simply hugged. As he drove off, she waved goodbye and entered the house alone.

Chapter 17

As if life was preparing her for a great loss, Grandma Victoria decided it was time to leave this earthly plane. It was a sad time, made more difficult by the absence of Robert who was travelling around Europe. The funeral was also taking place on Trudi's birthday, so not only did she have to attend a funeral without her husband, but she was also to celebrate her birthday alone too. A degree of sadness was removed when, early on the morning of the funeral, he phoned her to wish her happy birthday. Her heart glowed as he told her how much he loved and missed her. He said how he wished he could be there and that he was thinking of her. Then he was gone, leaving her alone crying tears of grief for the loss of her grandma, the absence of her husband and tears of joy for the love she'd received. A knock at the door brought her a big bouquet of flowers from him. There was a tender loving message tucked inside, which prompted water to fall from her eyes once again.

Trudi was travelling with Fran and Paul to the funeral, which was being held in the Church close to her aunt's home and where her grandma would be reunited with her husband. The sun shone down and lit up the Church as the ceremony took place. It continued to shine as they stood beside the grave, watching the coffin as it was lowered into the ground. One by one, members of the family threw a handful of soil onto the coffin below. Some dropped flowers and others simply stood in silence, keeping their thoughts to themselves. The wise old lady had gone. Gone to join her husband and daughters. Family and friends gradually moved away to the front of the Church where some said goodbye and others made their way to the house, where a small buffet offered the mourners a selection of sandwiches as well as ever flowing tea. Memories were shared and stories told. Mourning became laughter as descriptive phrases used by Victoria were expressed and the place became filled with loud voices as the family reminisced. Like an over filled cup, the room overflowed, not with tea but with love and affection as they celebrated Victoria's life.

Trudi sits back in her chair and raises her glass of wine as a toast to her grandma. It's as she sends wishes to the Heavens above, that her heart is filled with love for her aunty. It was Aunt Betty who'd entered the room carrying a single cupcake with a lighted candle on top. 'This might be the day we buried our Mum, but it's Trudi's birthday too. Happy birthday,' she said and the chatter was replaced with a booming rendition of Happy Birthday to You as Trudi blew out the candle. She feels her heart brimming with warmth as she remembers the love that was given to her on her birthday, the day they'd said goodbye to a very great lady. 'Yes, despite everything, my birthday turned out to be very special and certainly one I shall never forget!'

The weeks passed and soon the day she'd been longing for finally arrived. Her husband was coming home and would be staying home until the next round of British weekly tours began in the Autumn. She was elated to have him back and all suspicions were swept away by a tidal wave of undying love. Swept away, or swept under? Were they and all her shadows lurking in the dark recesses, biding their time until internal pressure forced them to present their ugly heads once again? In spite of that, Trudi was happy to swim in a sea of contentment and ignore any waves that were creating ripples on the surface. The tension between the pair had subsided and a stronger bond was developing. They were happy together, happy in each other's company. 'Perhaps it's true, absence does make the heart grow fonder,' she says to herself, albeit unconvincingly and with a slight hint of sarcasm.

Their spare time was spent decorating and a new carpet was bought for the lounge, hall and stairs. They finally had a three-piece suite. It was a long, corner suite which made it possible for the couple to curl up together whilst they watched television. They spent many cosy evenings snuggled in each other's arms and Trudi was back, once more, inside her bubble of bliss. Weeks of enjoyment, love and passion sped by, ending with sorrow and despair as they said goodbye once more.

Albeit there was the initial heartache as he left, Trudi was more at peace and feeling more relaxed about his oncoming weeks away. She maintained that they shared a love that was deep, that penetrated to soul level and that they were soul mates.

So, she chose to ignore the doubts when they arose once more and disregarded the previous dream when it returned. She paid no attention to the recorded film being played back, taunting her with the face and teasing her with scenes of two united bodies. It was a waste of time and energy worrying about imaginary people and scenes especially as she had reality to consider. She was pregnant. They'd agreed to try for a baby when he finished the European tours, she just hadn't expected to fall quite so easily, or quite so soon. She was over the moon and hoped that Robert would be just as enthusiastic. She waited with bated breath for him to make his nightly phone call and as soon as the first rings of the phone were heard, she leapt to her feet. Unable to wait for him to say hello, she blurted the news down the receiver: 'you're going to be a daddy!' It was received exactly as she'd hoped. From the elation she heard in his voice, she could easily imagine him jumping for joy as he told her how much he loved her and thanked her for making him a daddy. They were going to be a family, a family filled with devotion.

The wait for him to come home was intolerable and the days dragged by so slowly. Trudi was unable to restrain herself when he finally walked through the door and was on imaginary sprint blocks, ready for the 'go'. His face was alight with joy and the broadest beam stretched across his jawline. His hands were empty, having left his luggage in the car, and his arms were reaching out, ready to scoop her up as she sprung forward. Her tummy was felt, questions asked about how she was and little presents were showered upon her. One present showed her just how much Robert thought of her and the baby. It was a china mug which was decorated with a picture of a couple sitting on a carousel holding a baby. The words 'love and happiness make the world go round' were written in gold around the bottom. Life was perfect.

Trudi's attention drifts back to the first months of pregnancy. 'No one can really prepare you for them,' she states to the empty room. Yes, people had mentioned sickness, dizziness, tiredness, moods and cravings yet no one can possibly appreciate it until it is being experienced. She recalls the nausea in the mornings, rushing to the toilet on several occasions and Robert bringing her tea and biscuits before she got out of bed in a bid to ease the queasiness. She recollects it helping slightly, only the nausea then decided to creep into the afternoons, usually whilst preparing the evening meal and fizzy sweets had been the only thing to calm it. She thinks of the profound tiredness that made the days at work appear endless. Of course, in addition to that, there were the emotional outbursts brought on by changing hormones and the worry about another miscarriage until she successfully passed the twelve-week mark.

On top of all of that, there were the cravings! To begin with, a craving for melon dominated her mind, body and soul. No other fruit would suffice, only big succulent slices of melon, which dripped juice down the chin as they were bitten into. Juice that needed to be sucked with each bite, filling the mouth with a sweetness that oozed from the tender flesh. It couldn't be a watermelon. Oh no! Honeydew preferably, but Cantaloupe or Galia could be used as a substitute, as long as the melon was sweet. Sliced melon was kept in the fridge, ready for when the urge set in. The memory surfaces of how she felt like a cat burglar as she silently got out of bed and made her way downstairs to the kitchen to raid the fridge. 'Why though,' she asks, 'was it that if there was a store of melon, the craving wasn't stirred? Why was it only when the house was empty of all traces of melon that I was beside myself?' She'd behaved like a small child throwing a tantrum when they'd been denied something they really wanted.

She's reminded of how, later in the pregnancy, the craving changed to Mr Whippy ice-cream. The longing would not be satisfied with any other and it was adamant that it must be a whirly-whirly ice-cream, preferably with a chocolate flake, but it would be content without. On one occasion, just before the baby was due, Robert drove her round many shops looking for a whirly-whirly ice-cream. The quest was in vain! It was a Sunday, as well as slightly off season, making it all the more difficult for the yearning to be fulfilled. 'Oh dear! I went home feeling cheated, grumpy and with a strong urge to punch something!'

She's finding the memory quite comical and she recollects the same impulses during her other pregnancies, the doctor nearly being on the receiving end of one of those punches. He dared to suggest that she replaced the chocolate bars with a carrot or celery stick! How idiotic! Since when did a carrot or celery stick taste like chocolate? Only a fool would have the audacity to suggest such a thing to a pregnant woman! Then there was the occasion when an elderly lady, whilst queuing at the supermarket checkout, asked if it was possible to go in front of her. Without a second thought, the word 'no!' blurted from her lips, followed by helpfully suggesting that the lady went to the basket only checkout, admittedly uttered through gritted teeth. She has a sense of remorse about the way she'd spoken, although easily justifies it. 'I was nearly nine months pregnant, had a trolley filled to the brim, a toddler sitting in the trolley and a four year old walking beside me. What did she expect?' Pregnancy certainly brought out an evil side and she knows that she wouldn't normally behave in such a manner. She sends apologetic energies to the people concerned, but she can't help being amused. 'After all, they should think twice before crossing a pregnant woman!'

Some women enjoy pregnancy, but she never did. She felt uncomfortable, huge and completely unattractive. She disliked the bulge that protruded like an alien attachment and endeavoured to cover it with maternity clothes that hung loosely over the increasing protrusion. She admired it at first. The baby bump was stroked and talked to affectionately yet it was later viewed as an obstacle. It was a huge hard rock that prevented her from seeing her toes and definitely from touching them! It made turning over in bed nigh on impossible and even moving was difficult at times. The suffering endured from pressure on the sciatic nerve which triggered the pain to shoot down her leg and, as it travelled along the nerve line, clenched the buttock, forming a tight excruciating ball inside. Fingers, ankles and feet that swelled from the extra fluid that her body was determined to accumulate, causing stiffness and aching within the joints. All symptoms of pregnancy that she had to endure but the discomfort was overridden by the joy of knowing that there was a little soul growing inside. There was the thrill as movement was experienced for the first time. Those little butterfly sensations that induced twitches inside the stomach. The little flutters and ripples that felt like bubbles popping. It was then that she truly registered that there was a tiny being growing inside her. The realisation brought with it an air of awe and wonder. She adored every movement she felt, each twist and turn, no matter how uncomfortable. Every kick and punch brought love, provoking the love within her heart to be sent to the one inside her womb. Yes! It was all worthwhile, even the process of childbirth itself. Every contraction which brought tightness to the belly, forcing it into a hard dome shape before relaxing once again. The pressure placed on muscles hidden inside as they helped the baby make its way slowly through the channel. The relief as the tension released and the first cry heard. The immense delight as the baby was placed in her arms. A feeling of fulfilment, of oneness, of being complete. Nothing could replace it.

Trudi's reflections are swiftly taken back to when she was three months pregnant. 'Hmmm. Perhaps I was so caught up in the pregnancy I missed something,' she voices knowingly and pours herself another glass of wine.

Chapter 18

Trudi looks up at the moon questioningly, as if to check that he really wants her to face the looming shadows. The answer is given as the memory begins to be portrayed below, opening with the morning that they'd both set off for work as usual, giving each other a hug and kiss before leaving.

Little arguments had recently resurfaced and she calls to mind them having a slight argument the night before and how Robert's unusual 'see you' had struck her as a bit strange. She also recalls that his hug had been a little empty, his kiss too fleeting, but there hadn't been any indications to warn her of the pain that she would later have to face. Life had given the impression that all was normal and filled with the familiar working routines.

Whilst driving home from work that day, she thought about the meal she could cook for them both that evening and decided on something special to make up for the previous night. As she pulled into their road, she was pleased to see Robert's motorbike parked outside; it was unusual for him to be home first. Delighted that he was home, she rushed through the door calling his name. There was no reply, no warm hug to greet her. Instead, the house was cold and empty except for the sense of foreboding which was gradually filling the space like water with no exit route. As if being pulled under and drowning in the invisible water, she began to gasp for breath as terror took over her whole body. Her sixth sense was screaming and telling her something wasn't right, but she was pinned to the floor. Held down by an invisible source, unable to move, as if stuck in an oozing pool of mud. Only her eyes were free to scan the room, to fix on the envelope. A white envelope on which her name had been written in writing that she recognised as Robert's. Lifting her feet from the invisible mud in which they were stuck, she forced her legs to walk over to the table. With shaking hands, she picked up the envelope, her gut already having told her what she would find inside. She somehow managed to persuade her unwilling fingers to pull out the note. The note which told her that he'd left – no explanation, no address, only that he was sorry and that he would be in touch.

Misty eyed, Trudi looks back on that fateful day, feeling the pain, the sickness and the anxiety. The familiar abandonment, the unjustness. It's as if she is experiencing it all again for the first time with emotions that she has suppressed for so many years being pushed up from the depths. Tears begin to roll down her cheeks as the unstable foundations inside are shaken by a threatening earthquake. Debris is being forced to the surface through a volcanic hole creating a lava flow of emotions that bubble as it courses its way through, searching for release.

The scene plays before her eyes: alone, pregnant, rejected by her husband and with no idea of what she was going to do. Questions that weren't answered at the time rush into her mind. How could he have done it to her? What had she done wrong? Was she that bad? Had she really deserved to suffer the torment that had been inflicted upon her? Her stomach begins to churn as nausea takes over, her guts wanting to empty. This time she will not swallow. She'll allow herself to empty, not physically, but spiritually. She becomes the healer, not the victim. She becomes the observer, not the thinker. As she watches, she asks for healing and for all to be released. An energy engulfs her whole being, inside and out, swamping her with love and comfort. Gradually, the nausea subsides allowing the gentle tears to fall freely, soothing away the past, bringing enlightenment and touching her soul. Missing pieces of the jigsaw puzzle begin to be put into place. She was the facilitator, not victim. She paved the way for Robert to begin his journey of facing himself, of acknowledging his weaknesses and learning how his past affected his future. Images of him searching for fulfilment, gratification and success dash in and out; she can finally acknowledge that she hadn't been to blame. She, too, has learnt from the experience and has, more importantly, been given insight, spiritual awakening and strength. Strength to fight. Strength to survive.

The story returns to the point where she discovered the note. She sees herself throwing it to one side and running around like a headless chicken in search of clues, just a morsel, a grain and in hope that it was all a practical joke. The emptiness inside told her that it wasn't, which was confirmed by the wardrobe vacant of Robert's clothes. There was no sign of him, apart from one lonely jumper that he'd discarded in his hurry to leave before she got home. After picking it up, she held it close to her nose, breathing in the perfume of his deodorant, the aroma of his body. Pulling it to her chest, she sat down on the bed and sobbed heart wrenching sobs as the reality hit her. Insanity, fuelled by anger, forced her into action as her manic eyes hungrily searched for something to hurl at an imaginary Robert. Anything that symbolised the betrayal, the lies. She ran downstairs, the growing madness leading her to the thing for which she'd been searching. The mug. The one that he'd given to her in celebration of their expected baby, proclaiming that love and happiness makes the world go round. As she held it in her hand, tears formed deep pools in her eyes before they gave way and flooded down her cheeks. As they splashed on the ground below, the innocent wall received the full impact as a screaming maniac threw the mug with brute force. A crash, followed by the sound of broken china as the fragments hit the floor. Unsatisfied, the search continued. Ornaments that he'd bought from the places he'd visited, joined the pieces of mug on the floor. Then she sat in silence with fragments of her life, the lies, scattered around her and helplessness replacing the anger.

A vacant body which felt as if its life force had been sucked out, finally glided weightlessly towards the phone. An unfamiliar hand lifted the receiver and fingers not belonging to her dialled numbers automatically, not registering the person they were contacting. A voice she knew jolted the spirit back into the physical body. She mustered up all her strength to utter the words 'he's left me. Robert's gone,' before her tears took hold once more. Instructions were given. 'Don't move. We're on our way.' She wasn't able to move even if she'd wanted to. She was transfixed, surrounded by tiny pieces of china and trapped inside a body that was shaking with terror, anger and exhaustion.

Her parents arrived, with a 'tut tut' from her dad and 'oh no' from her mum as they took in the scene before them. Their daughter standing there, shaking, as pale as a ghost and surrounded by the after-effects of the manic attack earlier. The debris was left and Trudi removed from the crime scene as quickly as possible whilst insisting that she stayed the night at their house. Dinner was placed on the table, only she was unable to face it; her stomach heaved as she forced a mouthful down.

Her mum wanted to know the whole story, the ins and outs, the whys and wherefores. If only she knew herself! Her dad, on the other hand, didn't say much. He just listened before offering his opinion. After having to endure the 'I never trusted him,' 'there was something about him,' 'you'll be better off without him' and 'at least you're financially independent,' plans were laid out on the table. There were bank accounts to close, the house and her work arrangements to consider, the baby to think of – was she going to keep it? Her head was going to explode. They were expecting her to plan her life, a life without Robert and maybe without a baby. She hadn't had time to absorb everything that had happened and it was all still too raw to consider the future.

She feels the deep despair of that moment in time, and how she thought that life wasn't worth living. She was hurting to the core and didn't care less about the money or the house. Her parents wanted her to think about her future, except she wasn't ready. 'Why couldn't they see that?' They were happy to manage her life, and because she was unable, she let them. 'Not for long though!' she shouts into the air.

That night, she was restless in her old bed, tossing and turning as she attempted to make sense of it all. She mulled over the suggestions made by her parents and knew it was sensible to close the bank account. As for the house, if Robert had any decency in him, he would let her have it. Work would be sorted, although she didn't think she would be able to cope with that on top of all that had been thrown her way, so decided to phone in sick. And the baby? That was a different matter altogether. She would definitely not be able to abort, as her parents had advised, but was uncertain how she would manage as a single mum and whether she would still be able to work. There was so much to consider. Before she could address anything, she needed to go home; there was a mess to clear up, one that was easier to sort out than the one that she had to face.

Her parents took her home after breakfast, offering to stay to help tidy and keep her company, but she wanted to be alone. A desire to wallow in self-pity had kicked in. She promised not to do anything silly, that she would drive down later and then sat herself on the floor to give herself a few moments to breathe. A calmness took over allowing her to function again and to digest the incident of the day before. Was that all? A day? Time had passed so slowly yet it all seemed a lifetime ago. She set about tidying the house, doing any washing that was lying around and made sure she cleared up the debris from the day before.

It was whilst she was in the midst of all the mind focussing chores, that she came across letters Robert had written to her when he'd been away. The imagery of her sitting alone with the letters in her hand is so real that Trudi wants to reach out and touch her younger self. She glimpses again, through water filled eyes, each sentence, every word, which she studied so hard in search of any indications of when he'd stopped loving her. There were none. The sorrowful figure in front of her then contemplated photos taken of them together, hand in hand, arm in arm, only love between them. At that moment, totally unaware of what she was doing, the letters became tiny pieces around her, in shreds, torn to pieces, no more. Then, as she began to destroy a photo, she hesitated for one more glance at the man she loved. In that instant, the awareness of how they were one, joined at the soul, overwhelmed her. She felt a strength that had risen from deep inside, bringing with it a voice, a voice that was emphatic. She had to find Robert, but how?

The following Monday, Trudi phoned in sick, informing the Head of the situation who was very understanding, allowing her time off to sort things out and recuperate from the ordeal. Her family helped to take care of practicalities, closing and changing bank accounts and contacting solicitors for advice. The baby was mentioned and, despite her parents' arguments, she was adamant and stood firm – no one would change her mind. She was going to be a mum, with or without a husband. She already felt great love towards the baby and would love and care for it to the best of her ability; that was all that mattered.

The time off gave Trudi the opening she'd been yearning for, time to concentrate on finding Robert, much to the dismay of her family. Trudi thinks back to how she took on the character of Sherlock to help her in her new adventure and how no stone would be left unturned until she found the missing person. She'd no idea what would happen if or when she did find him, or how he would react, she just knew that she had to try. She couldn't let him go. A woman possessed, she put all her energy into the investigation, gathering as much information as she could.

Only a few days had passed since her husband had left, yet it seemed like weeks and there was still no word from him. He'd disappeared from the face of the earth. A numbness formed inside and the simplest of tasks became difficult, mainly because her attention was fixed on finding her husband. She was functioning like a robot that had been programmed to find a missing person. Trudi thinks back on how Sherlock stepped in, and how he felt so real, advising her to phone acquaintances and Robert's colleagues in the hope of gleaning some piece of information, no matter how small. She is prompted of how, little by little the jigsaw began to take shape and the dream that she'd dreamt all those months ago began to become reality. She discovered from one of his colleagues that Robert was having an affair with one of the girls, Amelia, who worked in the hotel at which he stayed whilst on tour. She knew instinctively that it was the girl in the dream. She'd been warned and had chosen to ignore. 'There again,' she voices to no one in particular, 'how was anyone in their right mind supposed to make accusations based on a dream? They would be laughed out of court!'

At least the truth had come to light along with where she might find him. All she needed was the hotel's phone number which should have Amelia's address. Robert's address book popped into her mind which she'd discovered in his bedside table when searching for clues. Stomach in mouth and shouting 'elementary,' she was pushed up the stairs by Sherlock. With no regard for taking care or leaving fingerprints, he encouraged her to ruthlessly cast the contents of the drawer aside until the offending item was found. A little book, full of names and addresses. Eyes feverishly searched, looking for the names of hotels, until they found the one they were looking for. Luckily, Robert had the forethought to tell her the name and she actually remembered it. Sherlock stepped aside as, clutching the book tightly, she hurried to the phone.

Apprehensive fingers dialled the numbers written on the open page and her ear waited anxiously for a voice on the other end of the receiver. Alarm rose as she heard a man say the name of the hotel. Taking a deep breath, she said 'hello. I wonder if you can help me. I need to get in touch with a member of your staff, Amelia. Would you be able to give me her address or number?' The man apologetically told her that he was unable to divulge personal information. Dismay set in even more. No! She decided to explain the reasons why. The man was very sympathetic, almost giving the impression that he knew all about it, but he unfortunately was still unable to help. There was nothing more she could do. She thanked him and hung up.

Even with an uncontrollable tiredness and desire to give in, a sudden light switched on in her head as she recalled having seen another hotel listed. It was a name that she'd considered odd for a hotel and now realised why. Hotel Amelia! Frantically turning the pages of the book, she came across the address with no phone number. Not to be deterred, she overcame the problem by sending a message via the only means left open: a telegram addressed to Robert, asking him to phone. She'd no idea whether he was there, or if he would reply. She could only hope and wait. The phone rang sooner than she expected, causing her to jump and her stomach to find its new home, her mouth. Uncontrollable shivers rippled over her as she walked towards the phone. 'It's most probably Mum,' she said silently, half wishing it would be. Sick with nervousness and weak at the knees she lifted the receiver. Her ear registered the voice, Robert's voice. She'd found him. He was more than a little surprised to have heard from her, although curiously didn't ask how she'd tracked him down. Unspoken questions formed in her mind: had someone warned him? Or had he suspected that she would search? In his heart, had he hoped that she would?

They didn't talk for long, but she clung on to every word he spoke, the sound of his voice causing her stomach to roll, twist and turn as if it was a roller coaster. Sheepishly, he did bring himself to ask if she was okay and promised to phone again so that plans could be made to sort everything out. There was no apology nor a hint of future contentment. Despite that, she wasn't ready to give up and was prepared to fight, no matter how much of her strength it took.

Trudi knows that other people had felt she was heading towards a painful fall but she is also aware of how much she was convinced that Robert would return and how this belief had given her a strong and powerful determination. She visualises herself praying, asking for guidance and support from God, angels and anyone who was willing to consider that her intuition was correct. As she is reminiscing, she thinks of her mum's friend, who was a spiritual lady, full of wisdom and wise words. She'd written Trudi a letter in which every sentence gave insight and support, but it was the words of wisdom and unconditional love that awakened her heart. Trudi recalls the words as if they were engraved in her mind:

*'If you truly love him, you will love him enough to
let him go. If you are willing to let him go, you will
set him free, free to make the right decisions. If it
is right that he returns, it will happen. If it is right
that you are destined to be as one, it will be so.
First you must let go, set him free, set yourself free
and trust.'*

'Let him go! Easier said than done,' she says out loud as if to remind herself of the difficulty of the task, except she had, even back then, understood the meaning behind the words. It was simple: set him free to make his own choice instead of trying to force his hand like an over emotional maniac. She must trust that the right thing would happen, not just for him, not just for her, but for the two of them. If their destiny was to be together, then it would happen.

The letter helped Trudi to make the decision of putting her mind to thinking positively about the future instead of the torture she was feeling. She began to concentrate on the little baby growing inside and to venture out more instead of moping alone at home. There were times when she felt as if she was going crazy, although her belief that all would be well was becoming stronger by the day. The horror of a future without Robert was replaced with hope. Light was appearing at the end of the tunnel, only she didn't know what would be illuminated.

Robert began to phone two or three times a week, at a time arranged previously. Whilst waiting for the call, Trudi paced the floor as if she were a cat on a hot tin roof and had to remind herself that coolness was the way forward! There was no need for him to phone as regularly and she found the cooler she became, the more frequent the calls. Light-hearted banter passed between them. Comings and goings of the day were shared and harmless flirtation bounced between them like a ping pong ball and so it was very difficult for her to keep her composure when, one night, he suggested talking about future plans: the house, maintenance and bills. This would be a sign of defeat which she wasn't prepared to acknowledge and so suggested that it might be better to discuss it next time as she needed to gather information.

The number of calls then increased to every night, with Robert admitting that he looked forward to them. Then it happened. Trudi has to quickly remind herself that she is reliving a memory and release her teeth that are digging deeply into her bottom lip, just as they had on that day to stop herself from screaming. Her fingers pinched her arm to make sure she wasn't dreaming and she told herself to keep calm so that the effect of his words wasn't evident to him. The words 'can I come home so we can talk properly?' Yes! Yes! YES, was what she wanted to shout out. Instead, she ignored the euphoria building inside, breathed deeply to put a lid on it and said 'that sounds like a good idea. When were you thinking?' Her heart, head and body were close to exploding when she heard that he would be able to come the following day if that was okay with her. Swallowing the screams of elation that were resting in her vocal chords, she told him she would look forward to seeing him sometime the following evening. The call over and the receiver left dangling, she allowed the sheer joy to erupt. She was unsure whether to laugh or cry and so she indulged in both. The news wasn't received with the same enthusiasm by her parents and she immediately felt as if a bucket of water had been emptied over her. They thought she was mad; she would never be able to trust him, but if that's what she wanted. Of course it was! She didn't care what others thought. After four weeks of separation, they were going to be reunited. Robert was coming home, the first big step in the right direction.

Chapter 19

The narrative resumes on the day of Robert's return. She woke tired after a restless sleep due to the previous four weeks flitting in and out of her consciousness and forcing her to battle with the accompanying thoughts and emotions. However, Robert's impending homecoming fuelled her with the energy required to get through the following hours and she distracted her thoughts by keeping busy to help the time pass more quickly. The house was spotless! The cupboards were filled with food that Robert liked and a bottle of wine was chilling in the fridge but her movements were slowed by the hefty bag of emotions she was carrying. A bag that weighed heavier with each step and pulled her down as if her legs were buckling under the weight of the hidden confusion, pain, anger, love, excitement. As if emptying a bag of shopping, Trudi decided to hide all the items she didn't need to access at the back of a deep imaginary cupboard where they could sit, untouched and forgotten. She only kept those she wanted, allowing the love and elation to carry her through the day. She couldn't quite bring herself to add forgiveness, not yet. There was room for it to be added later. After all, she didn't know how long he was staying.

Alice suggested that Trudi joined her and Stuart at the pub that night instead of staying at home alone impatiently waiting for the reunion. It would also give Robert the experience of returning to an empty house, not knowing what to expect. He could be left alone, back on home territory, to mull things over whilst surrounded by reminders of what he'd been willing to destroy. Appreciating the sentiment behind the words, she agreed. She was also going to make sure that she looked as attractive and irresistible as she could, pregnant or not!

A steaming bath was run, full of relaxing bubbles that smelt of lavender and tickled her naked body as she lowered herself into the inviting water. She lay back, enjoying the sensation of the water as it slowly rippled across the tiny bump that had begun to form. A trail of bubbles, resembling that of a snail's silvery trail, was left across her stomach as the gentle flow caressed the weeny bulge. She softly smoothed them away with her hands and whispered, 'daddy's coming home.' Then, several minutes later, dressed and ready she waited for her lift.

She spent a pleasant, but anxious evening with her sister and brother-in-law who then dropped her outside her home, just late enough to have kept Robert waiting. She was able to see the lounge light shining through the curtains and hear music playing as she walked up the path to the front door. Shaking fingers made her attempt to put the key in the lock more difficult than it should have been, but finally, with a heart beating its way out of her chest, she managed to open the door. Trying to appear cooler than she felt, Trudi walked into the house where she found Robert stretched out on the lounge floor. It was obvious that he was trying to look composed, yet his eyes and voice said otherwise. He looked very uncomfortable and suitably embarrassed. As she walked into the room, he raised his eyes to fleetingly look at her, smiled and said 'hello.' A knife would have had difficulty cutting through the tension in the atmosphere as pleasantries were spoken, comments made about how well she looked and how he'd expected her to be bigger. Not once was his absence mentioned, instead it hung above them like a big black cloud. The elephant in the room settled in position to which neither dared draw attention. She offered Robert a drink and something to eat which seemed to ease the discomfort. They began to relax in each other's company, but they still avoided the subject that needed to be discussed. All the time they talked, she managed to keep a physical distance between them and he didn't make a move towards her. No hug, no kiss. She held out for as long as possible, then the love for him and the need she had, finally won. She moved over to sit beside him. She took his hands and gazed into his eyes, seeing love reflected in them. Acknowledging it with a gentle kiss, her arms pulled him into her body and she whispered into his ear, 'welcome home.' His arms tightened around her and his lips pressed firmly on hers. Taking her by the hand, he led her up the stairs to the bedroom, to their bed where they gave themselves to each other with an ease and passion that surprised Trudi herself. Any thoughts of finding intimacy difficult was outweighed by the love she had for him. They didn't sleep much that night. They chatted and lay in each other's arms well into late afternoon of the following day. She was content and, though not set in concrete, had an irrefutable knowing that all would be well.

The illusion of living within that bubble of bliss creeps into Trudi's mind and she thinks back to how the translucent balloon carried her through the week that followed. The endless week which culminated with the icing on the cake, the crème de la crème when Robert told her how much he loved her and admitted what a fool he'd been. Her bubble hovered a little higher until she heard him say that he wanted to stay which made it levitate to another level. She floated like a feather through the air, although hanging on the sides, like the weights on a hot air balloon's basket, was the awareness that there was always the possibility of it bursting, POP, without warning.

The threat of the vulnerable bubble vanishing into thin air happened a few days later. The phone rang which she answered in her usual manner, not expecting to hear a woman asking to speak to Robert. Undaunted by her rising agitation, Trudi calmly asked 'who shall I say is calling?' 'Jane, Amelia's sister,' came the reply. She decided there and then to be in charge, saying, 'I'm sorry, but he can't come to the phone. Can I give him a message?' 'I just need to know if Robert's coming back soon?' the woman said. Trudi feels, once more, that imaginary knife which twisted menacingly between her fingers, waiting in anticipation for the right moment to strike a penetrating blow. She hears her voice, marked with an icy coldness, as it forcefully uttered, 'this is Trudi, Robert's wife. He **won't** be coming back.' A bemused voice retorted, 'oh! I didn't know he was married.' 'Oh yes,' she affirmed between clenched teeth, 'married with a child on the way.' Jane, evidently shocked by the news, gave the humble and apologetic response of, 'I'm sorry', traces of embarrassment showing in her voice. 'What does Robert want to do about the things he's left here?' After consulting her husband, who was beside her the whole time, Jane was told to keep them and not to contact them again. Trudi takes a deep breath and exhales slowly. 'Well done me. I took charge and I was strong. I deserve a medal!'

Trudi contemplates for a while, giving thought to the fact that Robert had omitted to share that he was married. She realises just how much she'd been left reeling from the knowledge and how it added to the deceit. 'How important was I in it all?' she wonders. She takes note of the questions she'd asked about whether he truly loved her, if she was living a lie or not, all these and more flit in and out of her mind like dancing bees scouting for a new home. Her head buzzes as the thoughts swarm in, creating a deafening noise which vibrate around her head as they search for a means of escape. The building energy forces her to revoice the questions for which she needed answers at the time. She then marks his answers as they flood back into her memory, scoring them out of ten with ten being acceptable. He was defensive at first, scoring a one for the excuse he gave for not wearing his ring, which apparently might have been damaged on the steering wheel. He scored a further one for saying that 'all the tour guides did it.' She detects the discernible disgust as she hears her loud retort of 'so that makes it ok then, does it?' She witnesses the tension that was starting to build between them, an argument based on fear and guilt brewing, something that Trudi wanted to avoid. Drawing in a deep breath, she explained that she needed to know why, to help her understand so that she didn't feel responsible. Her husband raised his head, his eyes veiled with an unhappiness she hadn't seen him show before. Taking her hands in his he said, 'I really don't know why, apart from being an idiot. I can't give you any other reason. I'm so truly sorry and deeply regret everything that has happened. I know I've hurt you badly. I really love you and truly hope you can forgive me.' His response earned eight out of ten and, back then, made her again consider adding forgiveness to her bag of items, but she still wasn't quite ready to add it to the mixture. Her response may have been partly driven by not wanting to lose him, but she'd made her decision. She looked him in the eye and said, 'It'll take time. I'll try if you can promise you won't ever hurt me again.'

She trusted him totally when he said he would never do it again. Her family were not as convinced, but were willing to tolerate her choice, even if they didn't agree. There were moments when the dismay and hurt emerged from the depths like a submarine shooting through the surface of the water and she knew it would take her a while to fully trust him again. As if to make it harder, her dream came back to haunt her, only now the girl had a real face. She'd found a photo in Robert's wallet and was in total disbelief when she saw the face staring at her. It was the same face she'd seen so clearly in her dream, positioned on a body which was flaunting itself in one of Robert's shirts. It was no longer part of a dream. It had become reality, there in her hand, the face smiling seductively. Her dream had been trying to warn her. She'd been warned by her Spirit friends but she'd chosen to ignore.

Trudi is reminded of the promise she made to herself: to listen to her inner feelings and follow her gut instincts as much as she could, or dared, but she realises that the promise hasn't always been kept. She decides to retake the vows. Standing in front of the mirror, she gazes into her soul, takes a deep breath and makes a pledge. 'I promise to put myself first and have faith in my intuition and what Spirit is telling me. I promise to try to protect myself from being hurt in the future.'

Trudi settles herself down for the next instalment with a contented smile on her face as she knows that this is bringing great joy, the birth of her darling little girl. She was doing her best to put the past behind her and move on, except this was sometimes made difficult by her family who occasionally made their disapproval evident. On the whole, they were civil and agreed to let bygones be bygones, although she now recognises that they had concealed their anxiety that Robert might let her down again, just as she had. Burying all unwanted feelings gave her the space to throw herself into her pregnancy and prepare for the little one's arrival.

The following months brought a larger stomach, a deepening relationship with Robert and a new job for her husband who was returning to his original career as a central heating engineer. The couple also decided on a new house for a completely fresh start, leaving the previous months behind to become part of the shadows of the past. The house was a new build which meant they could fill it with their own love and vibrations. It was a small modern detached house, with a winding, enclosed staircase that climbed up from the lounge to three bedrooms and a bathroom. The main bedroom had a small bay window that captured the character of the little cottage that she'd always dreamed about. The lounge was of average size and full of light, thanks to the natural brightness pouring through the window, which filled every corner of the room. The kitchen was fitted with ample units and there was a dining area just to one side of the kitchen. A door led from the kitchen into a long and narrow back garden which required a great deal of work. Then there was the pièce de résistance, a downstairs cloakroom! She had total faith, believing that this was the beginning of a new life together; they'd been given a second chance and nothing would destroy it.

They moved into their new house two weeks before the baby was due. The move wasn't easy with a large bump to transport, but family members lent a helping hand. Everything was going to plan until their bed refused to go up the narrow twisting staircase which was determined to prevent it from happening. Try as they might, the bed wouldn't go past the first step. Exhausted and frustrated, she sat on the bed, which had been positioned in the lounge, not knowing whether to laugh or cry. As if empathising with her frustration, the baby began to turn in what had become a very tight space, pressing on every organ in her body. In desperation she looked around at the people who were busy arranging things where they were able, emptying boxes and filling her cupboards with the removed contents. Anger replaced the frustration as resentment set in. No one had consulted her about her preferences and in fact, they seemed totally oblivious of her presence. It was her mum that noticed how close her daughter was to tears and suggested that it was time for her daughter to rest. Trudi laughs at the suggestion her mum had made because of the absurdity. How could she have gone for a rest? She didn't have a bed in a bedroom! 'Luckily for me, Carol, came to the rescue,' she recalls. Her sister in law had a spare double bed which split in two, making it possible for the bed to be carried into her bedroom. The problem was solved and Sleeping Beauty did have a bed that night.

It took a few days to arrange their new home to their liking, and then there was the nursery to prepare in readiness for the arrival of the baby, the day for which was drawing ever closer. A wicker crib, with a beautiful blue flowered cotton cover and a matching quilt, was placed in Trudi's bedroom in anticipation of welcoming the new arrival. The nursery was decorated and all the necessities for a newborn had been bought. Sat in the corner of the room, eagerly waiting for the off, was the packed hospital bag. All that was needed was the first signs of the new arrival.

The due date fell on the day after an important football match and, jokingly, Robert asked her not to go in to labour until after the match had finished. Much to her annoyance, Robert invited his dad to watch the match on the television. She'd managed to have a restful day, with no signs of the baby's arrival, but she wanted to spend a quiet evening with her husband. As the evening wore on, her intolerance increased and she resented every breath that her father-in-law was taking. She became restless, huffing and puffing as she waddled around the house with her bump leading her which occasionally 'accidentally' blocked the view of the television. Her house didn't feel comfortable. It was as if it had been invaded by intruders who were breathing in all the air, leaving her stifled and gasping for oxygen. She smiles, as now, she completely understands why. At the time she was ignorant of the hints her body and emotions were sending.

The football finally finished, the intruder left and the expectant couple made their way to bed. It was in the early hours of the morning that she woke with small intermittent pains in her stomach. She gently prodded Robert and said, 'I think it's started!' As if he'd received an electric shock, he jumped out of bed and ran downstairs to phone the hospital. Being Trudi's first experience of giving birth, she didn't know what to expect. Apprehension and agitation dominated her every thought but was lessened by the eagerness of meeting their new baby. There was also the bonus of getting rid of the bump that had hindered her movements, and view, for several months.

The hospital told them to head straight down. The half hour journey seemed interminable and the pains started to become more frequent. On arrival, she was taken to a cubicle for examination which was when the baby decided that it wasn't quite ready to face the world. As she'd shown that she was in the first stages, they thought it best to keep her in. Robert was sent on his way and told to return later. The hours passed slowly, with no imminent signs of a birth. The expectant father arrived, but, as all had slowed, he made his way home when visiting time was over. Of course, that was when the baby decided it was time to make its entrance! No sooner had Robert reached home, he had to turn around and wend his way back to the hospital.

Her husband was standing by her side in the delivery room, caressing her face and telling her that it would be okay. She took his hand and squeezed it, the force of which became stronger as the pains grew in intensity, gripping so hard that her nails dug into his hand making it impossible for him to leave. She desperately wanted to push despite the midwife telling her that it wasn't time, but the baby inside had different ideas. Trudi yelled 'I need to push!' Realising that she'd been incorrect in her assumption, the midwife sprang into action; their baby daughter entered the world and was placed in Trudi's arms. Robert leaned over and kissed her, before placing a kiss on his daughter's head. The love for her and the baby and the joy at having shared the special moment with her was evident in his eyes. Despite the initial reluctance, he was glad and felt privileged to have witnessed such a miraculous event. Their marriage had turned yet another corner and her shadows from the past were slowly disappearing and making room for happier memories.

Trudi looks down on the moonlit path below where their life as a new family is being presented to her, highlighting how she cherished every moment she spent with little Naomi before she had to return to work. She always knew, albeit reluctantly, that she would have to return to work after the baby was born because money was very tight. Robert's mother had agreed to look after the baby, about which Trudi had mixed feelings but at least the baby wouldn't be left with strangers. The memory still feels raw as she relives the emotional tug she had leaving Naomi. She wanted to share in every moment of the baby's life, to be there to care for her, to love her and to watch her change and grow. However, finances dictated that her income was needed.

It was difficult juggling work and home life. Every morning, Naomi was dropped off at her grandma's, with all the necessary equipment, before Trudi headed off to the challenges of the teaching day. The weekends and holidays were precious when she was able to devote her time to the cherished family addition, but she began to fear that Naomi would see Freda as more of a mother than Trudi herself and resented having to leave her. The suppressed feelings of the past decided to revisit and mix with the new, resulting in a lethal mixture that she refused to acknowledge. She became more and more unhappy, lost weight, looked gaunt and tired and felt completely unable to cope. Before long, she became ill and was unable to work any longer. For the sake of her health and sanity, they decided that they would manage financially the best they could and she handed in her notice.

Naomi was changing every day and Trudi was now able to be part of it. She saw her take her first step and heard her speak her first word, all the precious moments to a mum. There was no denying that money was tight, but they managed and life was finally more at peace. Contentment had replaced doubt and her trust in Robert was gradually building back, though she doubted that she would ever trust fully. Slowly, wounds were healing and in spite of experiencing another miscarriage, she was feeling much stronger within herself. Yet, that small voice inside was continually whispering warnings, but would she be strong enough to be guided by it? The test was not long in coming.

Chapter 20

Robert wanted to open his own plumbing business using their home as collateral. Trudi, yet again, ignored the old familiar alarm bells ringing out. She wanted to help and please her husband in every way she could, but it was the dread of losing him that was really driving her decision. It all seemed so feasible, so easy with no major risks involved. Advice had been taken, so there was nothing obvious to worry about. They went ahead and the business didn't take long to get off the ground, with them both working hard to make sure it would be successful. Still those warning bells were incessantly ringing.

It was just after Naomi's second birthday that Trudi discovered she was pregnant again, the baby being due just before Christmas. The pregnancy, itself, was easier than the first, although water retention and nausea did decide to return. The bump was also larger and made moving even more difficult, especially as she also had a toddler to run after. Her craving was different too, only wanting fizzy cherryade. Not orangeade or lemonade, it had to be cherry! Robert was often sent out to buy some. She laughs as she thinks of one of the occasions that she sent him out for her fizz fix; he took so long that her craving had gone. In spite of that, she still felt annoyed that her fancy hadn't been satisfied, especially when she found out where he'd been. He'd popped into see his new mates, the local firemen. Earlier in the year, he'd become a retained fireman and quite often found the need to stop off at the station, but her need on that night had been far more important! 'How on earth did I resist the urge to empty the bottle over him?' she asks herself.

It was always all or nothing with Robert. No one could ever accuse him of not being dedicated, for he always put everything into all he undertook. However, it was Trudi who suffered from his enthusiasm, often being left alone to cope. He'd had to undergo fire fighter training and was required to attend drill evenings once a week, but it was fire calls she found the most disruptive. Being a retained fireman meant he had to answer a call wherever they were and whatever time of day it happened to be. There were calls in the middle of the night and when they were on their way for a family day out which was suddenly put on hold. Sometimes he dashed off in the middle of a supermarket shop, leaving her with a trolley load of shopping, toddler and bump and praying that she had the means to pay.

As she'd not had complications with Naomi, she was allowed to give birth at a local maternity hospital which was only a ten minute drive from their home. The baby decided to arrive a week early. She instantly recognised the signs of the baby hinting that it wanted to meet its parents, but she held back until the signal became too frequent to ignore. The hospital was informed of their impending arrival and Freda was called to babysit. After six hours of labour, their second baby was born. A beautiful, lively, noisy and demanding baby girl. Trudi visualises the little baby that was placed in her arms, a few years ago now. A little girl making soft contented noises, almost purring like a kitten, as she snuggled in her mother's arms. She looked so different to Naomi. The feature she recalls about Naomi as a newborn is her hands – small, dainty and beautifully shaped. With Phoebe, the name they decided to give her, it's her face. From the time she entered the world she had a proud and stubborn look with mischievousness later shining in her little eyes and smile, a trait Trudi hoped that Phoebe would never lose.

Mother and baby left the maternity home two days after the birth. The opportunity to stay longer was there, but she wanted to return to her other daughter and welcome the new one into their home. It was within minutes of being home that Robert had a fire call, leaving the new mother to cope on her own. There was no dinner prepared, the baby wanted feeding and Naomi was in need of her mum whom she'd naturally missed. At the moment that tears began to fall, brother Thomas walked in to save the day. Her superhero! As he rustled up something to eat, he made his feelings towards Robert quite plain, for that moment and also for the past betrayal. Needless to say, her husband was very surprised when he returned to find Thomas carrying out the duties that he should have done. Unfortunately, he couldn't understand why the help was needed and became very defensive about his movements when confronted by a very hormonal woman. She was hurt by his response and, as the previously heard warning bells came to mind, began to wonder if there was something more behind it. Later in the evening, the reason for his abrasive attitude, and the alarm bells, became apparent. The business was in trouble and the only way out was to sell. Old friend numbness stepped in and switched off the anger that threatened to strike. Guilt also set in, for it wasn't just them that it would affect, it would also be her brother-in-law Paul and her dad, who were both working as part of the business. The writing on the wall became as clear as day with the words, written in black and white by her family, 'Robert is to blame.'

Sadly, Trudi affirms how correct her instinct was. 'It may have taken a few years to become clear, but they definitely blamed him.' Now, as she reconsiders events, she realises that Robert had been the easy target. He'd become the object of attack by people who were driven by unspoken anger and hurt about his past disloyalty. They'd allowed their opinion and response to become clouded by the past, a past that Robert had helped to darken.

Despite all efforts, it was necessary to sell the business with many unpaid debts. Thankfully, Robert was fortunate enough to find a job almost straight away, which gave the family another arrow to shoot. The job was with one of the builders he'd dealt with previously and some members of the family were convinced that Robert had steered proceedings in a way that made sure his needs would be met and provide him with a job. They assumed that he was looking after number one, without any regard for anyone else. All accusations, assumptions and beliefs were totally unfounded, but people were very quick to judge and accuse without any real proof.

Trudi allows herself a break to consider the last statement in more depth. Over time, she has come to realise that there is a family trait of jumping in with both feet and being unwilling to listen to facts which could enlighten, or alter, their judgement. 'Maybe they're afraid of admitting that they're wrong because it would highlight the fear of failure,' she considers. She also decides that ill-informed judgements provoke her defence mechanism and the need to justify her actions which, in truth, is a complete waste of energy. 'What's the point in arguing with someone who isn't prepared to listen? It's best to walk away confidently in silence with an inner knowing of the truth. Yes, there should be no expectations of apologies, just total unconditional acceptance of what is.' Her thoughts come to an end and she wonders where these words of wisdom have come from as they simply appeared in her mind. As she glances at the moon, he seems to smile knowingly and, at that moment, she becomes aware of an energy around her; she knows that she is being helped by her mum's angels. They are encouraging her to face the shadows, to learn from them and leave them behind.

The story resumes. Unfortunately, the only way to clear off all debts, was to sell the house, which proved harder than they'd hoped as the market was very slow. They cut back on expenditure where they could and it was just as well that Robert had the money from the firefighter job coming in. It meant that he had to answer as many calls as he could, but it was a small price to pay for the extra money, especially when Trudi discovered that she was pregnant. She was in total dismay. Aside from the impact on the finances, there was also her ability to manage with three children under the age of four. How would she be able to find the time to care for another baby? Her husband told her not to worry, that they would find a way to manage and so she began to come to terms with the arrival of a new baby. Whether it was the worry, or down to fate, she started to show signs of a miscarriage. As she was twelve weeks and had only a small amount of spotting, the doctor told her to rest. Her mum and mother-in-law stepped in to help and made sure she was able to get as much rest as possible. She thought everything was going well until her five month hospital check-up which showed no movement and no heartbeat. The pregnancy had to be terminated, and as she was over fifteen weeks, the only way was to give birth. Before she was able to come to terms with the news, the process of inducement began and the hours that followed were emotionally agonising. The physical pain of labour was nothing compared to the knowledge that there would be no baby. It would all be pointless. Even knowing that the foetus had died at around twelve weeks didn't ease the hurt. She felt angry that she was told to rest and, for several weeks, was trying to save a baby that had already decided to not enter the world. There was no relief found in the fact that she wasn't full term and she was able to empathise with any woman who'd experienced the ordeal of a still born birth. To her, the emotional torment of loss felt just as acute. It was also having a profound emotional effect on Robert who was by her side the whole time. Through tears of pain, he vowed that he would never allow her to go through anything like it again.

Once home, the emptiness increased, as if part of her was missing and the loss was reinforced by the maternity clothes she had to continue to wear. As if to rub salt into a very raw wound, milk started to enter, accompanied by a yearning to place her nipple into the mouth of a hungry baby. She was full of milk which had no place to go apart from seeping into her clothing until it finally realised that it wasn't needed. The loss was followed by grief which emphasised the empty space as she watched Naomi and Phoebe playing together, with the undeniable impression of another soul sitting in between them. This brought a desire to fill the void, but both she and Robert agreed that there would be no more children. Neither of them wanted to risk experiencing a similar ordeal. So, she took it as another of life's blows and placed all emotions in her bottomless bag.

Trudi's attention is taken to the time when they desperately needed someone to buy their house due to the mounting debts. As if life was giving them a reward after all their suffering, they were presented with a potential buyer. The house was sold and they bought a three bedroom terraced house which was perfect for their little family. She began to socialise with the neighbours, Robert was enjoying his new job and the girls were making friends with the children who lived in the street. Life was dealing them a decent hand of cards at last, yet Trudi had no trust in life and was waiting for the next smack in the face. As if it had been hiding in wait, lurking in the shadows, the clenched fist came out of the darkness and punched its next blow. Robert was made redundant.

To find as much cash as they could, they decided to sell items they no longer needed, including all baby equipment. All the items were gathered up, cleaned and advertised and didn't take long to sell, giving them enough money for food and essentials. Robert's salary as a firefighter added to the benefits they'd been forced to claim, all of which meant they were able to eat and live.

It was after all baby items were sold, that the fist dealt another blow. Trudi was pregnant. They didn't know how they would feed another mouth, albeit not for several months, but she knew that the newcomer was meant to be. The space that had never disappeared since the loss of the last baby would be filled and anything could happen in a year, or less.

As their car had come with his job, they found themselves with only a pushbike and a pushchair for transport. Trudi smiles in amusement as she visualises the picture of the family trekking to the local supermarket to do a weekly shop, with Phoebe in the pushchair and Naomi sitting on the bike as her dad pushed her along. Once the shopping was completed, they made the return journey, bags filling the basket under the pushchair as well as hanging riskily from the bike's handlebars. It seemed as if their life was turning into a black comedy with scenes added by the day. Life's humour then played another trick and removed the only means of wheeled transport from Robert. On receiving a fire alert, he positioned himself on the saddle, ready for take-off, but the tyre blew out, leaving her husband with a very frustrated look on his face. She chuckles as she is reminded of the incident which she found highly amusing at the time. She also recalls the look on Robert's face which was enough to stop the laughter before it had time to escape.

As money was tight, they couldn't afford a repair, but luckily, her mum had an old bike stashed away in the garage. With a little bit of work, the bike was ready for use and he, once again, had wheels. It was comical to watch him pedalling off on a woman's bike and the funny side of it brought relief from the despondency she would have otherwise felt. Except life wasn't content to leave it there, it decided to hit again. For Robert to have a quick response to a fire call, he left the bike under the kitchen window. Unable to fit a cat flap for their family cats, it was necessary to leave the small window at the top open as access in and out for the pets. She calls to mind the night when, as they were all sleeping, she was woken by the sound of Naomi's bike, which was kept in the hallway, being knocked. She put it down to the cats going in and out, except the morning presented a different tale. They'd been burgled. The burglar had used the bike to climb up and open the big window. Their only pint of milk had been drunk and her purse emptied of all they had. Then, as if they hadn't suffered enough, Robert lost the use of that bike too. As he responded to a call and rode off into the distance, the pedal fell off, leaving one leg moving frantically in circles as it searched for the missing object. Trudi remembers, despite not knowing whether to laugh or cry, giving in to the hysteria that was bubbling under the surface. She envisages herself laughing with tears streaming down her face, until she was unable to laugh anymore, praying that that had been the final test of endurance. She hoped, beyond all hopes that life had put down its glove and any further blows were halted.

She is then reminded of the first signs of something positive happening. Robert was successful in obtaining work as a kitchen designer and salesman, which also gave them new transport of the four wheeled variety. The pregnancy was advancing well, with a bulge that seemed to grow larger every day and ankles, feet and finger joints that collected fluid daily which, all combined, made it increasingly difficult for Trudi to walk. By the time she reached seven months she felt like one of the egg-shaped toys 'Weebles', Weebles that wobbled but didn't fall down. She plodded her way down the road like an elephant as she took Naomi to playgroup, using the pushchair as support, as well as to the many birthday parties that had suddenly become part of her daughter's life. She would have been quite content to have a wheelbarrow to carry the monstrosity, although Robert decided that she needed a car. They'd managed to clear their debts and things were more secure financially and so an old banger was affordable. It was a Godsend, making life a great deal easier. No more long walks to the supermarket. No more loading up the pushchair with numerous bags. However, she was so used to walking that on one occasion she forgot that she'd driven. She was on her way home before she realised and had to turn around!

The baby was nearly a week overdue. Trudi was feeling extremely uncomfortable and wished that she would receive a signal that labour was imminent. It had been a while since she'd been able to bend over, cuddle the girls without a barrier and move freely; she'd completely forgotten what her toes looked like. It was exactly a week after the due date when she finally had the familiar feeling of restlessness and the desire to crawl into a cave. There weren't any little niggles and so she carried on as normal, concentrating on preparing the house for the impending arrival of a new family member. She phoned Robert to warn him but didn't feel he needed to leave work. As the day went on, she became more intolerant and the first tightening began. A little while later, the small tightening began to increase and she knew it was time to phone Robert. Whilst waiting, she sat beside her two daughters, breathing deeply as she read them a story. By the time he arrived, the pains had intensified, indicating that it was time to make her way to the maternity hospital. Before dropping the two girls off at their grandma's, they were told that their baby brother, or sister, was on the way; a few hours later, the girls' baby sister arrived.

Unlike the other two, this baby had a mass of black hair. From her small dainty hands, long slender fingers, fit for a pianist, protruded. Her cry was distinct, sounding like a bleating lamb which Trudi was able to pick out from all the other babies' cries. There was a gentleness and sensitivity about her and she needed a name that suited her already distinctive personality. Ellie. The next day, two excited girls ran onto the ward, eager to meet their new sister. Climbing on to the bed beside her, they waited patiently for their turn to hold the baby and, as she watched the two girls cuddling their new sister, she felt, for the first time, totally complete. She had three beautiful girls, a husband whom she loved dearly and who loved her in return. That was all that mattered to her. Life could throw whatever it wanted at her for as long as she had Robert and her three daughters she would survive. It was a belief that she clung onto as if it was a case of life or death.

The scenes travel on, winding their way along her life's path, past happy memories, not shadows, chasing her, catching her and sometimes flying by. The film that has captured her journey is playing, displaying the years that followed the birth of Ellie. There are scenes of contentment, love and joy. The voices that she hears are filled with chatter and laughter. She catches flickers of many happy times, the family outings into the forest or the beach for picnics and walks as well as the frequent family holidays. She watches each daughter, in turn, as they start school, looking smart and proud as she told them how wonderful they looked in their uniforms. The movie portrays days of a sun filled life with no clouds hovering above waiting to dampen the happiness. Her heart fills with emotion as the images recapture the sensations that each experience brought: the love and joy within the family, the contentment she felt, the pride for each success the girls had. The film continues to play until it stops as another house move was about to take place which was followed by an unexpected and magical holiday.

Chapter 21

Two years after the arrival of Ellie, the family moved a short distance to a town where they would be able to buy a house that offered them about the same space for less money. Ideally, Trudi would have liked a modern house which, unfortunately, was just outside their budget and so they settled upon an older terraced house. She never really felt at home there. It had an eerie ambience which, at times, made her feel cold and unsettled to the point that she was sure that there was an unwelcome presence. The whole house required quite a bit of attention too, but it was handy for Robert's work and was also close to the school where she'd begun her teaching career which might offer occasional openings for supply teaching. With time and patience, they managed to modernise the inside of the house, yet she continued to feel uneasy, although ignored the impression of foreboding that was loitering in the background.

Financially, things had improved and for the first time they were able to afford a family holiday. They hired a caravan in Cornwall and spent a glorious time as a family visiting the local area and playing on the beach with the girls searching through the rock pools and building sandcastles. They'd enjoyed it so much that Robert thought it would be brilliant if they bought their own caravan and so they invested in an affordable second-hand van. It was used for the first time on Naomi's ninth birthday when, for her birthday treat, they went to a nearby Safari Park. The family thoroughly enjoyed experiencing all the animals and activities. The downside was the weather. It poured down, forming large muddy puddles all around the van which made it nigh on impossible to move it when it was time to leave. Everyone had to push the van and, when it finally moved, they were soaked through and covered in mud. They found it funny, Robert, on the other hand, felt that the weather had spoilt the whole break which made him change the plans for the summer. A holiday had been booked in Devon, but he remembered Trudi talking about the time she'd spent with the French family in the South of France. She'd described to him the clear blue skies, the bright sunshine and the blue sea that sparkled as the sun spread its rays across the surface. She'd told him of the sand that felt soft underfoot which had occasionally been too hot to walk on. Then there was the heat of the sea which, when entered, felt like stepping into a warm bath. The beauty of the mountainous area with its stunning surrounding and historic buildings had all been portrayed. It was the picture she'd painted in his mind that encouraged him to book a holiday in France, although for Brittany, not the South.

At first, the weather was good, then it changed and the rain was never ending with the forecast showing little chance of improvement unless they made their way further south. In no time at all, the caravan was packed, the girls hurried into the car and they were on their way, with no idea of where they were heading. Robert drove through the night and, nearly twenty four hours later they pulled into the campsite that Trudi had managed to find in the camping book. The office was closed and so it was the night watchman who squeezed them onto a temporary spot until the morning when they would be able to choose a pitch to their liking. The night pitch was tiny and the van so close to another that there wasn't room to swing a cat. The site was full of people bustling about their business and noise from the nearby bar echoed in the still warm air. Exhausted from the long haul, her husband broke as he said, 'what on earth have we done? This is awful!' Putting her arms around his neck, she said 'let's wait and see what the morning brings.' After an unappetising supper of beans on toast, they all collapsed into a deep sleep.

They were woken by glorious sun beating its way through the caravan windows and heat that was already indicating how hot it would get, even at eight in the morning. Unable to put off inspecting what waited for them, Robert apprehensively ventured out to explore the surroundings. The man that returned was not the same as the one who'd left. This man was beaming from ear to ear. On opening the door, he grabbed Trudi's arm and pulled her outside, calling to the girls to follow. The view that greeted them was out of this world. Just across the road, was another part of the site, positioned behind the beach. In the distance, they could see hilltop villages decorating the coastline, proudly displaying their medieval castles which called to have their history investigated by anyone who was willing to visit. The already building heat was drawing out the scent of the local shrubs and trees, a mixture of pine and spice with a hint of sweetness. Infront of them, the blue water of the Mediterranean Sea was starting to send out its invitations in the form of glistening jewels on the surface. As if they'd no time to waste, the family hurried to the office where they were given a selection of pitches from which to choose. They chose one situated on the edge of the beach and, in the blink of an eye, the caravan was moved and set up in what would be their home for two weeks. They spent two weeks of pure bliss lazing in the sun, swimming in the gloriously warm water and visiting the medieval villages nearby. It was a fairy tale place which brought a touch of magic into their lives and they decided that they would definitely visit again. The Cote d'Azur had lured them in, captured their hearts and cast its magical spell from which they would never be freed. She sighs happily. 'That place is still so magical and has given us very many happy holidays. Merci!'

Leaving the happy memories of their special place behind, she is taken to the time she returned to work and moved into the house of her dreams. A time that had been so exciting yet turned into one where she felt that her world was falling apart yet again.

Trudi was feeling that she had a great deal to be thankful for and relaxed into the comforting arms that life appeared to be offering. Naomi was at junior school and Phoebe had started at the infant school where Trudi had once taught. It wasn't long before she was asked to help at the school. To begin with, it was a few days here and there, although sooner than she really wanted, she was on a two-term contract. From then, there was no looking back and she found herself returning to full time teaching, albeit in a different school. Her mother-in-law stepped in to look after Ellie and collect the other two from school. As they were both in work, they decided that they might be able to afford a larger property and began to search for the house of their dreams. Also, Robert wanted to start his own business again. This time he wanted to concentrate on supplying and fitting kitchens, which would require space for deliveries. She was hesitant, but he pointed out there was a great deal of housing development going on locally which would provide him with openings. He already had potential clients, builders with whom he'd previously worked and he was certain that it would be a success. After many long discussions, she agreed.

The first time she saw the house, it was as if it was begging her to move in, so how could she refuse? It was a detached chalet bungalow, with three bedrooms, a lounge, a separate dining room and a large kitchen. The back garden was huge, with pear, plum and apple trees already firmly established; it also promised to be a wonderful suntrap during the summer months. There was a great sense of adventure as the girls explored the house. They ran out into the garden and, as if they'd never seen a space as big before, filled it with squeals of excitement as they chased around, investigating every nook and cranny. It was a happy house that wrapped its welcoming arms around the family as if to say, 'welcome home'.

Life was very busy, filled with decorating the house, work and family. Work had become more pressurised with the introduction of the new curriculum and she had to travel twenty odd miles to the school which, on a good day, she could do in thirty minutes. It meant she was later getting home than previously and no sooner had she walked through the door there was dinner to prepare. Dinner was quickly followed by homework and reading books and, once the girls were in bed, she had to prepare for the following day. It was hard to juggle it all and at times she felt as if she was being pulled in all directions with no time for herself. The scenario makes Trudi realise how many times since then she's had the same feeling. She's always found it hard to allow herself time, but she also realises how strong she's been, how strong she **is** and how her strength and fortitude has enabled her to deal with all eventualities.

Robert was working hard and had managed to obtain several kitchen fitting jobs. One night, they sat down to talk over their finances and the way forward. He wanted to improve the business which would need using the house as collateral. Trudi, on the other hand, felt the old tightening of the stomach and sickness creep in. Her friend panic returned. Her gut told her to say no, with guilt and terror of losing him doing their utmost to win the battle. Her instinct took over and she refused. A heated argument followed, but she was unwilling to budge and stood her ground firmly. It wasn't long after that the building industry hit trouble. Interest rates were high and the housing market slowed. Building stopped which resulted in work becoming hard to find. The business fell apart, leaving them with enormous debts once again. She, thankfully, was still employed and they also had the fire service money. Robert took on a job as a van driver, but it was a struggle to make ends meet. Their mortgage was large and soon they began to default on payments. They tried to sell the house, only prices had fallen dramatically and the market continued to be at a near standstill. In the end, the only choice was to make themselves bankrupt. Their house was taken. The family could have been separated and placed in a bed and breakfast by the Council. Thankfully, the Housing Association kept them together and they were given a temporary three bed terraced house, until a permanent one was found.

The day they moved out of their home, was November 5th and as she thinks back over it, she notices the same numbness she felt as a child on that date, nearly thirty years ago. The day her mum was taken to hospital. It also reminds her of the great big hole she experienced when Naomi went to university and the devastation she felt when Robert had left her. The pain, emptiness and grief she suffered on those occasions surfaced again as she said goodbye to the house, whilst putting a cloak of indifference around her in the hope of deflecting it. The same cloak that had shielded her in years gone by. She tries to understand why life has presented her with so many obstacles. She wonders if it was all her fault. Tears come, as if to wash away the agony, just as they finally fell that fateful November night when she and Robert were finally alone. Tears of grief over the loss of the house, tears full of suffering and heartache. He pulled her into his arms and, again, apologised for being the one to hurt her so badly.

Chapter 22

After only a few months in the temporary house, they were offered one on a new housing association estate which was ideal for the family, only to Trudi, it felt like the end of the world. She felt ashamed of where they'd ended up and the neighbours weren't the type of people with whom she would choose to mix. Some people may have classed her as being a snob, but she felt that she deserved better. As she contemplates her feelings at that time, it hits her how she'd behaved like her grandma all those years ago when she'd had to move into a Council house. Was it family karma, or was it a family thread that needed healing and cutting away so that it didn't pass down to younger generations? 'Only the future holds the answer to that, but I can do my best to stop it,' she answers.

The couple were determined to make the best of what they had and gradually work towards a better future. She held on to the fact that the family were still together, that she and Robert remained strong and that their relationship was even more secure. As a family, they would survive. Day by day, life began to look a lot brighter with the sun shining on the horizon once again. Robert found employment and Trudi began to study for an MA in Education. Financially they had never been better off. They were able to socialise a lot more and have frequent holidays to their magical place as well as exploring different places, making her aware that a down could have an up! Then the sun rose, casting its light on the future. Life presented them with a gift, the opportunity to buy part of a house and rent the remainder, with the option of buying the whole house when they could afford to. There were financial requirements to meet, a house with certain criteria to find and a mortgage to obtain. The first two didn't present any problems, it was finding a mortgage for ex-bankrupts. Nevertheless, with determination and grit, they finally found someone who considered their finances rather than the bankruptcy.

The house they acquired was a three bedroom end of terrace with an attached garage and a south facing back garden, a vital criterion! It felt like their home as soon as they saw it, as most of their previous houses had, each one having beckoned them because it held the next part of their story. Every brick of the house had an element of warmth oozing from it which enhanced the feeling of relief that was washing over her body. The weight of the world had been lifted from her shoulders and she started to view the future with a more positive outlook, ignoring the whispers within the walls that warned her of clouds forming in the distance.

At the same time as buying the house, Trudi passed her MA and was successful at gaining a post as part of the management team in a different school. Naturally, the promotion required more work, but the school was closer to home and the girls were older with different needs. The role gave her a new professional challenge and she enjoyed being opened to another side of teaching. She was experiencing fulfilment, contentment and satisfaction in all areas of her life. It was as if the cycle of destruction had finally been broken although she'd experienced far too often life giving and just as quickly taking away. It seemed to her that whenever life was showing signs of positivity, she was never allowed to feel totally secure. The shadow of doubt had its finger poised menacingly, ready to point out anything that might bring unease. This time, it returned its focus on Robert's job. He was made redundant once again. He was never one to sit back, he was a fighter, apart from on this occasion, when the stuffing was completely knocked out of him. His confidence, and morale, was broken and he was unable to see any point in trying. It was another blow from his friend 'failure' which, combined with all his other feelings of being unsuccessful, made him feel weak and useless. The picture of her husband sitting with his head hanging low is vivid in her mind and it is very clear to her just how badly he'd been affected. She wonders how much it had played in his future life and actions. 'No doubt it'll be made clear,' she scoffs.

Regardless of the despair she was feeling, Trudi did everything she could to bolster him up. She gave him emotional support when he was low, made him smile when he was feeling sad, whilst doing her utmost to make him feel worthwhile. She attempted to keep him positive, reassuring him that the right job would be found. As her mum always pointed out, 'things happen for a reason' and Trudi's instinct was saying that life was leading her husband in a different direction. She'd always considered that Robert wasn't suited to sales or office type work, the area in which he'd been employed. The role hadn't allowed him the opportunity to show his more empathic side. He was a very caring and sensitive man with the ability to keep calm under pressure, qualities that perhaps only she saw. She was accused many a time of seeing him through rose coloured glasses, but she knew him well and the things in which he would excel. Even though his role as a retained firefighter, to a certain extent, allowed this side of his personality to shine, it didn't totally fulfil him. One day, as she was glancing through the job adverts, her eyes were drawn to one which had Robert's name stamped all over it, one where his attributes could be used. Convinced that it suited him down to the ground, she encouraged him to apply, ignoring his argument of not having the necessary experience. Much to his amazement, he was successful and became part of a control room team in the Health Service. It meant shift work, which Trudi wasn't looking forward to, but it was something she was willing to live with for Robert to be fulfilled. Her husband embarked upon his new career with enthusiasm and his air of contentment increased with each passing day. Secure in this knowledge, Trudi began to feel at peace once more and have confidence in their life having finally turned a corner, after all, what more could possibly happen?

She brings her thoughts back into the room and sighs deeply. 'Unfortunately, I know exactly what happens.' She pours another glass of wine and prepares herself for the next part.

Mr Moon decides to do a detour and take Trudi back to the time when Naomi left home to start a new life at university. It was the most heart wrenching experience she'd ever felt, leaving a hole so deep it seemed as if she was teetering over it, ready to fall in. It was exacerbated by the fact that she had to endure driving her daughter there without Robert who'd hurt his back, making it impossible for him to sit in the car, let alone drive. She also had to tow a trailer, something she'd never undertaken before, loaded with student life accessories and personal belongings. Towing instructions were delivered to the panicking driver, farewells were said, and then she, Naomi and Ellie set off on the 100 miles drive.

It was a long haul, made harder by her unease about the trailer as well as the emotions she was swallowing every time she spoke. Driving on the motorway was less challenging, the straightness of the road calming her nerves, but the narrow bendy roads were a different matter. That required total concentration which, in some ways, was a blessing as it diverted her mind from the impending parting. All was good until she took the wrong road and needed to turn around, not an easy feat to undertake with a trailer. Trudi laughs as she remembers the look of dismay and embarrassment on the girls' faces when she drove on to a football pitch which gave her enough room to turn without reversing or unhitching. Even though it may not have been ideal, she'd succeeded! Embarrassment then turned into amusement, with all three laughing at the exploits of a virgin tower.

They arrived safely at the University complex, making sure that the car was parked for an easy get away. The three of them made their way to the admissions hall where Naomi was registered and given all the necessary information. Then it was back to the car, with its malicious trailer, to take her daughter to the digs she'd been given. The student houses edged a one-way street with many speed bumps which did their utmost to empty the trailer as it heaved its way over but, despite their futile attempts, the ensemble arrived intact. They were greeted by one of the house mates who gave them a guided tour before the belongings were taken from the trailer and placed in Naomi's new bedroom. They sat and chatted over a cup of tea until the time of departure couldn't be avoided any longer. Big hugs given, followed by a few tears and the homeward journey began, sobs being pushed down by Trudi so that Ellie didn't become upset. She can still picture Naomi standing at the gate waving, looking pale, young, lost and alone – or was it simply a reflection of her own feelings? She certainly felt as if the life force was being sucked from her and definitely felt pain deep within her heart. She somehow managed to take hold and concentrate on the drive home. She remembers how she broke down in Robert's arms, finally giving in to the built-up emotions, releasing them with heart rending sobs. She visualises him gently kissing her head and hears him assuring her that Naomi would be alright, yet nothing could relieve the agony she was feeling. The big hole inside her had opened again, bringing with it the torture she'd felt on previous occasions, her shadows from the past gradually filling the hole. She recollects recognising the pattern and similarities in all the experiences that life had thrown at her and how she vowed to learn from them and stop the pattern from repeating, to break the seemingly never-ending circle. 'I certainly made a good job of that!' she remarks sarcastically. She notices the moon looking at her, as if he is agreeing with her and he smiles encouragingly as she braces herself for the emotional turmoil that is heading her way. 'You're breaking me in gently,' she says to the shining object in the sky, 'but I know I can't hide from it forever.'

Life had finally changed for Robert. An opportunity arose offering him the opening to a career for which Trudi felt he'd always been destined. After all the rebuffs of the preceding years he had the chance to train as a paramedic, allowing him to use all those special qualities that she loved about him. The downside was that the training required him to be away from home for several weeks, although he would be home for the weekends. Even though old wounds and anxieties were coming to the fore, she knew it was the right move for him and would support him in every way she could.

On the evening before his departure, they snuggled in each other's arms, pretending to watch television. His mind was concentrating on the following week, hers was on the following morning when she would have to say goodbye. It was after the girls had gone to bed, that emotions took hold. She flung her arms around his neck with tears running down her face. He held her tight, his lips soothing the pain she was feeling. He looked at her and whispered 'I love you so much. There's nothing for you to worry about.' Then, he led her gently up to bed, where she cradled against his body, clinging on for dear life, knowing what the morning light would bring.

The night was long yet seemed to pass so quickly, the inevitable dawning with the light of day. Tears welled in her eyes as he held her close, promising to phone that evening. He kissed away the drops as her tear ducts overflowed, picked up his bag and was gone. Gathering all her inner strength she stood, with the girls, and waved him off. She watched as the car disappeared, wondering how she was going to endure the passing days, but then the normality of daily routines crept in. Work, the girls, cooking, but there was always space in her busy mind for anxiety. Each week brought the parting tears and the concerns she held within her; doubt and worry were ever present. He phoned her every night, full of the training and all he was learning. She loved hearing the enthusiasm in his voice and the fact that he appeared full of life. He always asked how she and the girls were, was interested in their day, but more importantly, he told her how much he loved her and how he was missing her. The weekends were special. They spent quality time together and she also helped him with his work, testing his knowledge in preparation for the ongoing assessment. She enjoyed being part of his journey and felt very proud of her husband. He'd finally found his vocation; it was just that persistent inner voice which was whispering warnings.

The October after he finished his training, they managed a few days away during half term, just the two of them, on a coastal campsite not far from home. There was an essence of freedom as well as togetherness as they shared the breath-taking views and relaxed in the sunlight as it flickered across the sea. Her feelings of unease were put aside, although they were still niggling underneath, but she was unable to put her finger on the cause. He did spend a great deal of time furtively on his phone which he quickly put down as she walked into the van. When asked who'd been on the phone, she was told that it was his work partner checking in on him, which was possible even if rather frequent. On returning home, a tension built between them. Robert became short tempered and intolerant. When questioned, she was told it was the change in job which was demanding and sometimes not very pleasant. Again, credible. On reflection, Trudi could kick herself. She'd seen the writing on the wall, why hadn't she read it? She'd heard the warning bells, seen the signs, why had she chosen to ignore them? Perhaps it had all been part of her life's lessons, her soul's journey. She'd ignored her gut instinct previously. Perhaps it was life presenting her with another chance which she'd chosen to disregard yet again! She knows she'd attempted to talk to Robert about her feelings and explain how she'd been worried they were growing apart. She remembers asking him outright, one night, if he was seeing someone else, only to be told that she was being paranoid; he loved her and when did he have time for an affair anyway? She notices the format of before when discussions had usually ended in a heated argument and her not knowing why or how it had started. The recognisable form of having no idea where it had all come from, or where it was leading to, and feeling as if she'd been going mad. She'd thought that perhaps she was, after all, there'd been no real reason to doubt him, only the unsettling feelings inside her which had rapidly become a gnawing, a gnawing that had eaten deeper and deeper into the pit of her stomach. Feelings that she'd experienced previously, had recognised, and still chosen to overlook. Why hadn't she remembered the promise she'd made to herself twenty three years ago? Nevertheless, as she looks back, she is conscious of the fact that she did follow her gut instinct to a certain extent, for without doing so the outcome would have been very different.

Trudi brings her thought to an abrupt halt and casts her eyes up at the moon, seeking comfort and reassurance as she starts to prepare herself for the biggest whammy in her life. She compares it to having had the heaviest textbook thrown at her by life which knocked her down, sideways and every which way. 'Surely there's easier ways to learn?' she asks the moon and tops up her glass as the next scene begins.

Chapter 23

The scene opens, shortly after their days away, with Robert returning home late one night, which wasn't unusual, except there seemed to be something different about his air. He appeared subdued, tears filling his eyes as he sat next to her on the settee. He took her hand as the tears ran down his cheeks, telling her how much he loved her. He told her how much he'd enjoyed their time away together and how he missed her whilst he was at home alone. He held her tightly in his arms, whilst Trudi, herself, was completely confused, not fully understanding what had prompted the emotional display. 'Hmm! More effective than a bunch of flowers,' she grunts, perhaps with a little too much scorn.

Those good old warning bells were clanging loudly and she felt the familiar knot tighten in her stomach, just as it had that fateful day twenty four years ago. The voice that escaped from her mouth didn't appear to be hers as the words 'are you seeing someone else?' squeezed into the room. Taking charge of the proceedings, she was calm and collected, even with the somersaulting butterflies in her stomach. She told him that she would rather know than live a lie and even talked about the possibility of loving two people. No blame, no pressure. Just the chance for honesty. He emphatically denied the suggestion of an affair and apologised for his emotional outburst, telling her he was just tired. The bells were ringing louder and louder, menacing shadows drawing nearer, but Trudi wanted to believe every word he said. She didn't want to contemplate the possibility of another woman, nor did she want to risk losing him. Swallow, bury and move on.

Over the ensuing weeks, tensions grew and nonsensical arguments became more frequent. Trudi felt as if insanity was truly creeping in and was completely oblivious to having experienced the same scenario in the distant past. Robert was spending an increasing amount of his free time at the fire station or having to 'pop out' for one reason or another. He was showering before his 'popping out' sessions, and dressing more smartly, although was always able to give reasonable explanations, such as 'it's a colleague's birthday' or 'I'm meeting some work mates'. She was becoming highly suspicious, but didn't have any proof, only gut feelings so all she could do was trust them and bide her time. Her intuition became her guide.

Phoebe's eighteenth birthday was around the corner which they were going to celebrate with a small party at home and they wanted to make it as special as they could, a day to remember. 'It was definitely that,' she gasps sadly, 'as it turned out, it was a day never to be forgotten.' It so happened that some of Robert's colleagues were going on the 'booze' run to France and he thought it would be a good opportunity to buy a supply of reasonably priced wine and spirits. This would keep the cost of the party down, as well as the fast approaching Christmas. She agreed. He promised to keep her informed of his whereabouts and, to ensure that he was able to, they swapped mobiles as Trudi's was set up for use abroad, his wasn't. She remembers how she considered her life to be a happy one and how in a flash her world was in turmoil, triggered by an innocent phone call, or was it so innocent? She summons up the sound of the sweet sickly voice coming over the phone, whispering words into her ear, words that were meant for the ear of someone else. She feels the excruciating torture, as the reality hit home. 'It was that small swapping of phones that prompted so many questions which had no answers. It shattered my dreams and caused so much insufferable pain. Why are you making me relive it?' she yells at the moon. Ignoring Trudi's outburst, the story returns to the disastrous afternoon.

After work, Trudi got into her car to go home, wondering if Robert was on his way to France. Suddenly, her mobile rang. She answered, expecting to hear Robert, only to be greeted by a voice mail and the voice she heard was not his. It was a woman, whose words and sugary sweet voice made her feel vulnerable, causing an inner turmoil of confusion and deep, deep pain. Those words spoken by this unknown person; the words so simple yet so destructive: 'hello. It's only me. I'm home now if you want to phone me. Hope everything's O.K.,' followed by a laugh, a girlish laugh, one that ran down Trudi's spine, chilling her through and through. Questions began to run through her mind: who was she? Why was she phoning? This time, she wasn't dreaming, this was happening in real time. She knew instinctively who was accompanying Robert on his trip to France and knew in her heart that a nightmare was about to unfold. Her husband of nearly twenty-five years would be spending the night in the arms of another woman. A simple message on a phone and her life was shattering around her. She felt anger, hurt, and sickness welling inside. Reason began to creep in with suggestions of it being totally innocent, except she knew from the heartfelt torment and the stabbing within her soul, that it was the exact opposite. With dread and vulnerability rising inside her, she prepared herself for the drive home. There was nothing she could do until Robert returned, when another dilemma would face her: should she keep quiet or confront him?

Shaking uncontrollably, Trudi started the car for the homeward journey, one that seemed to go on forever. How she got home she didn't know for her concentration was far away from driving. It was as if she was being transported by some invisible force, oblivious to the road, the surroundings and the car itself. Waves of emotions and thoughts engulfed her as the incidents of the past few weeks began to fit together like a jigsaw puzzle. The puzzle portrayed the images that had formed in her mind, but there were still a few pieces missing. Absorbed in the image, she suddenly became aware of the car pulling into the drive. She must pull herself together and brace herself for whatever the next few hours would bring. Mechanically she turned off the engine, stepped from the car and, like a true professional artiste, painted a smile on her face and walked through the front door. Ellie and Phoebe were in their usual position, lounging in front of the television, blissfully unaware of the turmoil churning inside of their mum. Greetings exchanged, she set about cooking the dinner and preparing Naomi's room, who was coming home for the weekend to celebrate Phoebe's birthday. There was also a Christmas function that she and Robert were supposed to be attending. Celebrations! She felt far from celebrating. Her whole life seemed like a farce. She felt alone and deserted by the one she loved and whom she'd thought loved her. Averting the temptation to scream and punch any inanimate object that was in her way, she put on a cloak of calmness and sat with the girls, forcing food into a body that was threatening to reject each mouthful. She allowed a fleeting sense of self-admiration, giving herself a pat on the back for her performance, which she believed was worthy of an Oscar. She'd been successful at keeping her turmoil at bay and hiding the truth from her precious girls but needed to perform an encore as she collected Naomi from the bus station. Another outstanding performance was achieved and she revelled in the standing ovation of her imaginary audience. Mission accomplished.

Her attention goes to the phone call he made that night and how he described the scene of the night lights reflecting on the sea as the ferry slowly made its way out of the port. He was on deck when he made the call and she could hear the rush of the water as the ship ploughed through the waves. She casually asked if he was alone. He ran off a few names and told her how much he wished she was there with him. The lies had begun or were being continued. She kept silent about the phone call she'd received, that could wait. For now, she must play happy families whilst sending evil thoughts to the pair in the middle of the ocean. She directed a tempestuous storm their way, imagining a tumultuous wave sweeping the offending woman overboard. Despite finding the picture of the woman being sucked under by an unforgiving wave pleasurable, it didn't bring her peace. If anything, she felt as if she too was struggling to keep her head above the ever increasing surge of water.

Sleep didn't come easily. Her head was filled with that sickly-sweet voice, with images of him and the woman, their arms and bodies wrapped around each other. Alone, she allowed the tears to escape, soaking the pillow beneath, as the pain welled up inside and mingled with the torment from years ago which had been reawakened. She felt the familiar knife twist inside her, the hate, the anger, only with greater intensity. The two events became one, doubling the anguish, the heart ache and despair. So great was the hurt inside her, she was incapable of moving. Cradling herself in her arms, she wished sleep would take her over and that she would awake to find it had all been a dream.

The morning didn't offer any relief from the agonising night she'd endured. She applied a cold compress to her eyes in the hope that the tear induced swelling would reduce and used make up to cover the redness and dark circles. Then, with churning stomach and as much positivity she could muster, she shouted goodbye to the girls and began to focus on the day ahead. Luckily, her class was an easy one and even though her mind was leaping continuously and tears constantly pricking her eyes, she managed to get through the day, pulling off another award-winning performance.

Work had brought some respite from the inner chaos, but, as she began the journey home, her stomach returned to the roller coaster ride and her mind whirled with plans on how to react when Robert got home. For the sake of the girls, she decided to be calm and act as if nothing was wrong, whilst discreetly gathering any evidence she could. It was easier said than done, for as soon as he returned, she felt defences going up, a shield of armour protecting her from any arrows that might wend her way. She withdrew, sucking her being into her shell and turning back into a tortoise hiding from danger. Robert, on the other hand, was bright and breezy, pulling her into a tight embrace. He was very pleased to see her, perhaps a little too much so, and seemingly unaware of her quivering body. She endeavoured to calm her anxiety as he gave his version of the previous night which was different to the one she was silently reliving. She listened as he recounted his shopping expedition, showing an interest in what he'd bought and felt more than a little smug when she discovered that the crossing hadn't been at all smooth. There was divine retribution after all! It was just a shame that the voice hadn't been washed overboard!

When the girls had gone to their beds, they snuggled together on the settee as if all was as it should be. Hoping to take him off guard, she found the courage to mention, as casually as possible, the strange phone call she'd received. Of course, Robert denied all knowledge – it must have been a wrong number. Even when she pointed out that he'd been mentioned by name, he still managed to talk his way out of it saying that it was probably someone from work trying to get hold of him. Yes! That was exactly what it was! The lies came too easily, as if he'd been prepped for the conversation, practised and well versed in what he was going to say. She suspected that the 'voice' had warned him of the phone call and she became convinced that the woman had left the message deliberately, knowing that the phones had been swapped. 'And I was right,' she says emphatically. 'It was all part of the voice's plot. After all, women can be very scheming when they want something – a skill at which I became very adept.'

Chapter 24

Despite deciding to lie in wait like an animal ready to ambush its prey, Trudi found it impossible to ignore the awakening inner cries of her old friend Sherlock offering to help with the investigation. Sherlock, once again, possessed her body and mind, pushing her in earnest to search for clues before Robert returned from wherever he was supposed to be. It was as if she was being driven by another force, fighting for her survival. A deranged woman began to search frantically for anything to prove that her gut instinct was right. The contents of the bedside table were thrown onto the floor and her fingers urgently rummaged unsuccessfully through the pile of rubbish before it was placed back in position. Undeterred, she emptied his briefcase, searching for anything, a glimmer of hope or despair. Nothing. Then her eyes fell upon the jeans he'd cast aside the previous night. There, protruding from the pocket, was his wallet that he'd inadvertently left behind. The memory of discovering the face of her dream all those years ago prompted her to open the wallet. Ignoring the lump rising from the pit of her stomach, she slowly began to search the inside. A five-pound note, a ten-pound note, credit cards, odd bits of paper with telephone numbers and then, hidden deep within a compartment, obscured by a card, was a photo. A photo of a woman. She held her breath. The 'voice' now had a face. As she focussed on the person being presented to her, her heart was pounding and her stomach churning, replicating the shaking of cream inside a butter churn. Her head was a ticking bomb, ready to explode at any moment whilst she sat contemplating the air of smugness and satisfaction that oozed from the photo. There sat the perpetrator, not an ounce of remorse visible, just a clear vision of triumph, the King of the castle. Anger rose, bringing with it a strong desire to forcibly wipe the self-congratulatory smirk from the face.

It was a face that surprised Trudi. She'd been expecting a young, attractive girl who exuded an air of sensuality. Instead, there was this middle-aged, plump woman who wasn't particularly attractive and certainly didn't emanate a morsel of sensuality. Appearances can be deceptive and there must have been something he found attractive about the dowdy looking person. She laughs smugly as she's reminded of her musings: perhaps the 'face' was good in bed, but looking at her, she had her doubts. She thought the face looked cold and hard with a tone of neediness around the person's aura. Trudi reminds herself of how she intuitively used the energy emanating from the photo to create a profile of the woman, like a medium reading a tarot card. It was a woman who appeared weak and needy yet very contriving. Anger rose within Trudi and, despite the self-doubt and low self-esteem, she knew that this woman would be brought down. She would fight and she would win! Sherlock had already helped her with the investigation, now he could help her bring about justice. Her searching was interrupted by the sound of a key in the front door. Realising that Robert had returned, she quickly placed the photo in her pocket, put the wallet back and made herself look busy as she heard him climbing the stairs. The actress within was summoned and she calmly turned as he entered the room with a somewhat suspicious look on his face. Smiling, she asked him if he'd managed to do all that he'd had to do and, when questioned about her activities, coolly told him she was tidying. Hiding the instability she was feeling, she kissed him as if life was normal. She had to rely on her acting skills to assist her through the day, until she knew how she was going to proceed. The girls were still none the wiser and she and Robert had the Christmas function to attend that night. It was imperative for her to keep her performance strong and convincing.

Time moves her forward to that afternoon when Alice paid her a visit. The two sisters sat alone in the wintery garden whilst Trudi's nerves were calmed with a cigarette. They were quietly talking about anything and everything when suddenly she couldn't keep her worries silent any longer. Without any warning the words 'I think Robert is having an affair,' escaped from her mouth. Astounded, Alice looked at her, as if waiting for the punch line. Realising that one was not to follow, she screamed 'what?' A trembling voice explained the suspicions, the phone call and the photo which, as if proof was needed, was surreptitiously shown. As the reality of the words hit, anger became visible on her sister's face. Her jaw clenched tight and invisible clouds of steam billowed from her flaring nostrils which grew wider with each intake of breath. Her fists screwed into an ever-tightening ball as she endeavoured to take charge of her fury and replace it with compassion. After making some uncomplimentary remarks about Robert, she asked how Trudi was and advised her to confront him with the photo but to find more evidence before making any decisions. She promised to be there and support her in any way she could.

After Alice left, Trudi began the first part of the attack. Holding the photo in her trembling hand she confronted Robert with the evidence, and still the denials continued. The photo had apparently been taken by him when he was away on training with her. He'd had it printed and put it in his wallet to give to her but had forgotten. He reinforced, once again, that she'd nothing to worry about, yet she knew he was hiding the truth. All she wanted was for him to be honest and then they might have something to work on, except he was unable. He was unable to admit the truth to her and himself. Appearing to believe his explanation, she set off to town to find an outfit to wear that night. She was determined to find something that was as alluring as possible, despite feeling unattractive, fat and betrayed.

Her mind not really on shopping, she wandered from shop to shop, trying on a variety of outfits before deciding on a pair of black trousers and a bright red top. She looked at the person reflected in the shop's mirror and didn't like what she saw. The hint of grey hair that had begun to show was highlighted. The wrinkles that had begun to form around her eyes and lips were emphasised. The skin on her body escaped in rolls more than she'd realised. Her eyes looked dull and lifeless, vacant of any spark of happiness. The image being reflected was one of despair, suffering, and foolishness. She didn't feel seductive or alluring. She wanted to hide, but somehow, had to face the world and fight for survival. Devoid of any excitement for the evening ahead, she slowly made her way back to the car with the shopping bag hanging heavy by her side as if it was carrying the weight of her emotions in addition to the clothes. Her mind continued to mull over the facts, the evidence and his futile explanations. She needed more proof, more bullets to fire.

When she arrived home, Robert was busy on the computer. He looked up as she entered the lounge and asked if she'd been successful with her shopping. She duly showed him her clothes which was quickly followed with the excuse of needing a shower, knowing full well that showering could wait for there was another mission to attend to first. Her Sherlock ego had taken on the persona of a dog digging for a bone, digging deeper and deeper until it discovered the buried treasure. She became that dog, frantically searching whilst knowing that the harder she dug, the more hurt she would suffer. Her bone digging was in the form of emptying drawers and piling the contents on the floor. Every piece of paper was examined once again, notes and letters read. She rummaged through every pocket on his clothes until she found the small piece of evidence for which she'd been searching. A note arranging to meet. Time, name and place, all visible in black and white. Tears of success and agony mingled together, stinging her already sore eyes and cheeks as they spilled over the folds of her lower lid. She became aware of another person close by and, as she turned, through her tear laden eyes, she saw Robert standing in the doorway. The look of desperation on his face revealed the guilt of someone having been caught in the act and prompted Trudi to leap into action. She menacingly waved the offending paper under his nose, daring him to deny it. He stood defeated, head hung low and unable to utter a word of denial. In that silent moment, the truth was unveiled. His silence was his confession. His body drooped as if relieved that the pretence of the past few days had been disclosed, a sign of his admission, an indication of his guilt. Tormented tears had permission to fall as she asked him for how long he'd been deceiving her. She pleaded with him for answers, needing to know everything, the ins and outs of it all, the nitty gritty, but above all why? Ignoring her pleas, Robert walked towards her and held her in his arms saying she'd got it all wrong. He gently wiped away her tears whilst insisting that she'd got hold of the wrong end of the stick, it was not as she thought. They were 'just friends' and nothing had happened. He wanted her to accept what he was saying and to trust that he truly loved her. He begged her to forget about it and to put it behind them. He wanted to concentrate on spending an enjoyable evening together, with the promise that he would answer her questions later. The hunger for the truth partially satisfied, vulnerability was permitted to enter and with her dread of losing him completely having been sufficiently enhanced, the fragile woman agreed.

Chapter 25

The moon shines his light on the emotional roller coaster of years gone by, that halted at her stop and invited her to climb aboard as if it was a long-lost friend. She remembers the familiarity as she clambered on and braced herself as the once abandoned journey continued. This time it gathered in momentum and inclinations, creating swirling rise and falls which viciously tossed the contents of her stomach. A shower brought some relief from the nauseous sensation that bubbled away inside as it searched for a route of escape in the hope that a little of the increasing pressure would be released. The water poured over her naked body with her face immersed under the constant flow. Tears added to the waterfall as the high powered jet beat away the anguish that was tying her in knots. Her hands gently caressed the shower cream over her figure until her arms formed a bear hug and squeezed tightly, in the hope that it would bring some form of comfort. Tighter and tighter she squeezed until her nails biting into her flesh brought respite from the torment inside. Inch by inch, her soapy body slid down the wet tiles until it reached the shower floor, where she sat under the cascade of water, arms wrapped around her knees. As she sat cocooned in her embrace, she whispered words of prayer, asking for help from God, from anyone. She asked for guidance, for the suffering to weaken. She asked for love, comfort, contentment and peace. In spite of the tightening knots inside, her body began to relax and, as the shaking subsided, she felt as if she might be able to face the world. Stepping from the shower, she wrapped herself in a large soft towel and gazed into the bathroom mirror. The condensation slowly evaporated and she saw unfamiliar eyes staring back, eyes that were hiding the anguish buried deep down. She didn't recognise them as her own. Her light, bright blue eyes had been replaced with ones that were dark, black and red. Realising that some work would be required, she took a deep breath, pushed all emotions into the depths of beyond and headed towards her bag of war paint. It was time to get ready for battle and the festivities of the evening.

Applying the mask of deception was a delicate operation, needing skill and determination. There were two objectives: one, to hide all indications of emotional surrender and, two, create a vision so irresistible that any ensuing combat would be one of love, not war. Just enough make-up was applied to subtly cover any evidence of tears and enhance her natural features. She then slipped into her battle dress, ensuring a deep valley was created between her two breasts and her waist pulled in as tight as she could bear. She carefully blew the headdress in place, styling it so that it swept back from her face and enriched her sculpted cheekbones. A squirt of intoxicating spray on her neck, stiletto weapons placed on feet and she was ready to go. Ready on the outside, but still not fully on the inside. She walked down the stairs where Robert was patiently waiting. He smiled warmly and told her she looked beautiful. Then, hand in hand, they left the house, making their way to join in the celebrations. Together yet apart, a space opening between them which, over time, would widen and make restoration appear impossible.

The memory of that evening is one of being outside of her body watching the proceedings with disbelief, observing an evening that had belonged to someone else. It conjures up a picture of a phantom looking quizzically on from a different realm, trying to make sense of it all whilst being cut off from all sensations. 'Or' she thinks, 'like watching a good old emotion pulling programme, but it was a complete façade of socialising, smiling, laughing and successfully concealing what was really going on. Yep, I pulled off another brilliant performance.'

She kept her distance from Robert who was laughing and joking with the men. She chatted and danced with the women, using alcohol as an anaesthetic to dull the throbbing ache in her heart and the swirling butterflies in her stomach. She threw herself around on the dance floor with sheer abandonment, all the time aware of Robert's eyes following her, making her all-the-more determined to show she didn't care. She skipped in and out, linking arms with other dancers as 'Cotton eye Joe' blasted over the speakers, throwing her head back in laughter as she proceeded across the floor. Her legs flailed out as she picked up the beat to the Can-Can, kicking them as high as she could. Then the mood changed as the music slowed and more people crowded onto the dance floor. It was the final dance. She began to walk away, leaving embracing couples moving their bodies as they swayed to the music. She felt a hand pulling her back. It was Robert. Held closely in his arms, she cried silently as the lyrics of 'Stay Another Day' echoed in her ears, with each word like a knife stabbing into every cell of her flesh. Her chin was gently raised by his hand. Tear-filled eyes met his from which love for her was pouring, intensifying the agony and confusion she was feeling. His finger touched her lip, gently encouraging her tears to cease and then, caressing her cheek and wiping away the wet trail, he whispered 'I love you. Everything will be okay.'

The celebrations over, they returned home where the old elephant in the room was back and threatening to come out of hiding but thought it wiser to remain under its camouflage cover. Once in bed, Trudi paid no attention to her resistance as Robert's hands ran across her body, just merely closed her eyes to block out the images of him kissing another woman, as his mouth searched for hers. Reluctantly her body responded to his touch. After, she lay cradled in the arms that had once given her comfort and protection but had now become a place which was offering discomfort and bafflement. Despite the exhaustion enveloping her, sleep wouldn't come. The elephant had silently crept in beside her, forming a thick grey wall between her and Robert who was sleeping peacefully, oblivious to the silent weeping as she called out to the night to bring her rest.

The morning didn't offer her a break from the turbulence and the storm still rode high waiting to make its brutal impact. Trudi was trying to carry on as usual so that the girls didn't become suspicious, only the storm was pushing ever closer. She wanted answers to all the questions that were exploding inside her head. Ignoring Robert's plea to let go, she decided to address the elephant that had woken and was accompanying her every move, demanding attention. The questions were fired one after the other and, if the answers didn't equate, more questions were asked, provoking Robert to become more intolerant. He insisted that he wasn't seeing 'the voice' anymore. She thought differently. He was adamant that if they were to find a way forward, she must forget and move on; she really wanted to try, it was just the pain of deception was too great. 'How can you forget when the suffering is always there to remind you?' she asks the moon. The answer is short: time, trust and love.

It was gruelling, and exhausting, over the following days putting on a brave face and concealing the tears that were for ever threatening to spill. The smallest mouthfuls of food were difficult to swallow and excuses for having to leave the room were becoming hard to find. Robert's impatience was growing; he was unable to deal with the situation around him and completely intolerant of her reaction and moods. A big black cloud was hovering intimidatingly above with the intent of causing more chaos.

Phoebe's birthday arrived which brought another opening for her acting skills to shine. Drama face on, deep breath and enter left….. Friends and a few family members had been invited to celebrate before her daughter ventured into town with her friends. The girls were their usual noisy selves and the party had gone off without a hitch, finishing with the bunch of friends falling chaotically into a taxi which took them away to continue the celebrations. No one suspected a thing. Only Alice, who put in a brief appearance to wish her niece a happy birthday, observed that behind the charade was a lonely, crying soul who wanted to scream out and tell the world the truth.

Time jumps to a few days after Trudi had discovered the truth. Only a few days had passed but it felt like an age ago. She was denying herself the right to speak freely, dodging the menacing clouds which were developing all around her, but her effort to avoid the storm on the horizon was in vain. Its ferocity had become more menacing, sending out fingers of electricity that tried to pierce her heart and soul, attempting to shred them into little pieces. It became a storm that she would have to meet head on for there was nowhere to hide.

The day after the party, Trudi left work at lunchtime for a doctor's appointment. Thinking that perhaps she could have lunch with her husband, she decided to go home as a surprise which was probably more of 'I'm checking on you' than 'I thought it would be nice to see you'. However, it was she who received the surprise. He wasn't there. She phoned him and a very guilty voice answered, asking why she was home. Trudi, on the other hand, knew exactly where he was. He didn't dare deny it when she stated accusingly, 'you're with her, aren't you?' 'Yes,' came the reply. Emotions running high, she hung up. It was then that Ellie, who was home for lunch, was informed of her father's whereabouts, in a way that Trudi later regretted. The answer given to the question 'where's Dad?' was a curt 'with his girlfriend!' Then, leaving her daughter alone to digest the information, she rushed out of the house and drove back to work.

She has an image of herself on the journey to work and is conscious of the rising emotional lumps that have risen into her throat, just as they had back then. The car itself had taken on its own remote performance whilst she heaved over the emerging lumps, just like the car going over the bumps in the road. She managed to keep them at bay until she stepped into the staffroom. It was then that the release had come. No longer able to carry on with the charade, she broke down. Her colleagues sat aghast as, through floods of tears she shared the events of the past days. She was taken into the Head's office where she was given time to compose herself. She was offered the chance to go home, but there was no point. She needed to keep her mind busy to avoid wallowing in the muddy swamp that was threatening to suck her under inch by inch. Once sufficiently composed, she left the office, taking comfort in knowing that her colleagues were there to support her. A smile placed on her face, she entered the classroom in the lively manner to which the children were accustomed. The busy chatter filled her head, taking her thoughts away from the darkness and into the lightness and laughter of her young pupils.

She looks back on the classroom and notices how it became her safe haven, bringing normality to the craziness in her life. She was able to find elements of joy and fun with the children, and colleagues, even though the days appeared endless and the minutes like hours. It was as if time was standing still, as if she was trapped in some sort of time warp. Her saviour was her work. There were many occasions when she felt unable to face the work world and was given compassionate leave, but, overall, she carried out her role like a true professional. She was even praised by her Head for the competent way in which she carried out her teaching role in spite of her turbulent personal life. Looking back on how she pulled through, Trudi can applaud her accomplishment and give herself the praise she truly deserves, for she was a star and, against all odds, she'd shone.

The story picks up as she drove home from work anxious about the scene she would be entering. She'd left Ellie with a bomb shell and didn't know if it had yet exploded or if Phoebe was there to share the explosion. She was also uncertain of how Robert would greet her now that she knew that he was still seeing 'the voice'. All was quiet as she walked into the lounge. Too quiet. Her daughters were sitting, as usual, engrossed in the television, only they looked withdrawn, especially Ellie. Her husband was in the kitchen, making a cup of tea. He sheepishly handed her a mug, brushing her hand gently as it was passed, and said 'I need to talk to you later.' She nervously nodded her head and set about cooking the meal, all the time wondering how she was going to swallow even one little mouthful. If she did manage to swallow, she wasn't certain it would remain in her for long.

Attempting to hide her trembling hands, their meals were placed on the table. The girls quietly ate their dinner, whilst a very strained conversation about their day passed between the two adults. Trudi's fork stabbed into the meal on her plate, twisting and throwing the food as if it was a mouse being teased by a cat. Hardly any ventured into her mouth, even the smell rising from the plate brought repulsion to the back of her throat and forced her to leave the room. When everyone had finished, she slowly cleared the table, putting off the 'talk' for as long as possible, knowing that it couldn't be avoided for ever. As if they were anticipating an eruption, both her daughters went straight out, leaving her and Robert alone with the elephant anxiously waiting to be greeted. Her swirling gut was telling her that she was about to be told the truth which caused her body to tremble as anxiety took hold. She was ready for fight or flight, a decision which would be made by instinct rather than reasoning. He took her by the hand and led her to a chair. He was subdued, his eyes not meeting hers as he spoke the words which stabbed into her heart, each one cutting a deep wound with its razor-sharp edge. After the lunch time phone call, he'd spent the afternoon discussing everything with the 'voice', who'd advised him to be completely honest. Finally, he admitted that they were more than friends and had been sleeping together, but it was over. He wanted to be with Trudi. It was at that moment that she found out whether it was to be fight or flight. All the pent-up emotions rose, turning her into a woman with such formidable strength that she lost control and erupted. The pressure built and the molten lava poured from her as the volcano inside exploded. Her limbs became the force of the lava as she hit out at the motionless person in front of her. Her mouth spat out fire as she hit, kicked, thumped, screamed and sobbed. There was no attempt to fight back or defend himself, he took everything that was hurled at him. Her strength was at hurricane force as pieces of furniture were flung across the room. Every movement she made intensified the torment she was feeling and her actions weren't bringing relief. She was being torn apart. Not only had he been unfaithful and lied, but he'd also put her at risk. No protection had been used. A feeling of defilement swamped her. It was as if she'd been raped, violated in every way and the only thing she could think of doing was to scrub herself from head to foot.

She ran upstairs to the bathroom, leaving her husband to pick up the pieces the storm had left behind. Discarding her clothes, she frantically jumped under the shower which was running as hot as she could endure in the hope that the heat would destroy the degradation. This time she didn't crouch in tears. This time the anger and pain served as a brush to scrub her body clean. She violently rubbed the soap into her skin until redness appeared on the surface. She used a nail brush to make certain that every part of her was cleansed. Her fists became pummel stones, punching into her flesh; she screamed out as if she were undergoing severe torture. The hot water beat down on her naked body, smashing out the ingrained dirt, but it was unable to reach the dirt inside. Her heart was breaking, her soul was in anguish and her inner body was in so much agony, yet she'd never-before felt such violation, not even at that party many moons ago. She knew that she would need to be checked for any sexually transmitted diseases, which added to the degradation she was feeling. Exhausted, yet with a nervous energy, she removed her aching body from the shower and used a soft towel to bring it comfort. As she dressed, an armoured shell slowly encased her body, pulling her in tightly to protect her from further harm. Her head protruded through the imaginary hole, ready to dart back in at the first sign of danger. She felt as if she was vanishing, never to be seen again and it was this feeling that she carried downstairs to encounter whatever it was she had to face.

Trudi is surprised at, after all this time, how emotional she is finding the memory and how easily she can tap into the suffering. She feels as if she's watched a truly moving film where the only choice is to give way to the emotions that the story has touched. She spurts out words at the invisible television screen: 'if only it had been that or someone else's story. The pain was unbearable and I wouldn't wish that pain on anyone. That was definitely one hard lesson!'

Chapter 26

The tale continues. Trudi found her daughters sitting quietly in the lounge with her husband nowhere to be seen. They looked at her anxiously, Ellie asking 'are you ok?' Trudi's gaze focussed on the imploring eyes, seeing questions and hurt forming behind the dark blue which turned into deep blue pools as the questions were answered. She couldn't hide them from the truth any longer. Quietly the story was relayed and their questions answered as best she could with her emotions unsuccessfully held at bay. She explained that she didn't know what was going to happen, that she loved them and so did their dad who, as if on cue, chose that moment to reappear. Phoebe removed herself from the room, her head already buried under the sand where it would remain for months to come. Ellie, on her way to her room, looked at her father as if he was something she'd trodden in. Trudi believes that that was the last time she looked at him for a long while.

Trudi was attempting to keep her balance on a ship that was fighting its way across a stormy sea, and at the same time, feeling as if she was living someone else's life. It all seemed so surreal. She was still the teacher at school, the mum at home and carrying out all the jobs associated with the different roles, but it didn't seem as if she was present. She was empty of expression, of life and was merely existing. Eating was difficult and what she did manage to eat usually left a few hours later. Naomi, who'd returned to uni before the storm, was informed of what had happened. She was concerned about her mum although didn't fully grasp the emotional impact on the rest of the family. She would be home for Christmas, until then, distance was protecting her from the emotional turbulence. Phoebe was staying away from the house more frequently and was obviously affected deeply by the trauma except unwilling to face it, as was her way. Ellie, on the other hand, was there, amidst it all, witnessing her mother's anguish, wanting to 'fix' it, but didn't know how.

It was a few days after Robert's revelation that he decided to move out for a while hoping that oil would be poured on the troubled water. He was going to stay in the caravan on a nearby campsite which would give Trudi space to calm and reflect, in the hope that she would forgive and forget. It was far from troubled water being calmed; it was more like adding fuel to the fire. Left alone with her pondering and hurt, her anger spread. She hated him for the hurt and pain he'd inflicted on her and their daughters. She couldn't forgive him. She couldn't forget. Night was as endless as the day long, with sleep avoiding her like she was the plague. Every night she pictured him in their caravan with 'the voice'. He said he was alone, but how could she believe him? Bewilderment mixed with the turmoil of emotions already swirling inside. How could he throw away twenty four years of marriage? How could he forget and defile all that they'd shared? There was no consolation to be found in the knowledge that he'd told the 'voice' he would never leave Trudi. The unbearable feeling of betrayal took over and twisted inside like a corkscrew. The words of advice and condemnation from her family helped the frenzied whirlwind to gain force, until it found its route of escape.

The weekend came and as promised, Robert returned home to discuss the way forward, only the time apart hadn't brought peace, it brought peace disguised as the calm before the storm. The whirlwind picked up momentum, forming a spinning funnel which was completely unruly. No holding back, her emotions, responding to the ever changing and muddling turbulence inside, hurtled towards him in the form of words. There was no stopping now. Question after question was hurled towards him and not one answer calmed her. Accusations were used like a tennis ball, constantly hit back in a long and drawn out match. Finally, game, set and match were hers as the words 'get out' shrieked out of her mouth. She could take no more. He didn't protest. He turned to her, saying 'I'll pick up my things tomorrow' and walked away, away from his wife and family.

She was left with an emptiness inside, reeling from the torrent of words she'd released. She was stunned and unable to fully comprehend the incident or connect with any sensation to which she imagined she should be responding. She became a cold machine that was programmed to carry out certain routines. Lost in her own robotic world, she waited for her daughters to come home from their Saturday jobs. Ellie was the first to return who, on observing her mum's appearance, immediately asked 'what's happened?' As she was told, she threw her arms around her mum in a tight embrace. They were in this position when Phoebe walked in who, on being told the news, said she was going out and would see them later. Trudi knew that it was her daughter's way of coping, but undeniably wished it was different. Their world was about to be turned upside down and there was nothing she could do. They all had to ride the storm in the best way suited to them as individuals, travelling through it in whichever vehicle was given to them. So, Phoebe must be given the space to deal with it in her own way along with the knowledge that she was loved and cared for.

It wasn't until Robert collected his belongings the following day, that the impact of the one before hit home. Little by little he put his things into boxes and suitcases until there was hardly any evidence of him left in the house. She silently watched him carry the luggage, one by one, to his car, until the last one was gone. No words were spoken. Not one touch was shared. She sat on the stairs and watched her husband walk out of the door, longing to hold him one more time, to yell stay, yet something prevented her. As the door closed, the sobs that had been building and threatening to escape finally broke through the wall of the dam. Her body shook violently, as the force gained in strength with her inner self contorting under the inflicted torture. Her life energy was being sucked out, leaving her like a deflated blow-up toy. The wrenching sobs deep within made breathing difficult. Arms encircled her body, the arms of her youngest daughter. Wrapped in each other's embrace, they stayed sitting on the stairs, in silence.

Trudi has the impression of time stopping, standing still as it did that day, stopped in its tracks. She has the image of herself wandering around the house in a complete daze with the eyes of Ellie following her every move and aware of nothing besides the quiet. Silence was filling the house apart from the occasional patter as her feet hit uncarpeted floor. Words were futile as both mother and daughter were caught up in their own thoughts and feelings, not ready for them to be brought out into the open. Alice, Fran and Thomas had already checked in and her mum had phoned to make sure she was alright. She'd wanted to yell 'of course I'm not!', but the deadness surrounding her heart and penetrating her soul had cut off any sensations and made it impossible to express what she was truly experiencing. The events of the day whirred inside her head like cogs in a machine as she attempted to cook a meal. She inadvertently placed a knife and fork by Robert's seat which, as they were removed, prompted the deep hurt to increase. Phoebe, who'd returned home to the news that her father had left, ate a few mouthfuls of food before disappearing once more, leaving Ellie and Trudi alone. Neither of them felt like eating. The table was cleared and they decided to remove themselves from the scene of the crime.

In some ways, like Phoebe, Trudi and Ellie were also running away, running from the house not the situation. They passed the evening in the company of Alice, who was a source of support to them both, in particular Ellie. They began to spend most weekends there as well as some evenings, soaking up the atmosphere of a complete family whilst their minds were taken away from the disturbance in their own. Respite was found in the comfort of a 'normal' family. Ellie chatted and laughed with her cousins, whilst Trudi lost herself in helping with the ironing, a mundane chore which she found extremely therapeutic. There was always a willing ear to listen, a shoulder to lean on and words of advice spoken. Although reluctant to leave the safety of her sister's home, the time to return to her empty and desolate house could no longer be avoided. There was school the next day and she needed to check in on Phoebe. Hugs of reassurance were given by Alice as they bid farewell and made their way home. When they pulled into the drive, the absence of Robert's car was blatantly obvious and penetrated like a wooden stake into her heart, awakening the anguish that had been held at bay for a few hours. Silently, the pair entered what seemed like a deserted cave, with the vacuum and chilling blackness forming a heavy cloak around them. Neither of them spoke. The darkness was illuminated as a light was switched on and the silence broken as a sudden voice on the stirring television spoke, but nothing was able to relieve the unvoiced desperation they were both feeling. After preparing for the next day, she sat with Ellie, waiting for Phoebe to return and wishing that Robert would phone. The door banged shut, announcing the arrival of her daughter who shouted 'goodnight' before thundering up the stairs.

Trudi instinctively knew that Phoebe was avoiding her and had no desire to discuss the circumstances in which they found themselves. She, on the other hand, needed to be certain of how her daughter was coping. Opening the bedroom door her daughter was found sitting on the bed, the daughter who just a few days ago had been full of excitement and celebrating her eighteenth birthday. The face that gazed up at her was pale and lost. Her eyes looked like a rabbit in headlights, full of turmoil and hurt, not knowing in which direction it should run. Reaching out her arms, she embraced her daughter in a warm hug but was told, 'I'm ok mum.' Phoebe, like her father, was burying her head in the sand, unable to admit the reality of her feelings. All Trudi could do was be there, though did she have the strength to carry them all? Her own emotions were draining her, leaving her body limp and lifeless, but she must support them, not vice versa. Placing a kiss on Phoebe's head, she left the room and headed towards her youngest daughter's room, whose whole demeanour appeared as if it was a building in the process of being demolished. She was so fragile, a little china doll, which fleetingly reminded Trudi of her special childhood doll that had been broken, except she wouldn't allow this little doll to be destroyed. She held her baby close, whispering how much she loved her and reassuring her that all would be well. Then, as if Ellie was again that little helpless child, she tucked her into bed and kissed her goodnight.

Adrenalin was now the only source of fuel which forced her legs to carry her down the stairs. They took her to the fridge where hands that seemed detached from the listless body, found a bottle of wine. Alone in the lounge, she made friends with a glass of wine, sharing her musings and feelings. More glasses of wine joined the new friendship, trying to answer the questions that were mulling around in her head. Why had it happened? Could she have handled it better? Why did she feel so guilty? After all, she wasn't the one who'd been unfaithful, yet she'd demanded that he left. Nausea swept through her being, bringing with it a belief that life was not worth living, but she had to – there were the girls. They needed her. Draining the remnants of wine from her glass, she silently screamed 'WHY?' With tormented hands twisting agitatedly in front of her, she forced herself to go to bed. She was exhausted but wasn't certain that sleep would grace her with its presence.

As she closed the bedroom door, her eyes caught a glimpse of his dressing gown hanging besides hers. She snuggled her face into the softness of the fluffy material, her nostrils catching the remaining odour of his shower gel. She removed it from the hook and held it close, taking comfort from the familiar odour of his body as her nose breathed it in deeply. She turned to face the bed where the sight of the space which, vacant of Robert's body, triggered another tearful outburst. With a cry of 'what have I done?' she collapsed on the bed in a silent, sobbing heap. It was at that point she discovered a distraction from the torment inside. Gently to begin with, her hands hit the side of her legs. Fists formed, hitting into her thighs and stomach, the force behind them becoming harder as she became aware of the release she was experiencing with each hit. Physical hurt was more tolerable than the suffering she had deep within. Harder and harder she punched, until, with all energy expelled, she wearily fell into a restless sleep.

The breaking of daylight brought with it the dawning of what had happened, as her hands searched for the familiar body which should have been lying next to her. The emptiness filled her fingers as she caressed the sheet, desperately seeking for a sign of the missing body, only managing to find a cold, vacant spot where her husband had once lain. As if being weighed down by a heavy object, she dragged herself from the bed and mechanically put one foot in front of the other. She made her way to the bathroom with her feet shuffling their way forward as if her body had aged overnight. She didn't recognise the face staring at her from the mirror, it was a shadow of the one she knew. Black circles under her eyes, skin pale and sallow, the already evidence of weight loss around the cheeks. She, unsuccessfully, attempted to wash colour back into her face and prepare herself for the day ahead which she was dreading, yet knew that work would keep her sane. Calling the girls for breakfast, she headed down the stairs. Every movement, every action, was unreal. It was as if she was outside of her body, a puppet being manoeuvred by strings above its head, empty of emotion, possessing a wooden heart.

She forced herself to eat a slice of toast but her digestive system had difficulty tolerating the foreign object as it attempted to find its way down. The cup of tea was kinder as the warmth of it helped to relax the contorting muscles inside and gave her enough of a boost to start her journey to work. Shouting 'bye' to the girls, she shut the door and reluctantly climbed into her car, praying it would start whilst also wishing that it wouldn't. As the key turned in the ignition, a whirring noise fired up the engine and the heater blasted out cold air until sufficient time had passed for it to warm and begin to melt the ice on the windscreen. She waited for an adequate gap of visibility to clear before slowly putting the car into gear and reversing off the drive. She strived to occupy her mind by planning the day ahead, but her concentration was rudely interrupted by words being sung on the radio about holding a lover. They drifted into her ears, rousing the threat of an outpouring of emotions which she'd managed to keep at bay thus far. She quickly changed radio channel only to be greeted by the usual song about being alone at Christmas, prompting her to switch off the radio whilst vowing to never turn it on again.

As the mist cleared from her eyes, she realised that she'd miraculously arrived at school. It was time to pull out all the stops for another acting performance in the classroom with no sign of weakness visible to children or parents, but first she must face her colleagues. She had to tell them that Robert had left. She wanted to feel that work was a place which would provide stability to the rocky foundations in her home life. Her needs were met. Trudi remembers with affection how her colleagues rallied round showing compassion and offering support, with those special few being there to pick her up when down. The special few who knew her inner most thoughts and feelings and who watched over her, ensuring that she was coping.

End of term was approaching and the little pupils were all fired up with Christmas excitement, but for Trudi it was an impending time of loneliness and gloom. Her colleagues were full of the festive spirit, sharing their plans and reinforcing that life goes on. They were totally oblivious of their joy acting as a knife which was twisting deeper and deeper into the open wounds. It wasn't just at work, everywhere she went happy couples appeared from nowhere, reinforcing her loneliness. Music that was played echoed her heartache and despair which, every day, was becoming harder to face. She attempted to be strong, to carry out her professional role, to be a supportive mum; truthfully, she knew she was struggling. Struggling to eat, struggling to sleep and struggling to live.

Trudi and Robert, who was living with his mother, decided to keep things as amical as possible, especially over Christmas, but she was finding the pretence of a normal life gruelling. Amazingly, she found enough energy to drag herself through most days, only surrendering to her emotions on the odd occasion. Usually, she was the victor in the Battle of Emotions, holding the force back; other times the enemy besieged her with such dominance that she had to surrender. It was then that she put herself under house arrest, hiding from the opposition in her room, where her rivals continued to torment her until she finally crumbled with her fists lashing out in an attempt to fight back. Fists that angrily beat into the opposing army, trying to destroy the advancing battalion but merely succeeded in her battered body succumbing to the persuasiveness of the enemy's emotional drive. A defeated woman, exhausted and drained, lay on the bedroom floor. The violence had abated and the flow of tears subsided, only the voice crying out for help conveyed the intensity of the pain she was carrying. She called out to God, to anyone and anything in the realms beyond to bring her peace, comfort and guidance.

Trudi slowly breathes in deeply as she sits back in her chair and exhales the breath with a gradual, deliberate force, a yoga technique she's learnt to help release stress and anxiety. She notices how she can empathise with the emotions and feel compassion, but there is a distance forming between now and then. She is stepping back and her story is turning into a different person's tale. She is becoming the victor instead of being the victim. Trudi gains power from the commanding realisation and can rejoin the story from a different perspective, one of a hero, for that is what she is.

Chapter 27

The Christmas holiday brought with it the compelling urge to meet 'the voice'. It was like an incessant itch that became more annoying with each scratch. She decided to be open with Robert, expressing her strong need to meet the other woman which she hoped would bring her a sense of satisfaction and closure. He was surprised but agreed to arrange it after Christmas, taking charge of a situation over which she'd wanted complete hold. Anger consumed her when she was alone and an impulse to reclaim hold of the reins came up from the depths. An invisible strength took over. Her mind became clear and her dear detective friend stepped in, leading her along the rocky road that was opening ahead.

Robert would definitely be angry and it would cause a heated argument, but she was unable to disregard the push she was being given. There was an unseen energy, guiding her and filling her head with unspoken words: 'trust and believe. I am here to support you. You are not alone.' This did give her cause to question her sanity even more, but the feeling of love that accompanied the silent words brought her comfort, removing all doubt. She wasn't insane. She was being helped and protected by some Spiritual energy that she didn't entirely understand, even so she was open to anything and willing to receive help from any source.

The investigative persona was already in place, finding it easier with the absence of Robert. There would be no sudden appearance as she trawled through old phone bills, searching for a number she didn't recognise. She scrutinised each one, until there it was, a number that had frequently been phoned, usually when she was at work. The bill was tossed in the air with a triumphant gesture, as if waving it under Robert's nose. Confidently, she picked up the receiver and pressed the corresponding buttons, listening as the number connected. It rang and a person picked up the receiver at the other end. Trudi instantly recognised the sickly voice. It was **the** 'voice', otherwise known by the name of Nicola, or Knickerless as she was fondly called by the family. The 'voice' was uncomfortably silent as Trudi introduced herself as Robert's wife and stated that she wanted to meet. Surprisingly, an utterance of agreement was given, the victor raising a triumphant arm into the air. They arranged to meet on the Tuesday night in a nearby pub. She knew that if Robert found out, he would want to be there, something she wanted to avoid. Taking a risk, she asked to keep the arrangement between themselves, but Nicola couldn't guarantee to this as she didn't want to keep things from him. Trudi bit hard on her lip to prevent herself from screaming 'you supercilious cow!' Instead, with an inexplicable inner calm and strength she bid her goodbye.

She knew full well that Nicola intended to inform Robert of their arrangement and was convinced that it was a deliberate ploy. It was part of Nicola's plan, just as leaving the message on the mobile had been. Only a few hours had passed before Robert phoned and as expected, insisted on being there or the meeting would not take place. He managed to take away the only grip she had over a very small part of her life. Fury stirred as she realised that her needs and feelings were being totally ignored. There was no regard for his wife, only for his mistress, the woman who'd assisted in turning her world upside down. He was concerned that Nicola would be at risk, a prospect she would have found highly amusing if it wasn't for the hurt penetrating her core. She was being cast aside like a piece of old rag that no longer had any use. Irate words were hurled back and forth, picking up from where the last tennis tournament had finished and became more forceful with each strike. The building anger mixed with all other emotions and pushed her to ensure that the meeting would take place. She agreed to a time and place of his choosing, but when he demanded to be present, she was adamant that he would not be given the chance to interfere. The compromise was that he would leave her alone with Nicola, whilst waiting close by.

The day of confronting the enemy arrived. Ellie and Naomi, who was home from university, offered to accompany her so that she wouldn't have to face the demon on her own; they also wanted to be there for moral support. How selfless of her daughters to put aside their own suffering to support her, especially as they would be sitting with their father to allow her alone time with the foe. The war paint was once again brought out for use and combat clothes chosen. She was going to look in charge of the operation and would leave the opponent defeated, or at least weakened. She created an air of superiority with careful application of the paint which also gave her pupils a piercing effect in readiness to cut through any lies or words of attack. Her fatigues were the pair of black trousers and low-cut red top she'd worn to the Christmas function accompanied by a pair of high heeled combat boots.

Although she may have looked as if she was ready to face the enemy, inside she felt as if she was about to embark on her very first tour of duty. She'd experienced nervousness, but nothing could compare to this. There was a sickness inside, her stomach swirled and she had considerable trouble controlling the shakes that were convulsing through her body. Jelly like legs wobbled their way down the stairs as she attempted to disguise the quivering wreck from the girls. They looked at her reassuringly, which gave her the strength to commence battle. Naomi whispered, 'you'll be fine Mum' and climbed into the car, followed by Ellie who kissed her mum gently on the cheek. Positioned behind the steering wheel, which she was clutching tighter than was necessary, the engine was started and she reversed out of the drive. Despite her shaking legs making gear changes a little more challenging than usual, they arrived at their destination in one piece. Taking a deep breath, she stepped out of the car. She smiles to herself as she looks back on the picture of her walking slowly and purposefully towards the pub's entrance. She captures the three of them walking, three ladies with heads held high. 'It looks like a scene from Charlie's Angels,' she chuckles. She envisages her husband waiting at the door who greeted them self-consciously and then led them to the bar where the enemy was waiting.

Nicola was sat in a bay which was just far enough away to give Trudi the privacy she wanted, yet close enough to feel the support from her daughters. Of course, it was also close enough for Robert to protect Nicola who at least had the courtesy to lower her eyes as Trudi approached and continued to evade eye contact throughout most of the evening. Despite having seen the photo, she was not as it had portrayed. The photo had been kind! It was even more difficult to fathom out what Robert found attractive in her. She looked no younger than Trudi, was plumper and certainly not as fashionable in her style of dress. She didn't emanate an air of sexiness or seduction whatsoever and her whole aura oozed unwholesomeness with elements of being pitiful, weak and needy. There was also something else that Trudi couldn't quite put her finger on. Nicola appeared on one hand to be a poor little defenceless creature and on the other, a calculating person who knew exactly what she wanted and what she was doing. As the evening progressed, it became clear. Nicola was manipulative. She'd found Robert's Achilles' heel: his ego and the need to feel important. Using a sob story of helplessness as bait, she'd reeled him in hook, line and sinker.

Most of the blame was being laid at Nicola's feet, except Trudi knew Robert had to share the responsibility, something that was quickly pointed out by the offender when the accusations were shared. That was the only time throughout the evening that she saw any spark of true emotion or life from the demon woman. The poisonous snake that was curled inside and waiting to attack was revealed as she hissed, 'he had something to do with it too.' Question after question was fired at Nicola like bullets from a gun in the hope of finding answers to a puzzle which appeared to have no solution. Little by little, Nicola shared her side of the story. It began, 'once upon a time there were two people who were very good friends....'

The relationship, according to the author, had started as nothing more than a friendship. Robert had *kindly* offered her support and guidance during the training which she'd found 'so difficult'. The fabricated story continued, with Trudi's mind silently adding her own words as she listened to the tale, which included a few derogatory terms and unsavoury vocabulary. Nicola described the wonderful caring qualities of Robert: his consideration, his attentiveness and good listening skills. It continued with the well-used excuse of 'it just happened' and stating that from the outset Robert was adamant that he would never leave his wife and family. 'So, you thought you'd help it a long,' her mind adds. Then the discovery of a partner who was completely in the dark, revealed a tantalising chink in the assailant's armour. Holding out the prospect of the partner being informed like an explosive hand grenade, the enemy weakened and pleaded for her partner not to be told. Like an animal playing with its prey, Trudi teased the woman with a sarcastic 'I may, I may not, but I feel it's only right.' As the verbal diarrhoea continued to spew from the enemy's mouth, Trudi's attention was alerted to the revelation that Nicola didn't know what the future held for her and Robert. Nevertheless, Trudi was certain that the woman wouldn't be happy until she had him all to herself. Instinct also told her that he didn't want Nicola, he wanted his wife. The emotional tug of war was beginning – a tug of war between two women, both wanting the same man. She became aware of a growing inner strength and the desire to fight a battle of which there would only be one winner and she was determined that it would be her. With more determination and courage than she had earlier, she stood, fixing her eyes on Nicola's assertively. She thanked her for meeting her and cuttingly said, 'you are both big foul lumps of stinking dirt and deserve each other.' Walking away, she displayed an air of confidence that she wasn't feeling inside.

Her daughters were waiting with Robert at the bar. Trudi was asked if it 'had gone ok' which she glossed over, wanting to reveal as little as possible. She wasn't going to give him any ammunition. He escorted Charlie's Angels to the car and said goodbye. It was agonising to stand so close to him. His face showed concern and she was yearning to be held, to feel his soft lips on hers, but all in good time. First, she had to make a battle plan. Operation Nicola! As she drove away, she caught a glimpse of Robert watching them go. He looked pale and lost, reminding her of when she'd taken Naomi to university. In that instant, the love for him washed over her and she was convinced that he was destined to come home.

Once on the road, the girls were keen to know how Trudi was feeling and what had happened. She didn't want to share all, especially her gut instinct of a reconciliation as her two daughters had made their beliefs quite plain. They were adamant that she would be ridiculous to even consider taking him back. Consequently, they were given a sketchy outline of what had been said and were reassured that she was fine. She felt pleased with herself for having had the guts to face the woman and also had a certain element of victory. Her adrenaline was running strongly and her exaggerated movements gave her the appearance of being intoxicated or high on drugs. She was over emphasising the bounce in her walk and the way she held herself tall. Her speech was a constant source of excited babble, especially when she shared the results of the combat with her sisters. It was later in the evening, when she was alone, that she began to come down to earth. With a celebratory glass of wine in hand, she contemplated the evening. There was a long road ahead of her with a multitude of mountains to climb. It wasn't going to be an easy journey, but she would come out the victor. She had faith that life would guide her, with the first obstacle being Christmas.

Chapter 28

The story reopens on Christmas Eve, a time when she and Robert had always wrapped the presents together and enjoyed a few glasses of wine in the process. She was determined that this year would be no different although was more than a little surprised when Robert agreed. He even said he stay overnight on the sofa so that he could be there for the opening of gifts in the morning.

He arrived later in the evening. The girls were out but took themselves straight to their rooms as soon as they returned, leaving Trudi and Robert alone downstairs. Everything considered, it was a pleasant evening and to an outsider it would have appeared that all was harmonious, despite the uncomfortable agenda hidden in the room. They sat close together, bodies touching as they finished the second bottle of wine; a hunger rose within her that needed to be fed. She took the lead with her lips gently brushing against his cheek. He was reluctant to begin with, saying it was inappropriate. She looked into his eyes, giggled flirtatiously and said 'we are still married. If this is going to be our last night together, I want to remember it with fondness.' His mouth tentatively responded. There was no awkwardness or resistance, only the same tenderness that they'd so often shared and, even though no words of love were expressed by him, she felt the connection. They surrendered to the electrifying energy that surged through their veins and, unable to ignore the emotion, she softly murmured 'I love you. Happy Christmas!' She hugged him tightly before reluctantly making her way to the empty bed waiting for her upstairs. There were no tears that night but sleep too was missing. Her mind was busy, full of ideas about the evening and what the future held. If his love for her had died, why did she feel it so strongly? Why could she see it in his eyes? Bewilderment about his true feelings began, presenting her with yet another puzzle to complete.

Christmas morning wasn't full of the excited noise that once echoed around the house, as was to be expected. Robert greeted her with a warm smile, although he appeared self-conscious when the girls came down. They, too, were obviously feeling uncomfortable. They wished him a Happy Christmas, missing out the hug and kiss that they affectionately gave their mum. Once breakfast was over, a small sign of excitement was evident as the presents were handed out which were all received with smiles and thanks. Trudi was in two minds whether to give Robert his present, a gold neck chain, but on receiving hers she knew she must. He'd bought her a beautiful gold bracelet, which added to the bag of bewilderment that had started the night before. If he had no feelings for her, why would he give her such a lovely present?

After a coffee, he returned to his mum's, who'd invited the family to join her on Christmas Day, something Trudi wasn't entirely looking forward to. His dad, after Robert's parents had divorced, wouldn't be there and so the bravado of a father being proud of his son's manliness wouldn't be inflicted upon her. Her mother-in-law, however, would have given Robert a lecture on the Christian values of marriage, but would also have shied away from facing the knock-on effect of her son's actions. Trudi believed that Freda had no concern for her daughter-in-law and granddaughters, despite the same thing having happened to her. As she gives this consideration, she realises how she'd allowed this to affect her relationship with Freda and built a brick wall between them. 'It's a shame I didn't know how much she'd cared until it was too late.' Trudi remembers being told, after Freda's passing, how highly her mother-in-law had thought of her and how she'd always asked after her and the girls. Her mother-in-law had, in her own way, cared, she just hadn't been able to show it. Knowing this helps Trudi to forgive and have compassion for her. As with her own dad, it's too late to do this face to face, all she can do is ask for love to be sent at soul level, releasing any resentment from the past. She can pray for peace for the two of them, freeing another shackle that is securing her to her shadows from the past.

Christmas dinner was calling and Trudi shouted out to the girls that it was time to go. The three of them ran down the stairs, more from hunger than enthusiasm. Grabbing their jackets, they climbed into the car for the five-minute drive to her husband's new home. Robert greeted them at the door with the bashful smile that was becoming a permanent fixture. Her mother-in-law was busy in the kitchen where, as usual, pots and pans covered every space; it looked as if World War three had broken out! There was no organisation which aggravated Trudi's need for tidiness and made it difficult to offer assistance, although the waft of the dinner cooking outweighed it all. The aroma of the basting turkey, the potatoes crisping in the oven, the warm ham waiting to be carved and the Christmas pudding steaming on the hob all mixed to create a mouth-watering smell that wafted around the whole house.

The girls walked into the kitchen to greet their grandma who turned with a welcoming smile on her face. She was very fond of the girls and they also held great affection for her. Kisses and Christmas greetings exchanged she continued to chatter as if all was normal. There was no uneasy atmosphere which allowed Trudi to relax. The dinner tasted even more delicious than the wonderful smell that had met their nostrils when they first arrived. The girls chatted to their grandma, laughed at the awful jokes found inside the crackers, all of which distracted from the persistence of the large grey mammal that had insisted on tagging along and was lurking teasingly in the background. Then, the Home Guard leapt into action as all hands were on deck to help clear the kitchen bombsite and once completed, they settled down to an afternoon of games.

The scene playing out is one where Trudi has two roles, one as a main character and another as a voyeur. Her character portrays being part of a happy family who were celebrating Christmas, with laughter and enjoyment all around. The spectator sees a farce where the trained eye would perceive the deception that was covering the cracks. Although she knows that she was more than happy to undertake any role and be a part of the scene for as many hours life would allow. She views herself sitting on the floor, leaning on her husband's knee, waiting for the cards to be dealt for another game. She notices the watchful eyes of her daughters, the intensity of which made their eyes appear like steel as they scrutinised her behaviour and sent sharp warning signals when they discovered something that made them feel uncomfortable. She thinks of how she began to feel on edge, a conflict raging inside her. The questions she'd been asking herself, revisit her mind: should she be behaving as she would have in the past, or should she be holding herself at a distance? At one point, she recollects, Robert's hand rubbed against the back of her neck, just as he used to, which added more confusion about the state of play.

Whilst tea was prepared, the girls sat quietly watching television. The only indication of a problem was the lack of conversation between them and their father. The misery of witnessing the divide growing between them sent sharp icy fingers stabbing into Trudi's heart, compounding the pain as if they were penetrating an open wound. On the flip side, she was enjoying the solidarity between the women, her girls being there for each other. Nevertheless, Robert was, and always would be, part of their lives and she didn't want them to lose contact with their father. The thought of her husband not accompanying her to their daughters' possible weddings or sharing the joy of any potential grandchildren filled her with an undeniable despair which travelled through every cell of her body. She didn't want him to live a separate life. The impact of what the future might hold hit her like a bullet and she realised that they all had so much to lose, including Robert himself. She couldn't envisage a future without him and would do all she could to stop the destruct button from being pressed.

Her thoughtful indulgence didn't prevent her from helping Freda lay the table for tea, whilst answering questions and talking about life in general. The conversation continued until tea was set out in all its glory and, despite being full to bursting, the girls hovered over the food like vultures. Trudi's stomach, on the other hand, had positioned itself on the roller coaster, waiting for the ride to begin again. The time was approaching for them to leave, for her to say goodnight to her husband and return to the lonely house. Robert watched them drive off. His eyes were like windows, revealing the figure of anguish standing behind them which tugged at Trudi's heart strings. She was right. He was hurting just as much as she was, which emphasised the futility of it all. She identified with the Christmas crackers that had recently been pulled, herself being wrenched in different directions, only there was no prize or ridiculous joke inside, just swirling and conflicting emotions.

Trudi's family wanted nothing more to do with Robert which added more suffering to the burden she was already carrying. She and the girls were spending Boxing Day with Alice and her family, during which time she would also visit her mum. She had, with some reluctance, left Robert and the girls for a short time the previous afternoon to visit her dad in the Nursing home. He'd already been informed of Robert's misdemeanour and, despite not being as alert mentally as he once was, she detected the disappointment in her dad's eyes. As she kissed him and wished him Happy Christmas, he lowered his head, shaking it from side to side, and gently patted her hand. He'd always been a man of few words, but so wise and she wished that he was there for her, to share his wisdom. Unfortunately, the dad she'd known was no longer present. He was another man she was losing.

It was a comfort to be amongst her own family which, although highlighting the missing person, gave the girls a chance to enjoy a day with their cousins. Trudi, though, was feeling agitated and wanted the day to pass as quickly as possible because she was supposed to be meeting Robert later that evening. After the dinner that Alice had provided, she took the young ones to visit their grandma. They spent the afternoon chatting amongst themselves whilst Trudi tried to dodge any questions about Robert that were being fired at her by her mum. It wasn't appropriate to discuss it at that time and she certainly didn't want to hear her husband being slated. 'But Mum, you became a tower of strength and support to me and I will never forget the words of wisdom you gave me that Dad couldn't.' Trudi sends a loving hug to her mum who is gone yet never far away.

They spent the evening back at Alice's until the urge to meet Robert couldn't be put off any longer. It was already ten o'clock and he'd been waiting at the house for about an hour or so; she made her excuses and left. When they arrived home, Robert was pacing the floor, not with worry but with anger. He was angry that she hadn't come sooner, pointing out that he had other commitments too. The evening was over before it had started. He left and Trudi tearfully raised a glass of wine and wished herself 'a happy blooming Christmas.'

New Year's Eve was another hurdle to conquer. She'd been invited to a family party to welcome in the new millennium and albeit she didn't feel much like celebrating, staying at home was not an appealing alternative. When they arrived, the house was heaving with family and friends who filled every space making the building bulge at the seams. Her daughter was already enjoying herself as she laughed, danced and chatted. Trudi endeavoured to involve herself in the celebrations, though her mind was determined to travel its own path, taking her to places she would rather have avoided. Robert was attending a work's function and Nicola was probably his plus one. Her imagination began to run wild. She imagined them mixing with people she knew, standing hand in hand for all to see as confirmation of them being a couple. She envisaged their bodies together on the dance floor, his hand rubbing up and down Nicola's back as they moved to the music. She pictured them leaving as a couple and heading off into the night with the likelihood of their bodies becoming one before the morning greeted them. The people around her didn't help to ease her images as she watched the couples happy in each other's company and their embrace as the clock began to strike midnight. Life must go on, but why did it have to stick the knife in? As Big Ben struck the final toll, she compared herself, again, to Cinderella, except the roles had interchanged. She was Cinders who'd been allowed to go to the ball, yet she was also the person who would search far and wide for the one who had parted so quickly. There was no shoe to match to the foot. All she had was her heart and soul, both waiting to be reunited with the one that had fled into the night.

The New Year celebrations were over and it was time to head home. Naomi and Phoebe had gone to their own parties and would probably stay out overnight, leaving, after Ellie had gone to bed, Trudi alone with Mr Misery and a bottle of wine which had become a frequent evening visitor. A glass in one hand and phone in the other, her fingers, with a life of their own, texted a Happy New Year message to her husband. She was uncertain if he would reply, but it was only shortly after sending the message that she heard the ping of her phone and saw a message from Robert, wishing her a Happy New Year. Taking comfort from those few words, she forced herself upstairs and tucked herself into the familiar foetal position on an ever decreasing amount of bed.

Over the days that followed, she saw more of Robert than she'd expected, who seemed to find excuses to pop in which raised Trudi's optimism very slightly. It was as if he wanted to be there, as though he too was having difficulty letting go. His visits were friendly and fun with them flirting like a couple of love-stricken teenagers. It was a game of cat and mouse, with their roles constantly swapping and, more often than not, the mouse was caught, surrendering their body to the captor. Trudi smiles coyly as she's reminded of the games she played and the role of seductress that she took on, all in the attempt to entice her husband home. A self-satisfied smirk stretches across her mouth as she looks back at the lengths she'd gone to, to ensure she'd win the battle, yet at the same time she finds it difficult to consider it as being her. 'I think I was possessed, but I really enjoyed the part I played!' she laughs with a grin that spreads from ear to ear.

For her own protection financially, she was encouraged by her family to seek advice from a solicitor, which she duly did, knowing in her heart that she would never divorce Robert. Several times, she invited him for a drink to discuss financial arrangements for an 'imaginary' separation, only for the meeting to go in a different direction. The seductress stepped in, having gone to great lengths earlier to make sure she looked the part for her new seductive role in this master production. The girls usually stayed out if they knew he was coming, so the stage was completely hers with all props in place that were necessary to aid her performance. His favourite wine was in the fridge chilling and the scene was set with paper and pens placed on the table, giving the impression that serious work was in store. She anxiously, yet full of excited anticipation, waited for his key to turn in the lock. He was tense as he walked in but became more relaxed with each glass of wine. The evening proceeded with chit chat, a glass of wine, 'we can talk finances later', more wine, flirtatious comments, seductive positions and movements and then the pièce de résistance. She slowly climbed onto his lap and sat in a provocative manner, before moving in for the kill. His unconvincing cries of 'no we shouldn't' soon dispersed and the temptress was successful. The first was just the rehearsal, there were further performances to come. There were times when she felt used and questioned her behaviour, yet she honestly believed that he wouldn't have succumbed if he didn't have feelings for her. It was her choice to become the mistress and she confesses that part of her had enjoyed the role. She laughingly congratulates herself on her seductive skills, then sighs deeply as she affirms that it was short lived. Like all good plays, the time came to pull down the final curtain, the finale being fireworks that burst into a fiery display of colourful emotions. Robert turned, doubtlessly swayed by Nicola, and decided that the only way forward was to separate. Verbal attacks resumed and soon the visits began to diminish. Robert stayed away, leaving Trudi in a complete state of confusion.

The evening when torment and desperation engulfed her, from head to toe, from heart to soul is presented to her. She observes herself as she secreted herself in her bedroom, trawling through photos as if to add insult to injury. She sobbed over the ones that portrayed them as a happy loving couple, their wedding photos and some of Robert with the girls. All meaningless. All a lie. Oblivious of the girls in the room below, she began to wail louder and more fervently, the inner turmoil being eased by her fists pounding into her fleshless thighs. A vicious storm swirled around the room, knocking the bedside lamp to the ground, violently followed by the table until its attention fell on the photos. With a ruthlessness that was foreign to her, she tore up the photos, screaming obscenities as she threw the little pieces around her, that fell to the ground like a whirling snowstorm. She came close to destroying all the photos she had of Robert but was stopped by the sudden appearance of her mum. She has a recollection of being so caught up in her own desperation, that she was unaware of her three daughter's downstairs listening to their mother going crazy upstairs. She pictures them huddled together on the settee, taking comfort in each other's arms and, not knowing how to handle the situation, phoning their grandma who immediately came to the rescue. Their grandma first checked that the vulnerable souls, who were sinking further into the sofa, were okay before she quietly walked up the stairs. Trudi sees her mum in the bedroom doorway, taking in the scene that was before her. Then, positioning herself beside her daughter, she comforted her as she listened to the words that she was able to detect between the wails. Words of wisdom followed: 'if you destroy all the photos, you'll be destroying part of your children's memories, their history, something you might regret later.' Then as quietly as she'd come, she left, leaving her daughter calmer, although guilt-ridden about the pain she was inflicting on her girls. Trudi remembers pulling herself together before going downstairs where she found her daughters still in the position that their grandma had found them. She glimpses once more the concern and tears in their eyes as they looked at her. She watches as her arms are put around them and she hears the words 'I'm so sorry I frightened you.' The picture closes with the four vulnerable bodies pulled in tight, crying silently together and the anxiety being soothed by the physical embrace.

She wipes away the tears that are falling as she relives the guilt and anguish and utters the words 'I'm so sorry my darlings. You should never have had to see me like that. Please forgive me. I love you with all my heart.' An anger sweeps over which makes her realise that she still hasn't fully forgiven, herself or even maybe her husband. With that thought, she returns to the story.

Chapter 29

From one day to the next Trudi didn't know what she was feeling, what the future held or even how to get through each day. Work was very supportive. The Head showed complete understanding whenever she phoned in sick at the last minute, unable to go through the front door let alone face a class of children. When she couldn't work, Thomas often came to the rescue. He removed her from the dark despair within her house and placed her in the warmth of his own home. He allowed her to talk, to cry or sit silently until sleep finally brought a short interlude from the turbulence. He was very supportive but had great difficulty hiding his anger towards Robert. Trudi loved him dearly and was thankful for his help, nevertheless, attacking Robert verbally was like attacking her. They were one. Whatever accusations or insults people threw at him, she felt. They were keen to give advice, share experiences and were also eager to point out that she would be better off without him. Yes, 'the future will be brighter', only with him, not without him. She wasn't ready to give up the fight, no matter the outcome. The one thing of which she was certain was that she didn't want to carry resentment, hurt and anger with her for the rest of her life. Somehow, whatever her future held, she would come out of it a better, and not bitter, person.

Matters weren't made any easier by Robert who was quite often at the house using the computer, causing Trudi to become more puzzled emotionally. She didn't want to see him yet at the same time longed to. Her heart leapt when, on returning from work, she saw the car outside and her stomach tightened with the uncertainty of how she would be greeted. She anxiously steeled herself in preparation, her swallowed emotions hitting the pits in an ever tightening knot, with the threat of vomiting continually present. She always attempted to be indifferent as she went into the room and resisted the urge to throw her arms around him, although it required enormous strength. On the other hand, if his car wasn't outside, despite her disappointment, it was a great deal easier to walk into the house. If present, he usually left as soon as she arrived and apologised for not having left sooner. However, her belief was that he waited deliberately and that he too required contact, just a soupçon, like an addict in need of a fix. It was this perception that encouraged her to orchestrate opportunities for them to be in each other's company, regardless of the possible self-infliction of suffering brought about by her deeds.

Naomi was due to return to university and Robert had agreed to the request of driving his daughter back. The journey was a quiet one apart from Ellie, Phoebe and Naomi chatting in the back and loud music from the radio which blotted out the words they were sharing. Quite often, it had been the norm to hold hands whilst he drove, not anymore. Trudi found it hard to resist touching his hand as he changed gear and sometimes had to look out of the window to avert her teary eyes, especially when music linked to their past played. Holding back the tears became more difficult when she related the music to their situation. It seemed relentless with one song being played after the other. 'Every Day I love You', 'She's The One', all forced her hidden emotions to the fore with the dam wall threatening to break at any moment. It was whilst she was absorbed in the musical turmoil that the words of the song 'I Have a Dream' filtered into her thoughts, awakening the sense of fight and the realisation that she wouldn't fight alone. A small inner voice was whispering in her ear, 'we are here. Ask.' Although, yet again, her sanity could be questioned, she knew she was being helped and would be given support by Spirit, God or whatever term people chose to use. She did have dreams and beliefs and, when the time was right, she would push through the darkness. The whole day was exhausting. Energy was spent on keeping her emotions concealed and giving the impression of indifference to Robert, as well as showing her daughters that she was strong. In reality, she wasn't strong, even with the recent revelation of invisible help. She felt vulnerable, was shaking inwardly and found it increasingly difficult to be civil towards Robert, who was constantly giving the inkling that he would rather be elsewhere.

Her attention is taken away from that moment and focuses on the last evening they'd spent together, just after the New Year's celebrations when they arranged for a real financial meeting.

Things were discussed in general terms, who was to pay what bill, bank accounts and such like. It was all amicable and Robert stayed the night. Initially, he stayed in the spare room, until she pleaded with him to join her, to cuddle her, nothing more. The ache to be held and the need to feel secure is brought back to her. She remembers how his arms enclosed around her, held her close, but it hadn't felt natural. There was a wall between them, a distance opening up like an ever-widening chasm. Unable to sleep, she slipped out of bed and went to the spare room where she found his clothes scattered across the floor. This time, it wasn't Sherlock or the need to inflict physical pain that drove her to search his belongings, it was a need to cause a deeper torment. A soul depth pain which would bring life into her empty body. She visualises herself searching through his pockets and wallet and finding the tickets to the New Year's Party. Wanting to ensure that the anguish was at its fullest, she looked for confirmation of his partner in his diary. There, in black and white, was the evidence and permission to twist the knife deeper. Not only had she found proof of that night, but also of all the other times they'd arranged to meet. Trudi watches her younger self as despair set in with an acknowledgment that she might be losing him after all. The other woman was gradually worming her way in to his life.

As her focus filters back to the scene of Naomi's lounge, her eyes pick out Robert who was hurriedly texting a message to someone. It was an act that confirmed her suspicion of him wanting to be elsewhere. He looked as if he'd been caught committing a crime, which, in Trudi's eyes, he had. The scene shows her with daggers shooting from her eyes and heading ferociously towards the intended target, when, on reaching it successfully, she sarcastically asked, 'texting your girlfriend?' He explained that Nicola wanted to know how the day was going and what time he would be back, which was like showing a red rag to a bull. Not wanting to create a scene in front of her daughters and Naomi's housemates, she buried the anger and politely asked him to refrain from conversing with his girlfriend until his family wasn't present. The anger waited for release until they were on the way home. It wasn't voiced nor physical. It came in the form of tears and choking over a burger that she was unable to swallow when they stopped for a meal and culminated in Robert walking to the car in frustration, with Phoebe and Ellie sauntering behind.

The memories continue to flood in and the suffering hasn't lessened. She looks back on the days as being so very long and the evenings longer. Minutes appeared to last for hours with the pain becoming more acute as each tick sounded, encouraging the invisible knife to be stabbed deeper into her heart. The agony increased with every passing day, fuelling the need to inflict the physical release she found through her fists more frequently, hating everything about herself and her life. One evening, as she was driving home from work, she banged her hands violently on the steering wheel, not in anger but in misery and despair. As the road disappeared in a wash of tears, she realised that she needed to compose herself. Pulling into a lamp lit car park, she allowed herself time to release the tears fully before going home. Not caring if anyone witnessed her emotional display, she surrendered to it all, screaming into the darkness 'why?' Then her awareness was drawn to her foot revving on the throttle and the brick wall situated a few yards away, calling her. For a second, just a second, the wall invited her to smash the car into it at full speed. Whether it was in the hope of putting an end to all the misery or to add more anguish to that she was already experiencing, she didn't know; whatever the reasoning behind her thinking, something stopped her. 'Well,' she gasps, 'it was either sense, or some Divine intervention, which brought me back to my senses.'

Mr Moon is relentless and continues the illustrated narration regardless of the trauma it might bring up in Trudi. It's as if he's determined that she faces her shadows from the past, learn from them and leave them behind.

She and Robert met to finally discuss the financial arrangements. He 'kindly' said that the house was hers, however she fought against all decisions made. This only created more arguments, pushing Robert to storm out of the house with nothing resolved and leaving her to beat herself for being so foolish. Ellie was distraught when she walked in to discover the emotional wreck, but Trudi was trapped in her own world of torture and was unable to protect her own child from the suffering. She couldn't perceive anything outside of her own little world of hell with Nicola as the Devil, who was burning her fiendish fire in the attempt to eradicate the beauty of the world Trudi had once known. Even if it was in vain, she wasn't willing to give in without a last attempt in battle. She was still convinced that she and Robert were meant to be together. Nicola was the one living in a fantasy world and she would make sure the fantasy was destroyed.

Trudi was taking one step at a time; her movements being led by how she felt on a particular day. She was receiving so much support from many different quarters, but it was the song, 'Rise' that helped her gain some direction in her life. It wasn't often that she listened to the radio because it was too painful, yet Fran was insistent that she listened to that particular song. She found the words inspiring, singing along forcefully and the louder she sang, the stronger she felt. She had the strength to move forward and, if needed, recommence battle stations. Her first positive move was to buy a complete new set of clothes. She'd lost so much weight that everything was two sizes too big and for the first time in her life she was able to wear tight fitting clothes and not worry about the bulges. Everyone told her she was far too thin and looked drawn, she, however, was going to make the most of the new set of clothing options that life had presented her. She bought a variety of outfits that flattered her new slimline figure and decided to finish the make-over with a change of hairstyle, settling on a very short, impish style, to accentuate her prominent cheek bones. The new woman was now in possession of a whole new set of combats for the next battle, when, or if, it commenced.

Her social life was also going in a different direction. She went out with friends, either for a loud social evening in a pub or to dance the night away in a club, sometimes hoping that a man, any man, would show interest in her. She wanted to feel attractive and believe that, if the worst came to the worst, she would be able to find another man. One night, she recalls, she was approached whilst she was waiting to be served at the bar. They chatted harmlessly and she probably could have encouraged more, but she didn't feel ready. Part of her wanted to dip her toes in the water, but, strangely, it felt as if it would be an act of betrayal.

She laughs as she thinks of how she always gave Robert the impression she'd succeeded!

Trudi embraced the newfound freedom with enjoyment but the credit should truthfully go to the adrenaline rush which made her feel alive and gave her a means of escape from the heaviness around her. It was on the return home that the loneliness and truth hit her once again. She put off going to bed because she didn't want to face the vast empty space next to her. When she finally succumbed, the empty space beside her seemed to envelop her and the physical longing for Robert deepened until the pain was so fierce it was difficult to bear. She craved for the comfort of his body next to hers and his arms around her. She longed to feel the caress of his breath as he gently kissed her neck and the sound of his voice as he whispered 'night. I love you.' Above all, she wanted the torture to end.

She decided to use her anger positively; it became the force behind the tools used to remove the wall tiles in the kitchen. It had needed decorating for quite a while and she detested the tiles beyond all measure. They were brown, old fashioned and worn. It was time to give it an overhaul. She chose a light yellow paint to bring sunshine into her life and pale blue tiles with a yellow flower to add more brightness. Before she could do anything, the old tiles needed to be removed. With great gusto, as if testing her strength in the strongman game at a fair, the tiles were hit with a hammer and chisel with no care given to the amount of debris being created. Every hit released a morsel of anger, helped by the visualisation that each tile represented Nicola's face. Grunts and groans often accompanied the thud as the hammer hit the tile, releasing more anger and bringing a sense of satisfaction. She took pleasure in watching the pieces of tiles fly from the wall, and even greater pleasure if a whole tile came away intact which was accompanied by a shriek of 'hallelujah!' Clearing the wall of the out-lived tiles was a portrayal of her life with an essence of casting away all that she'd outgrown as it crashed in pieces around her.

The smashing session when Robert appeared is brought to mind when he openly showed that he was offended by not having been asked to help. Unfortunately, he interrupted her at a very crucial hit and so, instead of the tiles receiving the full extent of her rage, it was hurled at him. She pointed out to him, quite plainly, that it was nothing to do with him and that she didn't want him interfering. After angry words were exchanged, he left and, regardless of being upset, she had a new strength about her. 'Yes, I had a feeling of empowerment, of being in control. I knew I would manage without him.'

Chapter 30

Trudi is reminded of how her life's journey led her along a spiritual path which activated at a time when she needed it most, mainly due to her mum. She was always conscious of the concept of life after death and spirit guides, as were her whole family, but it was her mum who introduced her to the realm of Guardian Angels and helped to activate her spiritual gift further.

Her mum was involved in Spiritual groups, meeting people who were kind and gentle through and through; she was of the opinion that her daughter would benefit from being in their company. It was when Trudi was at her lowest and her mum truly believed that it would help. Trudi remembers agreeing to accompany her mum to one of the meetings; she was willing to try anything that might ease the torment and help her towards a brighter future. The initial uncomfortable feeling comes back to her which, at the time, was accentuated by her mum freely sharing her daughter's anguish to all present. Then she remembers the love and kindness from the people that filled her with a soul touching warmth. They didn't judge, nor offer advice, they gave her unconditional love and ways to block out negative ideas. She definitely felt stronger and was given a light to help her find her way through the darkness. She knows that she learnt so much from those people and that it was being with them that helped her trust her intuition more. The already flickering light within her was encouraged to shine more brightly and her own spiritual awareness opened.

It was that, and acquired knowledge, which made her aware of Nicola attacking her on a spiritual level. Yes, people might say her belief was due to her mental state, but she knew that it wasn't. This felt completely different to any emotional outburst or anything she'd experienced previously. It was as if she was a puppet and Nicola the puppeteer. At times, she felt as if the woman was taking over her mind and placing ideas and doubts into any space available. The woman was fighting her subconsciously in an attempt to weaken her defences; it was like being taken over by an evil energy and a mind war taking place.

Someone suggested that she put a photo of Nicola in a box of inwardly facing mirrors so that all negativities would be reflected on her. Dubiously, she constructed the box and placed it under her bed, uncertain of the outcome or whether this was proof that she had totally lost her mental faculties. She photocopied the photo of Nicola several times and it became part of her nighttime routine to sit by the box of mirrors, tearing one photo into tiny pieces whilst chanting 'you can't hurt me. I am protected. I send you love.' The whole process gave her strength and gradually the tentacles, which resembled the wriggling snakes on Medusa's head, slowed in their venomous search of prey. 'Yes! the victorious battle had commenced, with me favourite as the victor,' she shouts out triumphantly.

It was whilst attending one of her mum's meetings, that she had the most spiritual experience she ever encountered. Her mum wanted her to attend a special healing service at her local Church. It was to be taken by an elderly Vicar who, according to her mum, was led by his soul and the unconditional love was evident as soon as she clasped eyes on him. They say eyes are the windows to the soul and his certainly were. She was able to see the kindness, the empathy, the wisdom and a divine sacredness that oozed from deep inside. He called her to the altar and, despite feeling self-conscious, she knelt in front of him. As he lay his hands on her head, the energy coursed through her, making her body shake. He prayed for her soul, for healing to be given, for love and protection to be sent and for peace to be hers. A warmth washed over her, entering her heart and soul and encouraged the pain to be released. All inhibitions cast aside, she surrendered to the emotions that had been forced up. Heart rending sobs echoed around the little Church as members of the congregation watched through moist eyes. She cried for what seemed like eternity. Tears and the contents of her nose dripped in a constant flow over the poor man's hands which held onto hers with a gentle firmness. Finally, the tears stopped, leaving her exhausted but at peace and with a belief that there was a God. A God, or energy, that could be presented in many different forms as well as different ways.

She was given a variety of Spiritual books to read. Some were information about the different aspects of spirituality, others were stories of people who'd been helped or how they'd been opened to this way of thinking. She found them all inspiring as well as helpful, yet it was the little books that contained words of wisdoms that she found most comforting. She has memories of how these books triggered a need to write and she began to use writing as a form of release, sharing her emotions with the paper, just as she had at college. She wrote poems which were for her eyes only, letters to Robert and Nicola which were burnt, not sent, as part of a releasing ritual. She hadn't realised she was blessed with a Spiritual gift, one of clairvoyance and guided writing, but as she became more in tune with her spiritual instincts, her awareness of guides and angels around activated. There was a presence of energy gently touching her to let her know that they were close by which gave her the shivery feeling of someone walking over her grave. The power that encircled her then, returns, and she feels the energy that has, then and now, encouraged her to go inwards, to ask for guidance and for words to write. Over the years, her writing has become more profound and taken on a form that has been unfamiliar to her, the writing flowing freely across the paper. She's relied on her intuitiveness to reveal the words, which, when reading back, she's had difficulty believing she's written. She's come to realise that she's been spiritually guided and how it has all formed a very important part of her healing process. She has been blessed and is able to give thanks. Hopefully, she can show her gratitude by using her gifts to help others in whatever way Spirit, or God, sees fit.

The evening is getting late. Trudi has been mesmerised by the moon since his first appearance at the beginning of the winter evening and has been unable to move. The story is not yet finished. There are still a few shadows to face and so it continues.

The days were starting to improve. She was finding it easier to concentrate at work and was stronger emotionally but was still hopelessly missing Robert in the evening and often aching just to hear his voice. She phoned him with any pathetic excuse she could think of and send flirtatious text messages. She used her recently found writing talent to create little ditties to make him laugh, usually at Nicola's expense which, to her surprise, he found particularly amusing; this raised doubts about all being well in Paradise. A glimmer of hope was reignited. He continued to find the occasional excuse to call in and to help tidy the garden or clear the garage. At such times, he reverted to his familiar role and referred to her as 'sweetheart,' touching her as he walked past, which sent shivers down her spine. Their conversation was effortless with their manner being as it used to be, laughing and joking. It gave her hope about their future though it quickly turned into turmoil when he said, 'I enjoy your company and receiving messages, but I can't really see a future for us.'

Hope rose again on Valentine's Day, when he gave her, and the girls, a rose each. It was something he'd always done, although under the circumstances, she wasn't expecting it and perceived it as a positive sign. She thanked him and asked if she could take it as a step forward, but the hope was brutally snatched away. His startled eyes and the words that followed, whipped Trudi up into an explosive frenzy. He showed true regret when he explained that there was no hidden meaning behind the rose. He'd bought them because he always had, without considering the implication. The hurt stirred up by his thoughtlessness propelled her into a vicious attack. She accused him of playing her along and keeping his options open until he'd made up his mind. She told him that it was too painful for her to be in his presence and asked him to keep away. He retaliated, informing her that it was still his home, but he would make sure that she wasn't there when he called. He reiterated that it was over and told her she deserved someone better. She did silently agree with the latter, whilst knowing full well that he was still the only one she desired.

When the passing storm had gone, she quietly deliberated over the words that they'd spoken. It was at that point she remembered the words of wisdom given to her over twenty years ago: 'when you love someone, you love them enough to let them go.' She, beyond all doubt, believed that Robert still loved her; he was just too stubborn, and ashamed, to admit it. If releasing him brought him to his senses, then that was what she would do. That night, she sent him a text telling him that she loved him but was willing to let him go if that was what he truly wanted. She thanked him for the happy years, for their wonderful daughters and bid him goodbye, unaware of the affect her words would have. Shortly after sending the text, he phoned, surprising concern noticeable in his voice as he asked if she was okay. Unwittingly, she'd given him the impression that she was about to end her life. Distraught at having given him that perception, she put his mind at rest and thanked him for his concern. Although she was upset that she'd worried him, she was unable to resist the tiny flutters of elation in her stomach as she convinced herself that he must still care about her. His concern was either triggered by guilt or by love and she was going to go with the latter. The battle that had been put on hold was revived. She was ready for battle stations. Operation Nicola would resume. It was time to put on her new combats and face the enemy head on, with the support and guidance of her unseen friends.

Trudi looks back on 'preparation battle' time and remembers how it was then that her mum, Grace, stepped up. She was her tower of strength and brought her peace and hope. She gave Trudi the comfort she needed, allowed her to be honest about her feelings and was, in return, truthful herself when they discussed Robert and the future. Grace became her confidant, her guru, sharing a once hidden wisdom, knowledge and spirituality that had been revealed for all those who were willing to see. Deep understanding and compassion were evident in her words. Yes, they related to the experiences of the lonely life as a Navy wife, but it enabled her to show empathy. She was able to give a different perspective and, whilst not condoning Robert's behaviour, she didn't berate him, nor think of him as a womaniser, just weak and easily led. In her opinion, he'd needed his ego boosted and Nicola, whom Grace suspected to be conniving and master of her movements, had latched on to it and lured him in. She'd played the 'poor little girl who was struggling' which had, in turn, activated Robert's ego. Trudi remembers finding confirmation of the struggling girl on the computer in the form of a poorly written email begging Robert for his help during their training. 'Manipulative and clever ploy,' she thinks sarcastically. It had fulfilled Nicola's need of support and satisfied his desire for intellectual recognition and feeling good about himself.

People, including Trudi, often mistook this characteristic of Robert's as being a 'know it all', yet she's come to realise that it was driven by a lack of self-worth, a realisation unveiled by her mum during one of the heart to heart chats. They were discussing Robert's qualities, Grace attempting to understand her daughter's reluctance to let go. She listened as his qualities were described, his sensitivity, his caring side, his love. On the other hand, there was also his self-centeredness, his intolerance and his belief that he was always right. His parents and childhood were discussed, with Grace interrupting the flow to ask questions to help her gain a better understanding of her son-in-law. She slotted the pieces of the puzzle together to create a picture in her mind with the final portrayal of Robert being a completely different person to the one she'd originally seen. Each puzzle piece helped her perceive what had driven him to make the choices he had. She was able to see the same qualities as her daughter, characteristics ideal for his chosen profession, but she also identified the weakness in his personality. The necessity to feel important, a need that would subconsciously use any means to be fulfilled. It was a magnet to those in search of comfort, support and love, pulling them into its invisible magnetic field, though it had also been the force behind his ambition.

As her mum talked, Trudi realised that she, herself, was one of those drawn in. She'd helped to nurture his weakness through her need for his emotional support in times of crisis, but, alongside, she used her negative childhood pattern of seeking recognition. Together, they acted as two like poles of a magnet, repelling each other, not meeting each other's needs which evoked emotional responses. Their subconscious desires were definitely at work over the past few weeks. Though, over the years together, they've also encouraged more positive elements to come through. They've helped each other grow but have, through no fault of their own, also succumbed to their shortcomings.

Lessons could be learnt from it all and changes could be made, a conviction which was echoed by her mum who was even more insistent that Robert was not a philanderer. It was his flaw that had allowed Nicola's own defect to tempt him. Grace gave her hope and told her that, from her experience, men usually returned to their long-standing wives. She was also realistic about it not being an easy task for either of them to tackle. Robert especially would have difficulty. He would be feeling guilt, as well as embarrassment, and would have to undergo reuniting with a very formidable family. There would be baggage, things to address and not be hidden away. There would be a need for honesty and change. She emphasised that the pair of them must learn from it all and take positive steps forward no matter what the outcome. She considered it of paramount importance to allow everything to run its own course and under no circumstances was Trudi to activate her emotional pattern and 'snivel and beg'. No matter what, she wanted her daughter to be happy and if that meant Robert returning, she was willing to accept it, but also pointed out that the rest of the family might not.

Trudi looks up to the sky and softly says, 'you were a wise lady, mum, with such a warm heart. Thank you for being there.'

Chapter 31

Three months of turbulence, loneliness, pain and hurt had passed. Three months of trying to hold the pieces together, but she was convinced that Robert would return, despite the possible volatile times that she'd have to face and the bridges that would require rebuilding. She knew that a big portion of Robert's reluctance to return home was the guilt, shame, embarrassment as well as the knowledge that his behaviour had caused pain to so many. He'd built a sturdy wall of protection around himself, but she had the determination and newfound strength to find a way through.

Trudi was walking on an emotional high and overload, unaware of what the future held, but hoped that it would be with Robert. She was tough when in the company of others, it was on opening the front door that she was still hit by the ever present space that had been created by the absence of the things that had always infuriated her. No shoes left in the middle of the floor, no papers scattered across the table, no dirty crockery left on the side or the tell-tale signs of lunch having been eaten. It was in this house, devoid of the man she held so dear, where the emotional tug became so strong, she felt sick.

In spite of continuing the nightly ritual with the photo and mirrors, and taking steps towards changing her mind-set, it was hard to ignore the conflict that was battling inside. People might have said that she was allowing her imagination to run away, but to her, it was very real. Nicola was inside her head, egging her on and demanding a fight. The woman persistently tugged on the chords like a demonic person, fighting for what she felt was hers. In Trudi's mind, an invisible tug of war had begun to take place between the two women, with Robert as the rope. They pulled as hard as each other and neither of them showed any signs of defeat. The tension of the rope tightened as it was heaved forwards and back. Imaginary blisters formed on the palm of her hands as she gripped on firmly, determined not to loosen her hold. Her eyes fixed earnestly on the braid, hoping to spot a forming fray or an indication of weakness in her opponent as a signal that her victory would be close at hand.

During the sleepless nights, her head brimmed with images of Nicola and Robert together, as they whispered words of affection and caressed each other fondly. She tormented herself wondering if he said the same loving words to Nicola as he had to her and if his hands touched her in the same way. She imagined her girls being invited to join the new family, leaving Trudi completely alone. The worry of losing them, of losing everything, overwhelmed her. Logically she knew that it would never happen, however, the combination of emotions and concerns were like a tumour growing inside her head, getting bigger and bigger. She hated the woman and wished her dead or some terrible fate to fall upon her, ignoring completely the teachings of love and forgiveness. Inconsolable grief consumed her, as if she was grieving for the death of her husband, thinking it would be less challenging to deal with if she was. Apart from having to endure the pain of loss and the loneliness, she would at least have closure knowing that he was gone forever. In hope of guidance and support, she turned to her books of wisdom. Solace was found in the words and she prayed, asking to be shown the way forward and the path ahead to be illuminated. Sitting quietly and going inward brought a sense of peace and clarity to her thinking, but, above all, the need to inflict physical pain diminished. Conscious of the fact that it wasn't helping her to move on and the only person she was hurting was herself, the self-torture ceased. Gradually, with each day that passed, Trudi became lighter in her mood and stronger emotionally. Save for the hope that they would be reunited, she was attempting to surrender to the ebb and flow of life which, if required, she would be willing to persuade to travel in the direction she desired!

The brightest glimmer of this happening shone one weekend; a light shining in a stormy sky. Initially, the sky was filled with a threatening storm as an inky blackness painted over any strands that indicated signs of light. Then, heavy dark clouds formed a stormy blanket which held its contents menacingly as it hovered above. White streaks of lightning suddenly ripped through the inkiness of the dark sky, tearing through it angrily as if it was paper. Explosive claps of thunder boomed as an indication of the wrath they were carrying and echoed constantly, concealing all other sounds. Tumultuous raindrops followed, hammering into the ground as if they were beating out the misery hidden beneath. Slowly, very slowly, they diminished and allowed the sky to clear, revealing a brightness on the horizon.

The threat of the storm appeared with the arrival of Robert, whom she'd agreed to meet to finalise details for his proposed separation. It wasn't something she anticipated with excitement, or joy, but she hoped it would show the way ahead. Shivering with an emotional coldness surging through her veins, she listened to the words spoken by Robert who remained standing in the doorway in a very confrontational and intimidating manner. His reluctance to sit was probably more to do with a possible quick get-away after he'd put forward his proposition. He suggested, again, that she should keep the house, with her being responsible for the mortgage payments. Bills would be shared between them and he would assist in any way he could. It was presented as a business plan, a done deal, to which she listened but was unable to agree. In answer to a previously asked question, he explained that he didn't know what the future held for him, though he doubted if Nicola would be part of it. He was concentrating on passing his assessment before deciding anything. The futility of the past months suddenly dawned on her and his words fuelled the anger which fired up the fight within her. He was willing to throw away all they had for nothing. The energy within forced her to stand her ground, her stature strong as she shouted, 'if you want to travel down the road without me, you'll have to be the one to instigate it because I don't want any part of it.'

The threatening storm had arrived and brought with it words that became angrier and more hurtful as the menacing deluge hovered overhead. She accused him of destroying her life and he, in return, laid blame at her feet. The storm became more violent as it picked up furniture and hurled it towards Robert. Chairs and tables became victims of the raging storm, their target motionless, making no attempt to dodge the flying debris. The dormant volcano inside Trudi chose that moment to erupt, adding to the destruction already created by the storm. Her hands flew out like fast flowing molten lava, picking up cushions or any item that blocked the way ahead. She choked on the words that spewed out of her mouth as if they were the smoky powdery ash that was being produced by the eruption. Abruptly as it had started, the eruption ceased, as she heard her husband agree to her threat of a divorce, if that was what she truly wanted. The lid then closed tightly on the volcano and pushed the stormy rage deep within. Then, the rain started to fall, slowly at first but, as the flow increased, it turned into a fast swirling river.

As if in defeat, Trudi allowed her body to weaken, and sink to the floor, surrendering as the final part of the tempest hit. Rocking back and forth, with her arms held tight around her, she gave way to the pressure of the distressed sobs as they brutally forced their escape. Choking and gasping for breath, she called upon the only way she knew to mask the pain she was feeling inside. She released her arms and began to use her body as a punch bag, beating herself to a pulp. Her hammering fists were like large hailstones which landed harder each time they came in contact with her body. She continued relentlessly, oblivious to the presence of Ellie or the pleas for her to stop. She was unaware of Robert reassuring his daughter and telling her that he would be able to calm the situation. Immersed in her own suffering, she had, again, ignored the distress she was inflicting upon this vulnerable young lady and not noticed the tearful exit as her daughter ran from the house in search of a friend from whom she could take comfort.

Trudi breathes in deeply to recover from the previous unveiling. 'How selfish emotions can make you,' she sighs, 'but they're all consuming. I remember it all so clearly and the person who brought me out of it!' She takes her contemplation back to the scene of the after storm destruction.

It was the sensation of someone's arms cradling her from behind and pulling her gently into their body that brought her back into the room. She slowly became aware of Robert's voice whispering soothing words into her ear. He was talking to her gently, rocking her from side to side like a parent calming and reassuring a young baby. Cradled in his arms, her sobs turned to a light flow of tears, gradually reducing with each kiss placed on her head. She felt his breath caress her cheeks as his kisses brushed down the side of her neck. His arms tightened fractionally as he held her closer. Tenderly, he coaxed her body round to face him and held her head against his chest, the closeness bringing her a sense of calm. His hand softly stroked her hair as he continued to murmur soothing words. He gave her the comfort and security for which she was yearning deep inside, encouraging her tears to cease. Regardless of an inner heaviness, butterflies fluttered around her stomach as she snuggled in closer and melted further into his arms, wanting the moment to last forever.

The fingers of one of his hands travelled the contour of her face, following the moist path created by her tears until they sat under her chin. They pushed it softly and persuaded it to tilt upwards. As the free hand continued to rub against her cheek, he examined her face with eyes full of compassion that locked on to hers. The intensity of his gaze sent shivers down her spine. His lips began to retrace the path of his fingers as if kissing away all signs of hurt and pain until they finally rested upon hers. Warm, soft lips moved with tiny movements, leaving a light impression as they danced across her mouth. The dance was uninterrupted, flowing from one side to the other with the pressure increasing as they travelled. No longer able to resist, her mouth responded, joining in the gentle, rhythmical flow. Cautiously, their lips stepped into a slow and delicate waltz. If they stumbled with uncertainty, they searched for reassurance that the correct steps were being used. Then, with confidence reinstated, the dance continued, the rhythm changing as it developed into a passionate Argentine tango. Their lips pressed harder; mouths moved faster as their tongues represented the swivelling legs that twisted around each other. The beat inside was stirred, increasing the passion and the seductiveness of the moves. Hands that had gently caressed her, slowly removed her clothes, item by item, and kisses placed on her flesh as it was gradually revealed. In response, her body pressed earnestly against his, with her breath deepening as it quickened in pace. The dance was in full swing with the crescendo waiting for its moment as they pulled each other to the floor. Their moves became more impassioned and the ignited spark grew into a fire which burned uncontrollably, melting their bodies together. As if smoke from the raging fire within secreted them from view, the two lovers became totally immersed in the performance. They moved in time, their bodies as one. The energy pulsed through their veins causing an exhilarating explosion which shook them both from head to toe. The dance had finished.

No words were spoken as they lay together. She snuggled in Robert's arms with contentment and peace filling her to the core as loving kisses caressed her face. She wanted to hold onto the moment for as long as possible, wondering if they'd just taken a step into the future yet too afraid to ask. The silence was broken by Robert, who, as if reading her mind, asked 'do you think it could really work? Shall we try?' The words were spoken quietly and warily, but they were the ones that Trudi had longed to hear. She was elated, the energy acting like the helium in a runaway balloon, forcing her higher and higher with only the ceiling to stop her travelling further. The storm had ended. The sky was clear and a small light was shining on the horizon.

Attempting not to overwhelm him with her enthusiasm and excitement, she replied. 'Yes, you know I do. I love you. This is all I've wanted. What about you?' The gut feeling that had prevented her from surrendering to the enemy was then confirmed as he uttered the words 'I've never stopped loving you and there's nothing I want more, but we really need to talk before making any decisions.' She knew in that moment that she'd definitely become the favourite to win.

Trudi calls to mind the conversation that followed. She pictures them sitting chatting over a cup of tea, sharing their views, hopes and concerns. Robert verified Grace's belief about him finding it embarrassing to face her family and she said that all that mattered was what was right for them. Trudi ponders over the words as they are presented to her and recaptures the strength and conviction that she had when she told him that they were worth trying for. She remembers how he looked at her affectionately and asked for space and time to think as his assessment was coming up and he needed to concentrate on that. Unofficial arrangements were made to meet at a later date for a chat and to hopefully celebrate the results of his assessment.

Despite the sun truly shining and the clouds having disappeared, she wouldn't allow herself to assume that the storm had passed permanently. There was light, only how bright it would shine she was uncertain. Hope had been given but it could as easily be taken away and so she wouldn't dare to share the possibilities. She would trust that the right thing for both of them would happen.

Chapter 32

Trudi looks back in awe on the week that followed the unbelievable experience and wonders how she managed to get through it. She thinks that it may have been the hardest week of them all. It appeared to be an extremely long one, in fact never ending, but she feels that it was made harder by not knowing if the 'happy ever after' ending would happen. It felt as if she was left dangling, hanging over the side of one of the rollercoasters. She'd already travelled on so many and wasn't sure she could face another. During that week, she anticipated the conclusion to the meeting with trepidation and excitement, the latter becoming increasingly difficult to hide. Nicola's grip on the rope had loosened and Trudi was beginning to walk with head up and a noticeable skip in her step. The previously unnoticed signs of spring caught her attention and the appearance of new life gave her cause to wonder if it was an indication of the start of a new life for her. She was aching to see Robert but was giving him the space he'd asked for. Instead, she compensated by returning to the use of texts, with no signs of anger, or pleading, just friendly chit chat. She relented once, phoning him to wish him good luck, which she considered a justifiable reason. He thanked her and promised to let her know the result as soon as he knew, making her feel quite positive about the impending meeting.

Result day arrived, along with conflicting notions that had gone into battle where one side of her brain was telling her that he wouldn't phone and the other saying he would. Her mind was so completely absorbed, that the sound of the phone ringing caused her to jump. She answered it, excitement bubbling under the surface as she heard Robert's voice. Squeals of elation were wedged between her larynx and mouth, waiting to be set free, but freedom didn't come until the call ended. A sense of pride washed over her as he told her he'd passed. She was delighted for him. Arrangements were made for him to come to the house around eight o'clock the following night, from where they would go to the local pub for a celebratory drink. A buzzing energy flowed between them as the conversation finished and the goodbyes said, the latter having been the signal for the trapped screams to work their way out of her system. They thrust their way to freedom, inch by inch, the force behind finally propelling them into the waiting silence of the empty house. She ran around each room and squealed at the top of her voice, like an excited child receiving a long desired toy or a teenager at a concert of an adored band. She attempted to remind herself that the coming evening was to celebrate his results and nothing more, but a strong expectation was in the spotlight, surrounded by the deep love she felt for him. Whatever the outcome, she considered it only right to celebrate his success. After all, she'd been the one to put him on his triumphant path, had supported him most of the way and so it was only right she was there at the end to share in his accomplishment.

Saturday, the day of the planned meeting, was interminable. The minutes dragged by as she waited for the arrival of her date later in the evening. The girls were out with their friends and plans had been made to visit her dad with Alice. During the journey to the care home, Trudi thought it only right to include her sister in the details of the plan for the evening. She explained about Robert's achievement, the celebration and the small possibility that there might be a reconciliation on the horizon. The two families had always been close and Alice was very hurt by Robert's exploits, feeling that he'd betrayed her too. Consequently, Trudi expected opposition to the news, as well as congratulations, nevertheless wasn't fully prepared for Alice's response which displayed displeasure both in her voice and her facial expressions. Alice did ask for her congratulations to be passed on to Robert but also said that she thought Trudi would be foolish to even consider taking him back.

Other words and opinions were shared, the impact of which left Trudi reeling as if she'd been knocked sideways. Despite understanding her sister's annoyance, it was hard to be at the receiving end and be reminded of the 'helpful' allegations that family members had made several months previously, pouring oil onto an already burning fire. The accusations spring to mind and she finds it hard to conceive that her family could have thought as they had, especially as they'd had no evidence, just word of mouth. Claims were made that Robert had 'tried it on' or 'attempted to kiss' them and the ensuing discussions had exacerbated the blazing flames, the light making the accusers' eyes gleam and emphasise their misplaced enjoyment. As she thinks over the allegations, she knows that they were totally unfounded and completely unnecessary. They merely showed how some people take pleasure from another person's misery and in watching the pain increase. Torturers without tools, except the cruelness of words. Torturers who were insecure, vulnerable people seeking for self-worth from a misguided source and Trudi realises that she now feels only pity. These peoples' actions were driven by their own learnt patterns. In time, maybe they would have their eyes opened, their heart and soul stirred and be encouraged to make changes for the better. There was always hope!

Trudi thinks of that afternoon with despondency. She feels sad that her sister felt the way she had about Robert, but also understands that Alice, after having witnessed her sister undergoing so much torment, was trying to protect her. There was also a need to keep the water as calm as possible, and so she chose to let it go. They'd already had to cross troubled waters, including the slow deterioration of their dad, and they needed to be there for each other.

As she sat by her dad's side that same afternoon, she wished she could tell him about the impending rendezvous with her husband and the hope she was feeling. She knew it would be futile. He would understand the words she spoke and shake his head from side to side to convey his concern, but he wouldn't be able to use his skill of discernment and speak his words of wisdom enabling her to clearly see the road ahead. If his mind allowed, he would point out the obstacles, his disappointment in Robert, the importance of loyalty and, also, how he wanted his daughter to be happy. She looked at her father and realised that she had at some level, held the conversation with her dad and intuitively homed in on the words he would have spoken. It was as if the conversation had really taken place. The way forward was clearly mapped out for her to see: the road of perseverance which she had to follow with great courage and strength until she reached her destiny. As she kissed him goodbye, he grasped her hand, squeezing it as tightly as his weakening body permitted.

His love and understanding emanated from him which gave her the strength to persevere along that path of destiny.

On the journey home, the two sisters chatted about their dad and laughed about some of the things he'd said. The evening ahead was also mentioned with all signs of tension gone. As they pulled on to the drive, Alice wished her sister luck but also advised her to be cautious about making decisions and opening herself up to more hurt. Trudi thanked her, promised to be careful and keep her updated with any news. She waved goodbye and went inside to feed the waiting hungry mouths, after which she was able to concentrate on preparing for her date.

The preparations for her evening out were similar to the initial blind date with Robert. There was the similarity of not knowing what to expect or what the outcome would be and her future was again in the hands of destiny. This time, however, there was no need for her sister to greet him or to run upstairs to tell her to put her shoes on, she knew exactly what to expect. Her mum's words of encouragement came to mind and they, alongside the still present touch of her dad's hand, heartened her. She was inspired to face the future robustly and unconditionally, without set expectations. What will be, will be. Even so, she was still in charge of her appearance!

Trudi took time to prepare for the evening ahead. After showering, she gently smoothed body lotion into her skin, her flesh purring like a pampered cat, thankful that it was receiving tenderness rather than abuse. After trying on several outfits, she settled on her tight blue jeans and a purple sequined top which tantalisingly divulged a small amount of cleavage. The outfit was finished with an accompanying jacket which she could remove seductively at an appropriate time, teasing him as her flesh was revealed. Fragrance that matched the body lotion was economically sprayed behind her ears, on her neck and in the ridge separating her two breasts. A final check and then there was just the agonising wait for Robert to arrive.

After what seemed to be a lifetime, Robert walked in through the door, with shyness and apprehension evident on his face, not only about the evening, but also the presence of Ellie and her friend. Overcoming the first hurdle, he bashfully greeted the girls who responded politely before returning their attention to the programme they were watching. Trudi kissed her daughter and reassured her that she wouldn't be home late. Then, she followed her husband out to the car. As the engine quietly turned over, he glanced at her furtively, her heart skipping a beat as he told her how nice she looked. Ignoring the thrill surging through her body, she thanked him and continued to chat casually as they made their way to the pub.

The pub was busy, full of people who varied in age from teenagers to pensioners, all having the common link of being out to enjoy a social drink. The couple found a table where they sat opposite each other and continued to chat like two old friends, with a smidgen of newness about them. It resembled a first rendezvous or a clandestine meeting, mixed with a trace of getting to know each other all over again. As they talked, her eyes scanned the room, scrutinising the people around. She wondered if any of them were on their first date and felt like she was feeling or had experienced the same as she. She saw delight shining on faces, heard laughter bellowing from mouths as stories and jokes were shared, the volume of voices increasing as each one fought to be heard. As her eyes roamed, her focus fell on the man sitting opposite, warmth and affection radiating from his eyes as they fixed on hers. His fingers tentatively reached out, their fingertips meeting across the table as if they were two lovers discreetly displaying affection. She felt his hand take hers and as he held it with a gentleness that she hadn't felt in a long while, a powerful energy travelled between them. Lost in the energetic exchange and the desire for it to linger, she was oblivious to the words he was speaking. An affectionate squeeze of her hand brought her back to consciousness and his words began to register, causing her heart to leap. 'I think I made the biggest mistake of my life. Trudi, I've been as sad and lonely as you and I've missed you so much, but before we can decide on anything there are things that need to be sorted.' Her eyes filled with tears, tears of happiness, of hope and her body relaxed as the turmoil was replaced by peace and the concept that victory was in sight. Even though nothing concrete had been put in place and no final decisions made, her soul was convinced that the war was almost over. Victory was around the corner.

Trudi and Robert left the pub hand in hand and made their way home, where they planned to continue the celebrations for a little while longer. Ellie and Phoebe had already gone to bed, leaving the couple free to carry on the evening with the bottle of wine Trudi had left chilling in the fridge. As she filled the glasses with the cooled sparkling liquid, she pondered over Robert's words, comparing the bobbing bubbles present in the glasses to her bouncing spirit inside. Despite the evening having given her far more than she could ever have hoped, she told herself to keep the bubbles under control. After all, he hadn't confirmed that he wanted to come home and there was still a chance of the bubbles being burst. For now, she must be content with the effervescence around and inside her with the indication of light appearing on the horizon.

It was around one o'clock in the morning when Robert said that he should leave and, as he'd been drinking, had better walk home. Trudi took this as an opportunity to suggest that he stayed the night, rather than walk the mile and a half in the pitch black to his mother's. At first, he was hesitant because he didn't want to upset Ellie and Phoebe but his reluctance to leave nudged him in to staying. He looked at her lovingly and took her by the hand. Easing her from the settee he drew her towards him, his arms tightly encircling her body. As they stood in each other's embrace, he kissed the top of her head affectionately before he gently led her into the hall and up the small flight of stairs. Under her bare feet, the carpet felt soft and inviting, contributing to the comfort that was already swirling inside which added a buoyancy to her step. The lightness she was experiencing almost made her dizzy, her mind woozy from the concoction of alcohol and jubilation. Her floating body seemed as if it was being transported by one of the bubbles she'd drunk earlier. She glided into the bedroom like a balloon on a string being pulled by Robert's hand. Silently, they undressed, the darkened room filled with an ambience of shyness and uncertainty, as if it was a new experience for their nakedness to be shared. She modestly slid under the duvet whilst attempting to hide her exposed flesh and the virginal vulnerability she was feeling. Her breathing became faster as she lay on the cool sheet and waited anxiously for the sensation of his body next to hers. The mattress dipped as he climbed in beside her and his hands cautiously moved towards her body. His arms wrapped around her and pulled her against his naked flesh. She melted into the embrace, relaxing more and more with each breath she took, feeling safe and comforted in his hold. They didn't make love; they were content to be in each other's arms enveloped in a bubble of warmth as they snuggled up close. Whispering 'this feels so right,' Trudi fell asleep in the arms of the man she loved.

Sunlight began to trickle its waking rays through the window, lighting the room with a pink glow as it mixed with the colour of the curtains, stirring the slumbering couple. The increasing sound of the dawn chorus broke the silence around, encouraging sleepy eyes to blink their way open and drowsily become aware of the surroundings. Clutching arms that had been released during sleep found their way back to the body they'd encircled previously and held it close. A raspy voice, sleep still evident in its sound whispered 'morning', awakening the realisation that it hadn't been a dream and that the arms she felt around her were real. She turned to face her husband and, smiling bashfully, murmured 'morning' as she crept closer into his hold. His hand swept against her face and a kiss placed on her head as he said, 'I've got to go.' Reluctantly, she released him from her grasp, saying 'Ok. What are you up to? Will I see you later?' Robert was noncommittal in his response. 'I'm not sure what's happening. I've got things to do so I'll let you know.' Confusion found its way back into her mind and mix with the already present anxiety, yet deep down Trudi felt at peace with her intuition telling her that everything was okay. The tension in the tug of war had eased and the rope had slackened but the time wasn't right to let go completely, there was still one last tug remaining before Nicola fell to the floor defeated. They said goodbye and, as she took comfort from the soft fleece of her dressing gown, she watched him drive off down the road and wondered what the day had in store.

The sunlight that had woken her earlier was rapidly disappearing and the sky was gradually being painted with a greyness that resembled her mood. Rain was threatening, even so she was determined not to allow the deluge forming within to escape and clung hold of the last bit of light present with all her might. As her daughters were out, she was alone in the house, trapped in her own prison of contemplation, trying hard to ignore the niggling doubts. After all, that's what they were, doubts, not instinct. There was also the concern about her family's response, for, if reconciliation was to come about, the reception wouldn't be warm and even met with hostility, yet it was something she was prepared to undergo. It was as if Nicola was handing her end of the rope to the family and another competition was taking place, yet, if she had to choose, her husband would win every time.

It was her mum's birthday. She'd arranged to spend the afternoon with her and was welcomed with a smile and an anxious, 'well?' Her mum was showing more interest in her daughter's well-being than her own birthday. Once birthday wishes and present had been exchanged, the story was shared whilst watching nervously for her mother's response. Her mum listened, conveying compassion and understanding as Trudi told of her feelings, her concerns and hopes. When the recount was finished, Grace's gaze penetrated deep into her daughter as if searching for the answer to an unspoken question. She looked at her and said, 'Trudi, you're meant to be together. Your soul's leading you and you must do what you feel is right. Just let it happen. No one can tell you what to do, only you can choose and whatever you decide is right. Don't let others stop you or stand in your way. This is your life. It'll be hard, but I'll support you and am willing to welcome him back.' Her mum's words were full of love, encouraging her daughter's hope to gather in strength to obliterate the hurt yet there was still uncertainty, and terror looming like a big black shadow.

As if on cue, her phone rang. It was Robert. Looking anxiously at her mum, she answered the phone, her voice trembling and hands shaking. The familiar churning of the stomach kicked into action as she heard a distracted voice speak. 'Can we meet up? I need to talk to you. I'm at home.' She detected a sadness as he spoke, making her heart sink. Her stomach swirled with more vigour and made her feel nauseous as all her shadows from the past came back to entice her once again. Her mum gave her a reassuring smile which helped her regain her composure. Calmly and coolly, she replied. 'I'm at Mum's.

I'll be back soon. Would you like to stay to dinner?' His acceptance of the dinner invitation allowed rays of light to shine through the menacing shadows. If he was staying to dinner, whatever he had to say couldn't be that unpleasant. Bracing herself, and with her mum's words of advice and luck ringing in her ears, she bid her goodbye and returned home.

Chapter 33

As she made her way home, the familiar vibration of an impending earthquake awakened the dormant tremors inside and activated the uncontrollable shaking she'd suffered from months ago. She breathed calmness into her being, whilst wondering if what she was experiencing was comparable to going cold turkey. She remembers that journey as if it was only yesterday and pictures herself climbing shakily out of the car. She recalls placing the invisible cloak of protection around her body which turned the fear to numbness and enabled her to walk through the front door. Her defence mechanism was in place, ready to receive whatever blow was waiting, but lowered when she saw the forlorn figure standing in the hall. There was Robert, his body hunched, his face pale and his eyes looking anxious and full of fear. His whole demeanour expressed nervousness as well as anguish and emphasised how uncomfortable he was feeling.

He took her into the kitchen, closing the door behind them. She detected tears forming in his eyes and could see he was in pain. Her immediate reaction was to hug him tightly but, as there was still the chance that he was about to tell her that it was all over between them, she ignored it. His head hung low as he began to explain that he'd spent most of the day with Nicola. Trudi's heart sank as she heard that piece of information, forcing her defences to rise once more against the impending knife attack. His voice trembling with emotion, he continued, but the words took a while to penetrate the protective armour that surrounded her. Then, gradually, the odd words such as 'Nicola, finished, love, home' echoed and bounced inside her ears until they managed to catch her attention. She wasn't under attack; she was being rescued. Knives weren't being thrown, it was a line of survival, of optimism.

The protective armour began to fall away, giving her the freedom to listen attentively to the man, her husband, who was telling her he loved her. 'I've told Nicola that it's over and that it should never have happened. You said last night that it felt right and I felt it too. I love you so much, Trudi and, if you'll have me,

I really want to come home.' She stared at him in silence, unable to digest what she was hearing. She was stunned, feeling as if she'd been given the most rewarding gift of all time and was incapable of expressing the joy she felt. She'd experienced a variety of emotions over the past few months, but this was totally different. Surprise, shock, overwhelming joy, love and victory, all rolled into one big bundle! Bursting with a fountain of love, she threw her arms around his neck, with falling tears of happiness. He pulled her in closer, his body relaxing in her embrace. Tears fell from his eyes as he softly murmured, 'I love you very, very much. I'm so sorry for everything. I'm so sorry for causing so much pain.' Locked in each other's arms, they silently wept as the battle finally came to an end. For now, they were quite content to ignore the rubble and debris created by the conflict for at least a few hours. He was home. They were together. Yes, they both had many wounds and, for Trudi, some could take a long time to heal, but the fight was over. Yet, like the end of every combat, there was the aftermath to follow.

Trudi's attention leaves the reunited couple and focuses briefly on the aftermath that followed the victorious battle. Life certainly wasn't plain sailing, as well she knows. In fact, she recollects feeling as if she was sailing across an unpredictable sea that was calm and peaceful and then unexpectedly transformed into a raging storm, with her clinging on to the side of the boat for dear life as it was tossed and turned by the crashing waves. She admits that, despite knowing that the journey wouldn't be easy, she hadn't expected it to be quite so hard or made even more difficult by others. There were times when she had to choose between husband and family because Robert wasn't invited to family gatherings. She's filled with sorrow as she is reminded of how they made it quite clear that they wanted nothing more to do with him and how she had to choose whether to go alone or not at all. Trudi laughs as she compares them to the mafia or a family from a TV soap! They are always there for each other, fight for each other, and amongst themselves, but woe betide anyone who steps out of line or even tries to worm their way into the family. She recollects the old tug of war game being back, with Nicola being replaced by her family, except they did gradually let go of the rope over time. Her mum though, regardless of everything, was completely non-judgemental, knowing that her daughter had chosen her own path. Her mum's words still resonate and she can hear her saying that important lessons had been learnt and how she could see a change in Robert. She understood that Trudi had been driven by her soul and followed her heart. Her mum maintained, beyond all doubt, that her daughter had been guided and protected by the Angels.

Looking back, Trudi is certain that she was helped, or guided, by some invisible source whether it be Angels, God or whatever a person believes. She can highlight too many synchronicities throughout the moonlit story for there not have been a Spiritual intervention of some sort. The inner guidance she'd felt at various times is undeniable, whether it was an invisible inner voice or her detective ego, she knows she was definitely helped. 'It's been tough reliving it all again, but I have learned a great deal about myself and my family,' she says to the orb in the sky. As she ponders over the story, the important moments which have enabled her to learn and grow as a person are brought into the spotlight. She is reminded of how her intuition has developed, how she has grown in strength, her spiritual gift that has evolved and how she has been helped along the road of self-understanding. She can now see the base from which Robert came and the games that they've both played throughout their time together; she also understands the games other people played and how she allowed them to affect her. The shadows of the past are brought to the fore, hers and the family as a whole, only now the emphasis is put on the past. It has been an expedition of life, where she has collected some good memorabilia and some bad, the latter rekindling behaviour which began in childhood. It has been an opportunity to learn from each experience, and if unheeded, it was presented time and time again. She has had happy and sad times, but she has allowed the happiness to be overpowered by the shadows. It is time to release the shadows and wave goodbye.

Although it has been extremely painful to revisit her life story, it has made her thankful for all the experiences she has had as she wouldn't be the woman she is today without them. All the pain and emotions have given her insight, wisdom and the ability to show empathy towards others. She has learnt the importance of not allowing painful emotions to control her life and the importance of loving oneself. Her bag of emotions has emptied, and the shadows dispersed, little by little, over the years, but facing her story has deepened the sense of release. This is all down to the full moon shining above, illuminating the memories that needed to be seen in a more positive light. She thanks him for shining his light and reminding her of how lucky she is. She smiles gratefully up at the moon and is certain that a smile appears on his surface along with the suggestion of a small wink.

A click of a door brings Trudi away from the memories and back into the moonlit room. She gazes at the clock and is surprised to see that only a few, but long, hours have passed. Robert, who has come back from an evening out, comes up behind and kisses her gently on the head. He slips his arms around her as he asks if she's had a good evening. An amused glint shines in her eye as she glances knowingly at the moon. Smiling affectionately at her husband, she sighs contentedly and snuggles into his embrace which still, after nearly fifty years of marriage, creates the same comforting warmth inside. Over twenty years have passed since the battle of Nicola. Yes, the pain and hurt are still sometimes there, although they are no longer shadows lurking in the background or taking control of her life. Their life has changed and the family has grown up. It has also expanded with the addition of wonderful grandchildren. She feels nothing except love and gratitude towards her husband but, more importantly, for life and for herself. Trudi pulls her husband's arms in tighter and looks up at him. 'I love you,' she whispers. 'I love you too,' he replies.

The moon gives a gentle, courteous nod before he starts to slowly fade over the horizon, drawing his curtains close as he bids farewell.